P9-DNS-945

THE GIRL THE SEA GAVE BACK

ALSO BY ADRIENNE YOUNG

Sky in the Deep

THE GIRL THE SEA GAVE BACK

ADRIENNE YOUNG

WEDNESDAY BOOKS
NEW YORK

This is a work of fiction. All of the characters, organizations, and events portrayed in this novel are either products of the author's imagination or are used fictitiously.

For information, address St. Martin's Publishing Group, 120 Broadway, New York, NY 10271.

www.wednesdaybooks.com

Designed by Devan Norman

The Library of Congress Cataloging-in-Publication Data is available upon request.

ISBN 978-1-250-16848-1 (hardcover)
ISBN 978-1-250-16850-4 (ebook)

Our books may be purchased in bulk for promotional, educational, or business use. Please contact your local bookseller or the Macmillan Corporate and Premium Sales Department at 1-800-221-7945, extension 5442, or by email at MacmillanSpecialMarkets@macmillan.com.

First Edition: September 2019

10 9 8 7 6 5 4 3 2 1

For Finley

I'm so happy the sea brought you to me

THE GIRL THE SEA GAVE BACK

13 YEARS AGO

The Headlands, Kyrr Territory

"GIVE ME THE CHILD."

Turonn's hands reached for the girl cradled in his wife's arms and she looked up, her swollen eyes glistening.

"They're waiting, Svanhild."

She touched her daughter's face, tracing the curve of her brow with the tip of her finger. "I will carry her," she whispered.

Her black hair fell over her face like a veil as her bare feet hit the cold stone floor and she stood on weak legs. When Torunn stepped toward her, she moved from his reach. The comfort of her husband would only turn the river of pain in her chest into an angry ocean. So, he let her go, watching her step into the ice-blue light of dawn spilling through the open door. He took the bow from where it hung on the wall and followed, his eyes on the hem of her white linen gown.

Below, every soul in Fjarra stood at the water's edge to witness the funeral rites. The bitterly barren headlands that had been the home of the Kyrr for generations were iced over, though winter was gone, and Svanhild couldn't help but think her daughter would be cold, even if she was dead.

The wind pulled the thin cloth around her slight frame as she walked the winding path down the steep incline to the violent waves crashing on the beach. There, her people waited. She looked straight ahead, tightening her arms around the girl's body, and one cold drop of rain hit her cheek. The clouds churned overhead, the rumble of thunder echoing the pounding heart in her chest.

She looked up into the blackening clouds, where the nighthawk was circling, and uttered a curse on her breath. She'd consulted the Spinners of Fate before her daughter was born six years ago and they'd told her what future lay ahead. But she still hated them for it. The three Spinners who sat at the foot of the Tree of Urðr weaving the destiny of mortals were as cruel as the cold waters that had pulled Svanhild's daughter beneath the waves. Her pleas to save her child had gone unheard, swallowed up by the raging sea that surrounded the headlands.

The boat was already waiting in the shallows. Its carved prow craned over the beach in the shape of a serpent's head and garlands of willow were draped over the sides, where a maze of runes and ravens' wings was burned onto the hull. Inside, long stalks of nodding avens and lupine were piled in an offering to their god, Naðr.

The people were silent, their eyes on Svanhild as she stood on the beach, peering down into the face of the girl. Her skin like milk, her hair like ink. The black marks that covered her skin wound around her arms and legs in patterns that Svanhild had made herself only a year ago. They were the same ones that covered the skin of every Kyrr standing on the beach, a labyrinth of ancient prayers that had been passed from one generation to the next and that signified her as a child of Naðr. But even the gods couldn't spare mortals from the hands of the Spinners.

Turonn set his hand onto Svanhild's shoulder and she blinked, sending hot tears falling into the fine linen. She waded out into the icy water, the gown clinging to her hips and legs, and the rain began to fall harder as she leaned over the side of the boat to set the girl down carefully, nestled into the soft violet-and-blush blooms.

Turonn took hold of the prow, shoving the boat out onto the water, and Svanhild swallowed down the sob in her chest until it was a heavy stone in her stomach. After all, what right did she have to cry out? The Spinners had told her this day would come. She'd known it the moment the midwife had placed the tiny child into her arms. And now that it was here, she'd send her daughter to the afterlife with strength, not with frailty. And when she saw her again, she would stand proud of her mother.

The boat's edge slipped from her shaking hands as it caught the gentle current and Svanhild stood there until the cold of the water crept into the center of her bones.

Until she couldn't feel anything but the biting wind on her face.

The sound of fire-steel struck behind her and she looked over her shoulder to where Turonn was nocking a flaming arrow, his face drawn with deep lines and his dark eyes reflecting the storm above. He looked to Svanhild, standing like a ghost in the gray water.

She gave a sharp nod and he lifted the bow, his fingers tightening on the draw. He pulled a deep, even breath in through his swollen throat and let the string creak before he released the arrow and it flew. It arched up over Svanhild's head and every set of eyes on the beach watched it vanish into the clouds before it reappeared, dropping from the sky like a falling star.

It hit the boat with a crack and Svanhild wrapped her arms around herself as the hungry flame caught and spread. The scent of burning elm crept toward them in a swath of smoke as the boat grew small, drifting into the thick fog until it disappeared.

And when Svanhild blinked again, it was gone.

The Shores of Liera, Svell Territory

Night still hung heavy as Jorrund opened the door to his small house in the Svell village of Liera, far from the frosted shores of the headlands.

Only the outlines of the tallest trees were visible, but he

knew the path well enough to walk it in the dark. He slung the satchel over one shoulder and took the bundle of wood under his arm before he set out, winding through the sleeping village. He rubbed at the ache in his cold hands, his boots crunching on the pine needles that covered the worn trail, and looked up to the dark branches, where even the birds had fallen silent.

In only minutes, the sun would rise up over the fjord beyond the trees and wake the world. But Jorrund didn't want to be there when the Svell chieftain knocked on his door. Not before he'd sought Eydis. Not before he'd asked for her guidance.

It had been only days since news reached Liera of the massacre to the east. The demon Herja had reemerged from the sea to spill the blood of the Aska and the Riki clans and for the first time in generations, it looked as if their gods had buried their feud. Now, the clans on the fjord and the mountain were weakened and the Svell people were hungry for the war they never could have waged in the past.

They looked to their chieftain, awaiting his answer. But Bekan looked to Jorrund, the Tala. Chosen as the mediator between the people and their god, he was interpreter of Eydis' will. But she had been silent, not a single omen or sign lighting the two dark paths ahead: one to peace and one to war.

The trees came to an abrupt stop, opening to the dew-covered meadow, and Jorrund set down the wood. He took the fire-steel from his robes and opened the satchel, pulling the bowl and herbs from inside.

But movement in the trees ahead made him still, one hand going slowly for the knife tucked into the back of his belt. His fingers curled around the handle slowly, his old eyes trying to focus. A streak of white moved through the dark forest like a floating torch.

But it wasn't a flame. It was a woman.

She stood between the trunks of two trees, wrapped in a dark robe. The length of her white hair spilled out from the hood, falling down her shoulder like a running river.

She watched with sparkling eyes as Jorrund stood, his faltering breath fogging out before him in the cold air. When her entire face came into the moonlight, he stopped breathing altogether, dropping the bowl at his feet. The look of her was too strange to be mistaken. Like the eyes of a hundred-year-old woman on the face of a child.

It was a Spinner. A Fate Spinner.

"Hello?" he called out, taking a careful step toward her.

But she didn't move. She didn't even blink. Her pale eyes only seemed to deepen and a chill ran over his skin, the tingling reaching down the length of his arms to the fingers that were still wound tightly around the handle of the knife.

He'd heard stories of the Spinners. His own mother had told them to him and he had, in turn, told them to the children of Liera. But never had he been visited by one. And if that was who stood in the forest before him now, there were only two things she could be bringing.

Life or death.

She reached up, pulling the hood of her robe down, and

stepped into the path with bare feet. Jorrund looked over his shoulder, to where the trail back to the village disappeared in the darkness. Maybe this was the sign he'd been waiting for. He'd called out to Eydis, but perhaps it was a Spinner who'd answered.

He followed her with tentative steps, the length of his robes catching the tall grass that lined the path. She moved through the trees like a creeping fog and the farther they walked, the colder the air grew. The smell of the sea blew through the trees, thick with the scent of a spent storm. The light of morning appeared in the distance, only beginning to illuminate the fjord in a blue haze that reflected off the thin crust of ice hugging the shore.

The Spinner stepped down onto the rocks without a sound, leaving the cover of the trees, and Jorrund stopped, the toes of his boots at the edge of the path. The beach was littered with a tangled maze of driftwood and rockweed, washed up by the violent winds that had blown in during the night. The Spinner walked among them, making her way into the fog that had gathered in the small cove ahead.

A faint cry twisted on the soft breeze, and Jorrund tilted his head, listening. It wasn't high-pitched enough to be a bird, but there was something unsettling about the broken sound. It rose above the sound of the water, coming in gusts with the wind.

He stepped onto the rocks and walked toward it, the beat of his heart matching his quickening pace. The Spinner disappeared and he pushed into the haze after her, following the fading echo. The fog thinned as he neared it, and the water calmed, lapping up onto the rocks under his feet.

On the beach ahead, the silhouette of a boat emerged.

He turned in a circle, looking for the Spinner, but there was only the cliff and the trees that encircled the cove. The sound rang out again and the chill that had found him on the forest path turned sharp. He eyed the boat, pulling his knife free and lifting it before him as he stepped forward warily.

His boots ground on the rocks and when the head of a wooden serpent appeared before him, he froze. His eyes focused to see the narrow face, an open mouth with an unrolled tongue reaching out toward him.

Naðr.

There was no mistaking it. The god of the Kyrr was the serpent that was carved into the prow, but what was a ceremonial boat like this doing so far from the headlands?

Sacred runes and staves were etched into the blackened hull. He took another step, his hands running over the carving of a flying raven half-erased on the charred wood. The boat had been on fire, probably squelched by the storm. And there was only one use for a boat like this—a funeral.

The wail echoed out again and Jorrund flinched, raising his knife again as he peered over the side of the boat. Inside, a small girl was crouched in a nest of wilted blooms of wildflowers. The black marks of the Kyrr covered her pale skin. Twisting, knotted symbols that made a patchwork of secrets began at her ankles, spreading over her entire body and reaching up her throat.

The breath caught in his chest as the girl looked up to him with large, red-rimmed eyes. Her trembling lips were painted the palest shade of blue, her arms wrapped tightly around her knees as she hugged them to her chest.

His gaze fell to the strange symbol on her chest, where her tunic opened. A large, open eye encircled by the branches of an oak tree. That, too, was something he'd only heard of in stories.

The mark of a Truthtongue. One who could cast the rune stones and see the web of fate.

He lowered the knife, letting out a long, heavy breath. It was no accident. After days of calling out to his god, the Spinner had appeared to him in the forest and led him to the beach. She'd entrusted the child to *him*. Surely it was Eydis who'd sent her.

He turned, searching the beach for the white-haired woman, but she was gone. There was only the sound of the water. The howl of the wind.

He reached into the boat, taking the girl's weak body into his arms, and she curled up against him, shivering. But he knew what would happen if he took a Kyrr child to Liera, especially one with the mark of a Truthtongue. The Svell would fear her. The chieftain may even kill her. But if Jorrund wanted to give the Svell leader the answer he needed, it was a chance he would have to take.

He set the girl onto the rocks and gathered the wildflowers into a heap before he hit the fire-steel in three clean strikes. The sparks caught the dried leaves and petals and the white smoke swirled up above his head as it spread.

The wind picked up and the fire found the hull, devouring the wood until the flames rose up taller than he stood, disappearing into the gray sky.

It was a betrayal. An ill omen. But it wasn't the Svell he'd answer to in the afterlife.

He'd answer to Eydis.

So he stood, his back to the wind, the girl at his feet.

And together, they watched the boat burn.

CHAPTER ONE

TOVA

The stones don't lie.

The call of the nighthawk rang out in the dark and I opened my eyes, pushing the furs back to sit up and listen. Hot coals still glowed in the fire pit, but the house was cold, the wind turning through the trees and making their trunks creak as they bowed.

The hawk's shrill song carved through the rumble of the sky to find me again and my bare feet hit the stone floor. I went to the window, watching the dark path that led through the forest to Liera. In the haze, an amber orb of torchlight bobbed through the trees.

Jorrund.

I let out a long breath, pressing my forehead to the wood plank wall, the weight of the rune stones pulling around my neck. The last time the Tala had come to my door in the middle of the night, I'd almost lost my life.

I pulled off my night shift and dropped it on the floor, working the twisting locks falling over my shoulder into one thick braid with clumsy fingers. As I tied off the end, my eyes focused on the pointed leaves and belled blooms of nightshade blackened onto the back of my hand. On the other, a bloom of yarrow. I held them out before me in the flash of lightning coming through the window.

One life, one death.

The pounding of a fist rattled the door and I slipped a clean tunic over my head, pulling on my worn leather boots as quickly as I could. I swallowed hard, steadying myself before I opened it.

Jorrund peered at me from beneath the hood of his robes, lifting the torch until I could see his slanted, silvery eyes. They were the only eyes I really knew the color of. The Svell were too afraid of misfortune to meet my gaze, convinced a curse would find them. I often wondered if they were right.

"We need you." Jorrund's deep, timeworn voice rose above the heavy pelt of rain on the roof.

I didn't ask why they needed me. It didn't matter. I was a Truthtongue, and as long as the Svell gave me a home and let me live, I did their bidding with the three Spinners.

I followed with quick steps, the nighthawk calling out again from somewhere high up in the trees. The sound of it pricked over my skin, the ill omen familiar. He, too, did dark work. The All Seer was the eye of the Fate Spinners. A messenger. And he only called out in warning.

Something had happened.

The rain ran in rivulets down the path and my boots sank into the mud as we made our way out of the mist of the forest. White smoke rose from the ritual house in the center of the village, winding like a snake into the clouds and my hand instinctively went to the stones around my neck as we passed through the gates of Liera.

The first time I'd passed beneath those arches, I was six years old. A trembling, terrified child, every inch of my skin covered in the ritual symbols of the Kyrr. The icy stares of the Svell had pierced before frantically finding the ground. I'd learned quickly that they were afraid of me. As I walked through the village at Jorrund's side, my arms wrapped around myself, a woman stepped into the path with a clay bowl clutched in her hands. Something hot hit my face and it wasn't until I reached up that I realized it was blood—a prayer to their god, Eydis, to ward off whatever evil I might bring. I still remembered the way it felt, rolling down my skin and soaking into the neck of my tunic.

Jorrund limped ahead, walking at a pace that was too fast for his old bones. As the Tala, it was his responsibility to interpret Eydis' will, but summoning me meant that there was a question that he couldn't answer. Or sometimes, that there was an answer that he didn't want to be the one to give.

As we neared the towering roof of the ritual house, the two Svell warriors standing at either side straightened, opening the doors against the roaring wind. Jorrund didn't even stop for dry robes, pushing the torch into one of the men's hands and making his way toward the altar, where bodies were huddled together in silhouettes against the fire.

I stopped midstride when I saw the gleam of eyes set upon me. They were faces I recognized, but half of them were smeared with dried blood, streaks of mud painted across their armor. The Svell village leaders had been called in and from the looks of it, some of them had seen battle.

"Come, Tova." Jorrund spoke lowly.

I looked from him to the others, my hand instinctively going to the leather purse beneath my tunic, where the stones were tucked safely against my heart. I knew what they wanted, but I didn't know why and I didn't like that feeling.

Their stares lifted from me as Jorrund led me to a corner and took his place at Bekan's side. The Svell chieftain didn't acknowledge my presence. He hadn't since the last time I'd been brought here in the middle of the night to cast the stones for his daughter's life.

But it was something else that drew the fury on Bekan's face now. He cast it upon his own leaders, something I'd seen more and more in the last years as the clans to the east unified. The shift in power had put the Svell at odds, and every year that Bekan didn't declare war only fed the division. The splinter that had wedged itself between the Svell was widening.

"You haven't left me a choice. Already a day and a half has passed. News will have reached them by now." His voice raked as he leaned forward to catch the eyes of his brother, Vigdis.

I'd seen the brothers argue many times, but never in front of the other village leaders. Jorrund, too, looked as if the sight unnerved him.

"You've always been foolish, brother," Bekan growled. "But this . . ."

"Vigdis acted when you wouldn't." A woman's voice rose in the shadows behind the others and the chill of the storm seemed to suddenly rush back into the room, despite the blazing fire.

Bekan's black eyes glinted. "We act *together.* Always."

I watched the others, studying the way their hands sat ready at their weapons, their muscles wound tight. All twelve of the Svell villages were represented, and more than half of the faces bore the evidence of a fight. Whatever mess they'd made, they'd done it without Bekan's consent. And that could only mean one thing—that the blood on their armor belonged to the Nādhir.

"Tell me exactly what happened." Bekan rubbed a hand over his face and I wondered if I was the only one who could see that he was a man coming apart at the seams. It had only been two full moons since his only child, Vera, died of fever. Every day that passed since then seemed to only cast a darker shadow upon him.

Vigdis lifted his chin as he answered. "Thirty warriors, including myself and Siv. We took Ljós in the night."

The leader of Stórmenska stood beside him, her thumbs hooked into her armor vest. "At least forty dead, all of them Nādhir, from what we could tell." She spoke carefully, measuring her words. Five years ago, they would have been her last. But now, the village leaders were united in what they thought should be done about the growing threat to the east and the ground the Svell chieftain stood on was crumbling.

"They are most likely calling in their warriors this very moment." Jorrund took a step closer to Bekan, his clasped hands before him.

"Let them." Vigdis eyed his brother. "We will do what we should have done long ago."

"Your fealty is to *me,* Vigdis."

"My fealty is to the Svell," he corrected. "It's been more than ten years since the Aska and the Riki ended their blood feud and joined together as the Nādhir. For the first time in generations, we are the most powerful clan on the mainland. If we want to keep our place, we have to fight for it."

The silence that followed only confirmed that even the most loyal among them agreed, and Bekan seemed to realize it, his eyes moving over them slowly before he answered. "War has a cost," he warned.

"Perhaps it's one we can pay." Jorrund leaned in closer to him, and I knew he was thinking the same thing I was. The scales had finally tipped out of Bekan's favor. He either agreed to advance on Nādhir territory or he risked a permanent division among his own people.

The others grunted in agreement and Bekan's gaze finally found me in the dim light. "That's what we're here to find out."

Jorrund gave me a tight nod, taking a basket from where it hung on the wall behind him. I stepped into the light, feeling the eyes of the Svell leaders crawl over the marks on my skin. They moved aside, careful not to touch me, and I took the pelt from the basket as Jorrund murmured a reverberating prayer beneath his breath.

"You tempt the wrath of Eydis, keeping that *thing* here," Vigdis murmured.

The chieftain's brother had been the only one to say aloud what I knew the rest of them were thinking. That Bekan's daughter, Vera, had died because of me. When Jorrund brought me to Liera, many said that Bekan would pay a price for the grave sin of letting me live. The morning Vera woke with fever, there were whispers that his punishment had finally come. The Spinners had carved her fate into the Tree of Urðr, but I was the one to cast the stones.

Jorrund ignored Vigdis, setting a bundle of dried mugwort into the flames. The pungent smoke filled the room with a haze, making me feel like for a moment, I could disappear. It wasn't the first time a Svell had referred to me as a curse, and it wouldn't be the last. It was no secret where I'd come from or what I was.

I hooked my fingers into the leather string around my neck and lifted the purse from inside my tunic. I hadn't cast the stones since the night Vera died, and the memory slicked my palms with sweat, my stomach turning. I opened it carefully, letting them fall heavily into my open hand. The firelight glimmered against their smooth, black surfaces where the runes were carved in deep lines. The language of the Spinners. Pieces of the future, waiting to be read.

Jorrund unrolled the pelt and my palms pressed together around the stones.

"Lag mund," Vigdis whispered.

"Lag mund," the others repeated.

Fate's hand.

But what did these warriors know about fate? It was the curling, wild vine that choked out the summer crops. It was the wind that bent wayward currents and damned innocent souls to the deep. They hadn't seen the stretch of it or the way it could shift suddenly, like a flock of startled birds. Fate's hand was something they said because they didn't understand it.

That's what I was for.

I closed my eyes, pushing the presence of the Svell from around me. I found the darkness—the place I was alone. The place I had come from. The call of the nighthawk sounded again and I pulled my thoughts together, sending them into one straight line. My lips parted, the words finding my mouth and I breathed through them.

"Augua ór tivar. Ljá mir sýn.

"Augua ór tivar. Ljá mir sýn.

"Augua ór tivar. Ljá mir sýn."

Eye of the gods. Give me sight.

I held my hands out before me, unfurling my fingers and

letting the stones drop until they were scattered across the pelt in a pattern that only I could see, reaching out wide to either side. The silence grew thick, the crackle of fire the only sound as I leaned forward, bringing my fingers to my lips.

My brow furrowed, my eyes moving from one stone to the next. Every single one was facedown, the runes hidden. Except for one.

I bit down hard on my lip, looking up to see Jorrund's eyes locked on mine.

Hagalaz, the hailstone, sat in the very center. Complete destruction. The storm that devours.

For more than ten years, I'd cast the runes to see the future of the Svell. Never had they looked like this.

But the stones never lied. Not to me.

My eyes drifted over them again, the pace of my heart quickening.

"What do you see?" Jorrund's voice was heavy when he finally spoke.

I stared at him, the weight of silence pushing down on me in the hot room until it was hard to draw breath.

"It's alright, Tova," he said, gently. "What lies in the future of the Svell?"

My eyes cut to Bekan, who stared into the fire, his gaze as hollow as the night his daughter died.

I reached out, the tip of my finger landing on *Hagalaz* before I answered.

"In the future, there are no Svell."

CHAPTER TWO

HALVARD

"How many?" Espen barked, the pounding of his boots hitting the rocky path ahead of me like a racing heartbeat.

Aghi struggled to keep up, leaning into his staff and rocking from side to side as we made our way up the narrow trail that led away from the beach. "More than forty."

Espen stopped short, turning on his heel to face us. "You're sure?"

"I'm sure." Aghi's eyes met mine over Espen's shoulder.

I'd known by the look on his face when I saw Aghi standing on the dock that something was wrong. But this . . . the entire village of Ljós was gone. Aghi and I had been there only a week ago, meeting with the village leader. Now, it was most likely nothing more than a pile of ash.

Espen drew in a deep breath, his hand tangling in his beard as he thought. "Are they waiting in the ritual house?"

"Yes," Aghi answered.

I looked up, feeling eyes on us. The people of Hylli were tending to their morning chores, but their hands stilled on their work as we passed. They could feel that something was happening even if they couldn't see it.

"It was the Svell?" I kept my voice low as a man shouldered around us, a line of silver fish slung over his back.

Espen's jaw clenched. "Who else would it be?"

A fire was lit in his eyes that I hadn't seen since the day I'd first met him, after the battle against the Herja that nearly wiped out the entirety of both our clans. It was something I recognized, the same fire that had lit the eyes of so many warriors I'd known as a boy up on the mountain. The hunger to spill blood was something that ran through the veins of both the Aska and the Riki, but we were the Nādhir now. And it had been ten years since that part of us had been awakened.

"What will you do?"

He didn't answer aloud, but I could see in his face the weary look of a man who'd seen far more death than me.

We'd spoken many times about the tensions growing along the border with the Svell. The call to act had grown more insistent in the last few months, but we needed another ten years before we'd have a strong enough army to defend our lands and our people with better odds. We'd lost too many when the Herja came, and now many of the warriors who'd survived were too old to fight.

As if he could hear my thoughts, Aghi's gaze drifted back to me. His leg had never recovered from the wound he suffered in the battle that defeated the Herja.

Espen led us up the path, an eerie quiet dragging behind us and covering the village in our wake. Spring had melted most of the ice on the fjord, but the crisp tinge of it still cut through on the wind that blew in from the sea. Beyond the rooftops, the mountain rose before a clear gray sky. My family had spent the winter in the snow-laden village where I was born and they wouldn't be back for weeks. But if war was coming, it would draw every Nādhir to the fjord in a matter of days.

Freydis, Latham, and Mýra were already waiting when we came through the doors, their armor oiled and their weapons cleaned. Mýra's red hair glowed around her fair face like fire, twisting down into a tight braid over her shoulder. She was wound as tight as rope, ready to snap. Beside her, Espen's wife stood before the altar, his axe sheaths in her hands.

He turned, taking them onto his back, and she buckled them as he spoke. "Tell me."

"More than forty dead." Freydis answered first. "They moved on Ljós in the night, about twenty or thirty warriors. A few survivors made it to Utan by morning and riders were sent, but the Svell were already gone."

"How do we know it wasn't raiders?"

"They're dead, Espen." Freydis' voice faltered under the words. "All of them."

I watched their faces, the silence falling heavy between us. If it was a band of raiders, the deaths would have been minimal. Whoever marched on Ljós had come for blood, not wool or grain or *penningr.*

Espen's jaw worked as he thought. Once, the Nādhir had been two clans, both bigger and stronger than the Svell, who had been nothing more than a distant people in the eastern forests. They'd survived by avoiding notice. It was after the Herja came and our clans united that the Svell gained their strength and advantage. Now, they were finally ready to use it.

"They've sent a messenger," Freydis said. "The Svell."

"A messenger?"

"Their leader, Bekan, wants to meet. In Ljós. He wants to make an offering of reparation."

Espen and Aghi looked to each other silently. Whispers of war had traveled across the valley for years. It didn't make sense that their leader would make an offering of reparation after their first attack on a village. Unless attacking Ljós wasn't Bekan's act of war.

"It wasn't Bekan," I murmured, thinking aloud.

"What?" Freydis' brow wrinkled.

I turned to Espen. "Bekan's men moved without him."

Mýra's head cocked to the side. "How do you know?"

"I don't. But we've known for a long time that their leaders are divided. It's the only reason they haven't moved against us before now. I think Bekan's men acted without him and he wants to put out the flames before he has to call the Svell to war."

"It doesn't matter. It's too late for that." Latham spoke through his teeth.

The oldest leader among us, Latham had never shed his taste for a fight. And he'd never forgotten just how quickly you could lose everything. He'd been the first to urge a strike against the Svell when the first rumors made it to the fjord.

Freydis' hand tightened around the hilt of her sword. "I can have every Nādhir warrior ready to fight in three days. We can take them village by village. The losses will be—"

"Too great," I finished.

Mýra's eyes cut to mine, her mouth pressing into a hard line. I stood a whole head taller than her now, but she was still as ferocious as the day I first saw her marching into our village with a sword in one hand and a shield in the other. "It's a trap. They're counting on the fact that we don't want war. They're trying to draw us in before they push to the fjord."

"I'll go," I said, avoiding her gaze.

She stilled, her hand absently drifting to the axe at her back and her voice rising. "What?"

"I'll meet with Bekan. They'd have taken at least two more villages by now if he was moving through the valley. He doesn't want war any more than we do. I think he does want reparation."

"You're not giving orders *yet*, Halvard." Latham spoke from where he stood beside me. His face was still engraved with the jagged scar from the battle that had crippled his entire village. He'd spent the last ten years rebuilding it. "Forty of our people are *dead*. Blood must answer for blood."

The leaders had been in agreement when they summoned me to the ritual house two years ago and told me I'd been chosen to take Espen's place as chieftain of the Nādhir—the once warring, now allied people of the mountain and the fjord. Since then, my days had been spent preparing for it. But I'd never seen war the way my elders had. I was among the first generation that didn't live to fight in a blood feud. And now, a wound that would never heal had been torn back open. I'd grown up the son of a healer, but no one could mend a break like that. And no one doubted me more than Latham.

"He's here to speak like the rest of us," Espen rebuked, reminding Latham of his place. He was the last person to hesitate drawing his sword, but he knew I was right. War with the Svell meant the same kind of losses we'd suffered ten years ago. Maybe more.

"Let me go," I said again. "It will take at least three days to gather and ready our warriors. I can make it to Ljós and back in that time."

Mýra glared at me from across the fire, her green eyes sharpening. "If he's going, I'm going."

"You're staying here," Aghi grunted. He was the only father either of us had, but Mýra wasn't one to take orders. "I'll go with Halvard."

She opened her mouth to object, but Espen spoke before she could. "So will I."

Freydis looked to Latham, stiffening. "I don't think that's a good idea." Her voice turned wary.

"We'll take twenty warriors. Latham and Freydis, you will call in the villages. Ready our people for war. Mýra will do the same here in Hylli."

But Freydis didn't look sure and neither did Latham.

"We leave at sundown." Espen squeezed my shoulder.

I nodded, stepping back as he made his way to the doors. His wife followed and as soon as they were gone, Latham turned toward me. He'd never hidden his uncertainty about my ability to take Espen's place, but he'd agreed anyway. He looked at me the way a disapproving uncle would his stubborn nephew, and I knew he didn't really believe I could do it. If I was being honest, neither did I.

He met my eyes for a wordless breath before I followed Aghi outside. The doors hadn't even closed behind us when Mýra was suddenly turning on me.

"What do you think you're doing?" She squared her shoulders to mine, looking up into my face. "I'm going with you."

"You're staying," Aghi said again, this time letting the edge slip into his voice.

"When they find out . . ." Her eyes went to the mountain behind me and I knew she was thinking of my family. They were her family, too. "Wait two days. I'll leave for Fela now. We'll ride through the night and—"

"We'll be back before they even know we're gone," I

said, but I knew she was right. Eelyn and my brothers would be furious when they found out I'd gone to meet with Bekan.

"I don't like this." Her voice softened, her eyes searching mine. She was eleven years older than me, but in that moment she looked so young. "You shouldn't go, Halvard."

"We'll be back in three days. Four at the most."

She nodded reluctantly and I knew that look. She was worried. Scared. I pulled her into me, wrapping my arms around her small frame and setting my chin on top of her head.

"I'm not losing any more family," she said. "Do you hear me?"

"If we go to war with the Svell, you will."

She pulled away from me, her voice hardening. "If you're not back in four days, we're not waiting."

"Alright."

"If I don't see you on that horizon before the sun sets . . ."

"Alright," I said again.

"Sigr guide and protect you." She drew in a deep breath, looking from me to Aghi before she shook her head, cursing under her breath as she moved around us to go back inside.

Aghi waited for the doors to close before he finally turned to me. I knew what he was thinking before he said the words. "Are you sure about this, son?" His deep voice carried on the wind pushing up from the sea.

I looked at him, searching the eyes I'd come to know so

well, now framed by deep lines. He'd taken us in when we came to live on the fjord and when my brother married his daughter, he'd made us his own. He'd opened his home to us when the feud between our people was still smoking like the embers of a fire, threatening to reignite. I couldn't lie to him. Even if I wanted to, he'd see right through it.

So I answered with the truth we both already knew. "No."

CHAPTER THREE

TOVA

THE ALL SEER WAS GONE.

I walked the path from the corner of the forest with the bow slung over my chest and two gutted rabbits cradled in my arms, their furs still warm. My eyes were on the treetops, my ears listening for the call of the nighthawk. But it was quiet, the songs of nesting birds and my boots on the fallen pine needles the only sounds. The rune cast still haunted me, my eyes drifting to the mark of henbane on the back of my left hand. But if the All Seer had left, maybe misfortune had, too.

"I couldn't find you."

I froze, my fingers tightening around the bowstring as Jorrund appeared beneath the arched branches of flowering maple on the path ahead.

The clusters of blooms had opened early, and I wondered if that was a good omen or a bad one. They were beautiful, pale green blossoms swaying in the wind, but a late frost would strangle them.

"I was worried."

I could see that he meant it. His hands wrung each other at his back, his smile crooked.

"I'm sorry," I said, stopping before him. Jorrund didn't like it when he didn't know where I was. He didn't like being reminded that he could lose me.

He took the rabbits and I followed him in silence. The warmth of the earth returning after winter meant fresh meat and green herbs. Both gave me excuses to leave my little house on the outskirts of Liera that at times felt more like a cage than a home.

We came through the door and I hung my bow and quiver of black-and-white-flecked feather arrows on the wall. I lit the candle even though the sun was already rising over the trees and my cold hands hovered over the wavering flame, the heat stinging my palms.

Jorrund watched me as he set the rabbits on the table. His white hair curled around his face, his beard twisting down his chest. He still hadn't slept and the tiredness pulled at his eyes, making them more slanted than usual. After I cast the stones, he'd spent the early hours before daylight behind the closed doors of the ritual house with the Svell leaders. Their voices had carried almost to the gates as I made my way back into the forest.

"What will they do?" I watched the melting wax drip and pool on the wood where it turned to a milky gold as it cooled.

"Bekan will meet with the leaders of the Nādhir. He'll make an offering of reparation."

I arched an eyebrow at him. "An offering of reparation?"

He nodded, his eyes leaving mine, and I realized he didn't want me to see what he was thinking. But I could already guess. Jorrund didn't want war, but the stones had convinced him that the time had come for it. He'd never say it aloud, but he thought Bekan was making a mistake.

I'd heard of offerings of reparation, but never between clans. It was something enemies did to squelch a blood feud between families before violence took hold as a heritage. It was an offering of peace in the form of a gift.

"When?" I sat down onto the stool, looking up at him.

"We leave tomorrow."

"You're going with them?"

"I am." He paused, looking at the ground. "I'd like you to come, too."

I pulled my hands back from the flame. "Me?"

He tried to smile, but the corners of his mouth betrayed him, turning down just enough for me to notice. "That's right."

"But why?"

"I will need you if I'm going to help repair this. We all will."

My fingers tangled into each other in my lap, beneath the table. "What does Bekan say?"

Jorrund studied me, his eyes running over my face, but he didn't answer. Bekan had barely acknowledged my existence in the weeks since his daughter died. Jorrund asked me to cast the stones for the girl, but the Spinners had given a different answer than the one they wanted. Bekan's only child was taken to the afterlife and there she'd wait for her father until he took his last breath.

Almost the moment I'd spoken the words, I'd felt it. The fracturing of the ground beneath me. In Bekan's eyes, I was no longer just a Truthtongue. Now, I was a bringer of death. And the ally I'd once had in the Svell chieftain seemed to have turned his back on me.

"What if it can't be repaired?" I measured my words carefully. Jorrund used the runes the way a healer used remedies, trying one after the other until he got the result he wanted. But the Spinners were more slippery than that. They were shrewd and cunning.

He stood, going to the drying branches of heather hanging from the rafters and inspecting the tiny pink petals nestled in the dark green leaves. He lifted a hand, pinching the tip of a stem from the branch. I watched him twirl it between two fingers before he held it out to me.

I took it, spinning it in the morning light coming through the window.

"This may be the very reason Eydis brought you here, Tova."

I tucked the bloom into the end of my dark braid. "How do you know it was your god who brought me?"

He looked surprised by the words. I never questioned Jorrund because I didn't want to give him cause to question me. But the world we'd carefully built together was coming apart. I could see it, and I knew he could, too. "Some god spared you and it wasn't Naðr. If the god of the Kyrr favored you, you never would have been in that boat."

I could barely remember it, but Jorrund had told me the story many times. My own people had tried to sacrifice me to their god when I was no more than six years old. He'd found me washed up on shore, a failed ritual sacrifice, but the only thing I could still pull from my memory of that day was the whiteness of the fog. The cry of the wind and Jorrund's long fingers wrapped around my arms as he pulled me from the hull.

"Maybe it wasn't the gods at all. Maybe it was the Spinners."

He looked amused, as if what I'd said was a joke between us. But Jorrund rarely answered my questions about the day he found me on the beach, his words always twisting into something other than an explanation.

"You were huddled in a pile of nodding avens and lupine, your lips blue," he said softly, the memory playing in his eyes.

I remembered that, too. The sound of water sloshing against the boat. The sharp scent of sour blooms and the serpent's head carved into the prow. And the cold. The cold was the only thing I remembered clearly.

"I knew when I saw the symbols inscribed on the wood what the boat was. And when I saw those"—he pointed to the stones hanging around my neck—"I knew it was no accident that the sea had brought you to us."

My hand went back to the flame, my fingers rolling over its heat. There was almost nothing I remembered about my life in the headlands. But there was a strange light that reflected off the sea I could still see in my mind. A pale, white glow that seemed too bright to be real. And the rasping hum of a woman's voice that still echoed within me. Deep and soft and low.

"Your people meant to sacrifice your life to Naðr, but Eydis is merciful. When the Kyrr sent you to the sea, she brought you here. She saw this day coming."

I swallowed hard, pushing that glimmer of gray light from my mind. Sometimes I felt as if the sting of it still lingered on my skin. The pounding of the drums still sounded in my dreams. I'd left the headlands, but the headlands hadn't left me. What and who I was was marked into my skin in the sacred staves and motifs with meanings that even I didn't know. It would never leave me. And because of that, I'd never had a place in Liera except for the one Jorrund had given me.

My hand went to the bracelet around my wrist and I pressed the copper disk between my fingers, trying to conjure the talisman's protection.

"*Hagalaz,* Jorrund," I said. "The cast was clear."

"The hailstone can mean many things," he said, but we both knew I was right.

"Only when there are other runes present. It sat in the center. Alone."

His hands fidgeted nervously. "I believe the time has

come for Eydis to use you. Sometimes, it's the most destructive storm that brings life, Tova. *Hagalaz* is coming. But I think we will survive it. I think it will make us stronger."

That was just like Jorrund, thinking he was wiser than the gods and Spinners together. Thinking he could outwit fate. But there was a deep line across his forehead that wasn't usually there and I wondered if he truly believed what he was saying.

"A spider. Walking the web of fate." His voice softened. "That's what the Spinners carved into the Tree of Urðr the moment you were born."

What little I understood of my marks said as much. Across my left side, a spider stretched over my ribs. But what was carved into the Tree of Urðr could be changed. It could be rewritten. The Kyrr had cast me off as a sacrifice to their god, and it didn't matter who'd spared my life, gods or Spinners. I was here. There had to be a reason for it and that was what plagued me.

"Will Vigdis betray his brother?" I asked the question that had been on both of our minds since we'd left the ritual house.

"He's already betrayed him."

"You know what I mean. Will he try to take his place as chieftain?"

"No." But Jorrund had given his answer too quickly. He wasn't sure. He'd dedicated his life to making Bekan the greatest leader in the Svell's history and he'd used me to do it. But one envious look from Vigdis could threaten it all. And it wasn't only Bekan's life at stake. It was mine. It was Jorrund's. If Vigdis became chieftain of the Svell, the broken ground beneath me would give way to the frozen depths. I knew exactly what the Tree of Urðr would say of my fate then.

"When do we leave?" I asked, knowing I didn't really have a choice.

He smiled widely, a gleam of pride in his eyes. "Tomorrow. Sundown."

His robes brushed the ground as he opened the door and when it closed, I went to the window and watched him on the path. The Svell had wanted to cut my throat when their Tala brought me into their village. For years, there was a guard outside my door to be sure no one carried out their god's wrath upon me. But Jorrund had been sure, and he'd convinced Bekan, speaking on behalf of Eydis.

He disappeared into the trees, leaving me alone in the forest. The little house he'd given me was the only home I remembered. No matter how hard I tried, I couldn't summon the faces of my Kyrr family or our home to me. They were like snowflakes, melting before they touched the ground.

I opened the pouch and let the stones fall onto the table, finding *Hagalaz* and holding it out before me. The rune was a dark one, the wrath of nature and uncontrolled forces. The hailstorm never left the earth unbruised even if it did bring water to a thirsty land.

I turned the stone over in my fingers, watching the sunlight slide over the shining black surface. There was only one way to know for sure what fate was coming, and that was to wait. Because no matter what Jorrund had planned, the Spinners were weaving. They were folding time and every one of us within it.

I pulled the sleeve of my tunic up, tracing the marks on my arm with the tip of my finger. They stretched across my skin from my ankles to my throat. I couldn't remember getting them, but whoever had pricked them into my skin had done it with precision. The winding, curling fins of a sea serpent, the unfurled wings of a raven. A wolf, teeth bared. The black stains crept over my shoulders, down my back and breasts in intricate, knotted patterns that honored Naðr, the god who'd once abandoned me. They were riddles. A patchwork of secrets. Only a Kyrr could translate them for me, and my people never left the headlands. They were born and buried in the frozen north. But if I never unraveled the marks, I'd never know my story. I'd never truly know myself. And I wondered if that was the punishment the Spinners or the gods had bestowed on me for whatever sins I'd committed on the headlands.

I opened the neck of my tunic, studying the open eye encircled by a garland of oak leaves. It was the only symbol I knew and it was the one that had told Jorrund who I was the day he found me. *What* I was.

A Truthtongue.

I wondered what he would have done if he hadn't seen

it. Would he have drowned me in the cold water of the fjord? Was this mark the reason my own people had sent me out as a gift to the sea? Maybe it was a penalty for bringing a fate down upon them too dark to survive. Like Vera.

I blew out the candle, taking my satchel from beneath the table. I would never be one of the Svell. I'd known that for a long time. But after all these years, I could still taste death on my tongue. I could still hear the echoes of its whisper and I recognized the shape of its shadow cast around me.

The storm of *Hagalaz* was coming. And if the Svell perished, so would I.

CHAPTER FOUR

HALVARD

The trail to Ljós was well-worn but silent. Tall, thin trees thickened as we pushed away from the fjord toward the border between Nādhir and Svell lands. Ten years ago, Ljós had been one of only two villages that wasn't attacked by the Herja. Possibly because it was so small. Or maybe because it was settled into the farthest reach of our territory. You almost couldn't even smell the sea this far inland, but there was still something about these forests that felt like home.

Aghi rode ahead, watching the slope that reached up to the ridge. The warriors walked in two lines of ten behind him, clad in the old Aska and Riki armors. For many years after we became the Nādhir, the sight had been strange to me. But now, the dark leathers the Riki used to wear seemed strange alone.

Rays of sunlight found their way through the treetops

as they walked, their attention on the trees all around us. If Bekan was planning to push across the valley and take Hylli, we would have seen traces of them by now. But the forest was quiet and there was no sign of an army. We'd guessed the Svell could have as many as a thousand warriors if all twelve of their villages were asked to fight. No matter the number, it was more than the Nādhir had, even if we called our youngest and oldest to the battlefield.

"Virki." Espen rode beside me, his gaze drifting over the shadows as he listed the order of acts in war. "Do you remember it?"

"Yes," I answered. I'd only been there once, but it was a place I'd never forget. While my brothers went to fight the Herja, I'd been taken to the old stronghold, a hollowed cliff face on a wide river. My mother and I had stood waist deep in the water, peering up against the sunlight as a warrior appeared with the news of victory in Hylli. I still remembered the sound my mother made, her hand pressed to her mouth and hot tears streaming down her cheeks. It was another three days before we learned that both of my brothers had survived.

"The young and old to Virki. Aghi will lead them," Espen repeated.

I nodded, looking again to where Aghi rode ahead. He wouldn't like being sent with those who couldn't fight. He might even refuse if it came to that.

"If defeat is imminent and Hylli is going to fall . . ."

"Send a messenger."

"Three messengers," he corrected.

"Three messengers," I said, remembering. In case one didn't make it. In case two didn't make it.

"Aghi will assume leadership of the survivors in Virki."

"And where would they go?"

"They will leave the fjord."

I pulled back on the reins, slowing, and Espen turned his horse to face me.

"*Leave* the fjord?"

"That's right. And the mountain."

"Abandon our lands?" The edge in my voice surfaced.

"If Hylli were to fall, it would mean the loss of most of our warriors. We would have no way to defend our lands. Those left would have to settle somewhere new." He spoke calmly, no trace of frailty in the words.

But the Nādhir leaving was like the idea of the sea rising up to flood the valleys, drowning the land until it disappeared. It seemed like something that could never happen.

"We have to be ready. *You* have to be ready," Espen said, his face stern. It was a reprimand—a reminder of who I was supposed to be. He was counting on me to lead after he went to the afterlife to be with those who'd gone before him. He'd watched his fellow clansmen fall in the fighting seasons and then again against the Herja. He'd been waiting a long time for death. So had Aghi. And it was my duty to give him peace of mind once he was there in knowing that I was doing what I'd promised to do.

He turned the horse again, but I didn't move, my eyes

on the reins wrapped tightly around my fist. "Why did you choose me?"

"You were chosen by all the Nādhir leaders. Not just me."

"But why?"

He looked over his shoulder, to where Aghi and the others were disappearing around the bend in the path. "You are every Nādhir coming behind you. Born on the mountain, raised on the fjord. A child of both Thora and Sigr. The people will look to you, Halvard. They already do."

"And Latham? Would he follow me?" I asked.

"Yes." He answered without hesitation. "Latham chose you like the rest of us did."

"He doesn't believe I can do it. I don't know if *I* believe I can do it."

"You'll do what you have to do," he said, simply.

I swallowed hard, forcing myself to look up and meet his eyes. I didn't want to admit it, but I owed him the truth. "I'm not ready, Espen."

A patient smile pulled at the corner of his mouth. "You'll have to be if we don't find peace with the Svell."

"You don't think we will?"

He thought before he answered. "I think our world is changing. But not fast enough to keep a war with the Svell from our lands. Our people will see more fighting before we're free of it."

A whistle echoed up on the ridge and I stilled, sliding my axe free as I scanned the trees. Espen did the same, his weapons hanging at his sides as his horse stamped the damp ground nervously. The whistle sounded again and I searched the shadows until a figure appeared and one outstretched hand lifted into a beam of sunlight.

"Halvard!" A voice I knew called my name.

I lowered my axe, letting out the breath I was holding as Asmund slid down the incline, a cascade of fallen leaves racing behind him.

"I wondered when I'd see you." His frayed, stained tunic was the color of the dirt beneath his furs and mismatched armor. "Espen," he greeted. But the chieftain didn't dishonor himself by acknowledging him, kicking the horse and taking off down the path where Aghi and the others had disappeared. He didn't approve of Asmund. Most didn't.

"You've heard?" I asked as he came through the trees.

Asmund stopped before me, his face heavy with his unspoken answer.

Above us on the ridge, the other raiders watched from the trees. As soon as Espen rounded the bend in the trail, they made their way down the slope on the same path Asmund had taken.

It had been six years since Asmund and his brother Bard left Hylli. Now, they made their living as raiders with the outcasts and exiled of the mainland, except for a Kyrr man named Kjeld. My eyes went to the black marks reaching up his neck and down his wrists to his hands. He was the only Kyrr I'd ever seen, but everyone on the mainland knew the stories about his people. It was the reason no one went to the headlands.

"We saw the smoke from the eastern valley." Bard took my hand in greeting as he reached us. "Svell?"

I nodded. "Have you seen them?"

"No, but Ljós is gone. Burned to the ground." His voice lowered. He may have chosen to leave his clan, but there were some things you couldn't cut from your soul. We would always be his people.

"Did you find survivors?"

Asmund shook his head, starting down the path, and I followed beside Bard. The brothers had been among the first friends I'd made when I came to Hylli, but they'd lost every member of their family when the Herja came, and though there'd been many who'd lost everything, some couldn't stay in the home they'd known with the people they loved. When they were only fourteen and sixteen years old, they'd left their past and honor behind in exchange for a life that didn't remind them of the one they'd once had.

"So, it's war?" Asmund watched my face carefully.

The years in the wilderness had weathered him in a way that made the pain he'd suffered easier to see. Maybe that was true for both of us. "We're going to Ljós to meet with Bekan."

"*Meet* with him?"

"He wants to make an offering of reparation."

"What does that matter?" His voice turned sharp and the strain in his eyes made him more familiar to me.

"You know we can't afford war with the Svell."

He leveled his gaze at me. "Then spill as much blood as you can before you reach the afterlife."

He had the heart of the old ways, fueled by all he'd suffered. We all did. "What did you see in Ljós?"

"From the look of the trail in the forest, it was maybe thirty warriors and it was quick. They killed whoever they found, set fire to the village, and left."

I reached a hand out between us and he took it, his worry not hidden. "You should go back to Hylli. Bring every Nādhir to the border and take them."

The same thought was written on the face of his brother, but Kjeld was unreadable as always, his deep-set eyes watching. His fingers wound around his wrist, where a copper disk and a string of bones were knotted in a bracelet.

Asmund sighed. "Be careful, Halvard."

The others followed him as he headed back into the forest, slipping in and out of shadows. Bard looked back at me once more before they disappeared over the ridge.

"Cursed, every one of them," Aghi called out from where he waited ahead. He grunted as he rubbed the heel of his hands into the knotted muscle above his knee. "Traitors."

"You know they don't raid on Nādhir lands," I said, catching up to him.

He arched an eyebrow up at me. To him, it didn't matter. They'd lost their honor and there was no coming back from leaving your people behind to take up life as a raider. He didn't understand them the way I did.

"You're quick to see good, Halvard," he muttered.

I looked down to my father's axe resting against my leg. The engraving of a yew tree gleamed on its blade, the same symbol that marked his armor. "You think it makes me weak-minded."

His brow furrowed. "It makes you stronger. Wiser than I, I think." Aghi was a man of few words, but they were weighted when he spoke. "You're afraid," he said. "That's good."

"Good?" I half-laughed.

He leaned in, meeting my eyes, "Fear is not our enemy, Halvard. You remember the fighting seasons."

I did. It was one of the only clear memories I had of my father, sitting beside the fire and sharpening his sword before he left for Aurvanger, where the clans met every five years to quench their blood feud. "But my father and my brothers weren't afraid to go to war."

"They weren't afraid of battle. They were afraid of losing what they loved. And that's what made them brave in battle."

I tried to imagine Aghi on the fields of Aurvanger, swinging his sword and roaring into the wind. He must have been a great warrior to have survived so many fighting seasons, but the Aghi I had grown up knowing was gentle, in a way. "What are you afraid of now?"

He blinked, his blue eyes as clear as the cold waters of

the fjord. "I'm afraid that one day, after I've gone to the afterlife, and my children come to meet me, they will tell me our people lost the peace we found when I lived in this world." He breathed. "There will always be war, Halvard. War is easy. It comes again and again, like waves to a shore. But I lived most of my life driven by hate, and I don't want that for my grandchildren. Or yours." He reached a hand out for me. "Now, help an old man get off his horse so he can take a piss."

I smiled, taking his arm against mine and leaning back as he slid down to the ground with a grunt.

Far ahead, Espen and the warriors from Hylli waited on the path where the land dipped down into the deeper part of the forest. The wind wound around them and up toward us, the sharp tinge of ash carried from beyond the trees, where Ljós was waiting.

CHAPTER FIVE

TOVA

WE STOOD IN THE BLACKSMITH'S STALL IN THE DARKENING light as he turned the sword over in the forge a final time. Vigdis' gaze was pinned to the dirt beneath the smith's feet, but Bekan watched patiently as the hilt of the weapon was set with a large stone of amber, the symbol for peace engraved on the tip of its shining blade.

The day had been uncomfortably quiet, the tension of the Svell leaders visible as they caught each other's sideways glances. I could see Jorrund watching them all closely, his eyes suspicious. He hadn't spoken a word since we stood outside the ritual house waiting for Bekan that afternoon.

Vigdis was furious when his brother ordered the blacksmith to take the sword he'd been crafting for Vigdis and finish it as the offering of reparation to the Nādhir chieftain. He'd called Bekan a coward after the others disappeared through the doors of the ritual house, but when Bekan threatened to take Vigdis' position as village leader of Hǫlkn and give it to someone with more loyalty, he agreed through gritted teeth to go with him to Ljós.

Now, Vigdis stood, staring into the fire with his thumbs hooked into his belt, his long black hair waving around his face. "And if they don't accept?" His eyes rose to meet Bekan's as he asked the question.

"They're not fools. They'll accept," he answered.

Jorrund nodded in agreement. "We'll make a sacrifice at dawn and ask Eydis to give us her favor."

The smith pounded the blade on the anvil and I flinched against the ear-splitting ring. The sword was almost as long as I was tall and the smith struggled to keep it steady. I'd never seen another blade like it, the intricate hilt and setting of stones was beautiful, the curves of the blade expertly crafted. It would have been a weapon of great pride for Vigdis. Now, it would serve as his humiliation in the hands of his enemy. If the Nādhir chieftain accepted it, the Svell would owe him a debt in exchange for peace.

When it was finished, the smith held it up for inspection and Bekan gave an approving nod. "Vigdis." He said his brother's name, gesturing toward the smith, who waited before them.

Vigdis' jaw clenched as he realized what was behind Bekan's unspoken words. He would still pay for the sword with his own *penningr*.

He met Bekan's eyes for a long moment before he finally reached for his belt, yanking his purse free. He didn't bother asking how much, emptying every coin into the smith's open hand. The man backed away slowly, the *penningr* clutched to his chest and his eyes averted as Vigdis' fury filled the wavering silence around us.

The others started for the gates and Bekan kept his voice low as he walked beside Jorrund, sliding the new sword into the second sheath at his back. They'd both get what they wanted if the Nādhir accepted the offering. The border village and any disputes with its leader would be gone now that Ljós had fallen. They'd made a show of force to the Nādhir people, cementing their position of power and strength. And war wouldn't take the lives of the warriors they may one day need for another battle.

But Bekan's faith in Eydis' favor was too great. Even after Vera, he still didn't fear the web of fate the way I did. He still couldn't feel the power it held over the days ahead. Even then, I could sense it shifting, its threads unwinding and then weaving into new patterns. It was in the feel of the wind. The silence of the forest. The Spinners were at work and I was the only one who could see it.

We reached the gates of Liera, where the Svell village leaders and a band of thirty warriors waited. A wordless exchange passed between Vigdis and Siv and I watched her fist tighten around her belt. As long as Bekan stayed chieftain of the Svell, he would value peace over war. And I wondered if Vigdis and the others could live the rest of their mortal lives without spilling more enemy blood.

The half moon rose up in the sky as we rode into the

forest and it cast a pale light on the earth that made me uneasy. It had been Jorrund's job to keep the divide between the Svell leaders contained in the last years and he was growing weary of it, convinced the tide was turning more forcefully than Bekan could control. But Bekan was more confident in his brother. He put his faith in all the wrong things.

"The runes were clear," Vigdis said, slowing until his horse fell into step on the other side of Jorrund.

Jorrund's gaze drifted to me, but I looked ahead as if I couldn't hear them. Staying below Vigdis' notice was the only way to keep my neck from his blade.

"Perhaps you changed the fate of our people when you took Ljós. This is your chance to right it." Jorrund waited for Vigdis to speak, but he didn't. "The Nādhir will find their end when Eydis wills it. Not a moment before."

Vigdis didn't argue, but anger still etched the dark circles beneath his eyes. He glanced over his shoulder to the man riding behind us. "Don't take your eyes off her until we're back through those gates, Gunther."

I froze, my hands twisting into the reins as I looked back over my shoulder to find him. Gunther rode on his horse behind us, his gaze cast over me, to Vigdis. He didn't argue with the order, but I could see in the way his jaw clenched that he didn't want the responsibility of watching me. No one would. There was more gray streaked through his hair since the last time I'd seen him, but in most ways, he looked the same as he had the day I first met him in the meadow as a girl. He'd never liked me then, either, but I knew that he wouldn't hurt me unless he had to. And that was more than I could say for any other Svell.

Jorrund looked between Vigdis and Gunther nervously. Vigdis didn't know about the deal he'd made with Gunther all those years ago and Jorrund didn't want him to. In fact, no one knew about those days in the meadow. Not even Bekan.

Gunther stopped his horse beside mine, holding his hand out before me, and his eyes went to the bow slung over my shoulder. I looked around me, to the armed Svell riding into the trees. I wasn't trained to fight like the rest of them. My bow was the only way I could protect myself. When I didn't move, he kicked at his horse, moving closer.

Jorrund jerked his chin up, ordering me to obey and I gritted my teeth as I unbuckled the quiver and tossed it to Gunther. He fastened it to his horse's riggings and let the small bow drop over his head.

Of course Vigdis would have me watched. He'd never trusted me, but it was the night his niece Vera died that I first realized that he wanted me dead. He'd wept over her still body, broken in a way that I'd never seen him, and when his eyes found me in the shadows, he'd made me a promise.

I'll kill you for this.

The same look was painted on his face now. He spat onto the ground between us, kicking his heel into the horse and moving ahead to catch up to Siv.

Gunther fell back behind me as we started again and I

glared at him, pulling the bear fur tighter around my shoulders. The wind picked up, winding through the trees as the village grew small behind us, and without the familiar weight of my quiver at my back, I shivered against it. I'd never been away from Liera and the feeling of leaving the forests I knew made my breath hitch. It curled around itself inside my chest and a feeling like eyes watching me from the dark crept up my spine.

Jorrund stared ahead, his face unreadable. "Why was there no other stone overturned in the cast?"

"I don't know." I gave him the only answer I had. In all the years I'd cast the stones for him, I'd never seen them fall the way they had that night. The future was always changing and shifting. The Spinners were always spinning. But *Hagalaz* had found the center, its parallel lines perfectly vertical. And every other stone had been turned down, erased from the web of fate.

He sighed. "Tomorrow, we will fix this."

But it sounded like a question on his lilting voice. For maybe the first time, Jorrund wasn't sure. He was more uncertain than I'd ever seen him and that's why he'd brought me. To see the things he couldn't see—fate, omens, and signs that were invisible to him.

He leaned forward, taking the clay bottle from the side of his saddle and uncorking it before he handed it to me. "It's a long ride and it will be a cold night. Drink. It will warm you."

I brought the bottle to my lips and breathed in the sweet

smell of the mead. It reminded me of being a small girl, perched in the rafters of the ritual house while Jorrund and Bekan talked below beside the altar fire. Even then, their conversations had been about the future and the generations that would follow after they'd long been in *Djúpr,* where the Svell went after death.

"The Nādhir changed more than their own fates when they ended their blood feud. Perhaps we should have listened to Vigdis long ago, when he first suggested we invade their lands. They were weak then. And for the first time, we were strong."

I still remembered the first time I heard the word Nādhir. Two clans, one people, who had buried the blood feud that had defined them for generations. It was something no one thought possible.

I took a long drink, thinking. Jorrund had never outright disagreed with Bekan. He'd only ever supported him. But I wondered how strong the bond of loyalty between them was. And I wondered what Jorrund would do if Bekan found a blade at his throat and his brother sitting in his seat before the altar fire. Jorrund believed in Bekan, but the hearts of mortals were dark. Darker than they wanted to believe.

I still remembered the night the news came about the Herja. They were called a demon army because the stories about them couldn't be true—that they had come up from the depths of the sea to attack Sigr's fjord and Thora's mountain. The people called it the work of some vengeful god, but it sounded more like the work of the Spinners to me. I only wondered what the clans had done to deserve such a fate.

The Svell had gathered when the messenger arrived, filling the ritual house until people were spilling out the door and into the village. That was the first time I'd ever seen the brothers argue and the last time I'd seen Jorrund sleep soundly. Since then, the Svell had been torn, pulled in two directions.

War and peace.

And for the first time, I couldn't tell which side Jorrund was on.

The cold sharpened, making my fingers numb on the reins, and I searched the sky again for the All Seer. But he wasn't there. Maybe there was a chance the future could change.

By the time the first breath of sunlight was painting the sky, the horse's hooves were crunching on the forest floor. It was at least three weeks after what should have been the end of winter. I watched the sparkle on the leaves and pine needles in the patches of dim light, a knot twisting in my stomach. When Jorrund looked over his shoulder from where he rode ahead, I could see that he was thinking the same thing—a late frost.

If he was waiting for an ill omen, we'd found it.

7 YEARS AGO

Village of Hylli, Nādhir Territory

"ALMOST THERE." FISKE WADED INTO THE SHALLOWS AHEAD, breaking up the thinning ice with the blade of his axe.

Morning was just beginning to warm the sky as Halvard followed his older brother away from the shore, holding his breath against the bite of the cold water. He lifted the barbed spear over his head, keeping his balance against the current. Winter had left the fjord, but it would be weeks before the days began to stretch and the sun finished melting the ice. Until then, they'd fish in the bitter waters.

"Here." Fiske stopped, sliding the axe back into the sheath at his back and turning to face him.

The water rose to Halvard's chest as he found even footing beneath him. "You promised," he muttered.

"After."

Halvard glared at him. "When you were my age, you started your day training. Not fishing."

"When I was your age, I watched my friends die in the fighting season." His voice turned sharp, his eyes narrowing, and Halvard relented. The only thing worse than standing chest-deep in the icy fjord was invoking the disapproval of his brother.

He took the spear before him, watching the shadows beneath the water. The clouds were thick enough to keep the glare from the surface, but he'd never been good at spearing fish. "My throw is bearing right."

"I know. And we'll work on it. After," Fiske said again.

Halvard clenched his teeth, his hands tightening on the spear as he brought it before him. When his father died, Fiske had become the leader of their family and responsible for raising him. But with ten years between them, Fiske had a different kind of life planned for Halvard than the one he'd had as a boy.

He stilled, following the movement of the fish until he saw the flashing gleam of silver scales below. The weight of his feet sank into the silt and the wind calmed as he raised the rod higher.

"It will be different for you." Fiske spoke quietly, watching him.

"I know." Halvard brought the spear down with a snap, pinning the fish to the sand. They were the words he'd heard his brother say over and over since the day they came to live on the fjord.

Fiske met his eyes as he brought the spear's end up out of the water. "I brought you here to have a different life."

The fish flicked as he pulled it from the two iron prongs and tossed it onto the ice beside him.

"But I have to know how to fight."

"You do. I've been teaching you since before you could stand on your own feet."

"Not like you. Not like Iri." Halvard lifted the spear again, his attention going back to the water. The sooner they had four or five fish to take home, the sooner his brother would spar with him.

He still remembered watching Fiske and his father work at their armor and weapons beside the fire in the days before they left for Aurvanger, where they fought against the enemies of their god in the fighting season. He had watched them disappear into the forest, wondering if they would ever return. And he'd wanted to go with them, but even then, before the clans made peace, Fiske's plans for Halvard had always been for him to take over his mother's duties as the healer in their village. He'd never wanted to see him step foot into battle.

"You'll get your chance," Fiske finally said, as Halvard brought another fish up out of the water.

"You think the Svell will come?"

He'd heard the people in Hylli talking about the clan to the west. Some thought they'd be on the fjord by the next winter. Others thought that peace was possible. Fiske and his other brother Iri had never said what they thought the future held.

Fiske set the fish onto the ice beside the other one. "I

think if it's not the Svell, it will be someone else. Peace is never long-lived."

Halvard lifted the spear again. "Then why are we fishing?"

A small smile pulled at the corner of Fiske's mouth, but he was missing the wry look in his eye that was always there when he baited him. "Because I want to believe I'm wrong."

Village of Liera, Svell Territory

Tova watched the cloud passing overhead, its shape wavering in her vision as her eyes filled with tears. Jorrund stood over her, squinting as he stitched the broken skin around her swollen lip.

He'd taken her to the healer, but she had refused to stitch Tova up, afraid that Eydis would bring a plague on the village.

Her blood shone on the needle as Jorrund pulled the thread in one long motion and tied it off. When a tear finally rolled down her cheek, he gave her another drink of the sour ale. She swallowed it down until the burn in her throat reached her chest. The sting of her lip was nothing compared to the bruises that were blooming over her back.

If the nighthawk had tried to warn her, she hadn't heard him. She'd only opened her eyes to the sound of boots hitting the stone floor and before she'd even been able to think, she was being dragged through the forest screaming.

It wasn't the first time someone from the village had tried to take her fate into their own hands. In the five years since Jorrund had brought her through the gates of Liera, she'd heard the whispers. She'd felt the stares pinned to her back. But no one had ever come so close to killing her.

She was a living curse. A betrayal to the Svell god. And even though she lived under the unspoken protection of Bekan and Jorrund, the disagreements over the clans to the east had fractured the people's resolve to trust their Tala and chieftain. In the eyes of the Svell, she wasn't just an eleven-year-old girl. She was a scourge. And there were many who wanted to see her dead.

The angry waves crashed onto the rocks behind her and she watched the water slide up onto the land, covering her bare feet. Jorrund opened his satchel and pulled a small bottle from inside. He dabbed the stinging oil onto her mouth and the cut across her forehead as he spoke. "Not everyone can see the will of the gods, Tova."

He'd told her that before. But it wouldn't be the last time a Svell from the village would come to her little house in the forest and try to take her life. The laws that protected the Svell from each other didn't apply to her. There would be no consequences for killing a Kyrr girl.

Footsteps hit the sand behind her and she turned to see a man standing against the trees. The worn fur draped over his shoulders wrapped around him like a cloak, the old Svell leathers hidden beneath it.

Tova stood, stepping deeper into the water. If she'd ever

seen the man, she didn't remember. He towered over her, hiding her in his shadow as he stopped in the sand before them.

"Tova, this is Gunther."

She waited for him to speak, but he only looked at her. His worn face was unreadable, his sharp eyes on Jorrund. "You ever tell anyone about this and—"

But Jorrund lifted a hand, cutting him off before he pulled the length of his robes into his arms and started back toward the trees. Tova watched him with wide eyes, looking from the man back to Jorrund as she realized that he was going to leave them.

She reached for the small knife at the back of her belt and pulled it free. The handle was slick in her sweaty palm as she stepped back, feeling the pull of the cold water against her legs. The waves soaked the wool of her dress as Gunther looked down at her, his eyes running over her small frame.

"You won't need that. A bow would be best," he said, taking it from where it hung across his back and unbuckling the strap of the quiver. It dropped to the sand beside his feet as he took a step toward her. "If anyone gets close enough for you to use a knife, you're dead already."

Tova stared at the bow in his hands, confused.

Gunther leaned forward, taking hold of her wrist and jerking her forward, out of the shallows. He squeezed hard until her fingers opened and the knife dropped to the water, the blade sinking into the wet sand.

"We'll start with the bow," he said again. "Then the knife."

He plucked an arrow from the quiver and held it out to her. She looked around them before she took it, running her thumb over the edge of the black speckled feather that made the fletching. "Why are you helping me?"

The wind blew the hair across his face as he looked down at the marks on her bare arms. He was old enough to be her father, but she couldn't find anything tender or warm in the way that he studied at her.

He turned into the wind, not waiting for her to follow. "First the bow. Then the knife."

CHAPTER SIX

HALVARD

WE GATHERED THE BODIES.

The broken skeletons of homes in Ljós jutted up from the blackened earth and dead Nādhir covered the ground like birds fallen from the sky. Most of them weren't even wearing their armor or their boots, cut down as they tried to flee in the dark. They'd been sleeping when the Svell came out of the forest and set fire to their homes. They'd never had a chance.

The sight was familiar, even if it had been ten years since the Herja came. They'd drifted into our village as the moon rose when I was only eight years old. It was the first time I killed a man and the first time I'd thought I was going to die. The bodies of people I'd known my whole life had been strewn through the village, bright red blood staining the crisp, white snow, and I'd never forgotten it. I never would.

I blinked the memory away and took hold of the wrists

of a man my age who lay at my feet. I dragged him down the path, his open gray eyes looking up at me, and lifted him onto the pyre we'd built outside the village gate. I straightened what was left of his burned tunic, crossing his arms over his chest.

The smoke of the fire lifted like a cloud into the sky and we stood before it in silence, watching it burn as Espen led the funeral rites. His deep voice carried over the sound of the wind and we spoke them in unison, the eyes of every warrior on the flames.

"Take my love to my father. Ask him to keep watch for me." I whispered the last words, "Tell him my soul follows behind you."

I wondered what my father would say if he could see what had become of us, those who were once enemies, mourning each other's dead. My mother said that he would be proud, but I didn't remember enough about him to know if it was true. I was six years old when he died of fever and even when I tried to pull the image of his face from where it was buried in my mind, he was only a shadow.

Footsteps in the gravel sounded behind us and we turned to see one of our men at the tree line. "They're here!"

Espen and Aghi met eyes before they gave the order and everyone moved, drawing their weapons and lining up before us. I pulled my axe from its sheath with my left hand and my sword with my right, letting their comforting weight fall at my sides.

"They're waiting in the glade ahead." He ran to us, shouting between heavy breaths.

Espen clapped him on the back as he passed and he took his place at the end of the line.

Aghi reached up, tightening the strap of my armor vest beneath my arm. He set his hands on my shoulders and turned me, checking the other side. "Stay at the back. Use the sword before the axe."

"I know," I answered lowly.

He reached up, taking the back of my neck with his rough hand and meeting my eyes. "Ready?"

I searched his face, a knot tightening in my throat. At the back, I wouldn't be able to fight beside him if he needed me. And he wouldn't be able to run. If a fight broke out, he was the most vulnerable of us. "Ready."

"Good boy." He let out a long breath, smiling.

He took his place beside Espen, and I went to the back as he gave the signal. We moved toward the trees shoulder to shoulder, taking measured steps and keeping the line tight. When we passed into the forest, the quiet swallowed us, the cool air like water against my hot skin.

I looked to my right, half-expecting to see my brothers there. Fiske's dark head of hair pulled into an unraveling knot and Iri's blond beard braided down his chest. Mýra had been right. They'd be angry when they found out that I'd come to Ljós without them. So would Fiske's wife, Eelyn. And now, Mýra's words echoed in my mind, making me wonder if this was a mistake. Maybe it had been foolish to meet with the Svell. Maybe it had been a desperate, weak move.

The glade appeared ahead, bathed in warm sunlight and the stretch of tall golden grass was aglow with it. It wasn't until we reached the tree line that I saw them.

Two lines of twenty-five or more Svell were on the other side, their elk-hide leathers making them almost invisible in the trees. A single hand lifted into the air and a man with long flaxen braids stepped forward, out from under the branches. Espen lifted his hand in response and we moved together toward the center of the glade. The wind blew through the grass and it rippled around us like the calm waves of the fjord when we stood in the shallow waters, fishing with spears.

Espen and Aghi stepped forward as we stopped and the blond man across the glade did the same. From the look of his armor and the brooches around his neck, he had to be Bekan, the Svell chieftain. A black-bearded man walked at his side and they parted the grass in a straight line as my heart kicked up, my pulse pounding at my throat.

Aghi's fingers twitched at his side, resisting the urge to lift his sword at the ready, and I counted the number of steps it would take for me to get to him if I had to. A bead of sweat trailed down from my brow, stinging my eyes.

"Espen." Bekan spoke, coming to a stop before them.

But it was a face in the distance that pulled my gaze, a raven-haired figure standing behind the two rows of their warriors. A cloaked girl stood beside their Tala, her eyes fixed on me. The telltale black marks of the Kyrr crept up and out of the neck of her tunic, where an unfolded wing spread across her throat.

The only Kyrr I'd ever seen in my life was Kjeld, Asmund's man, but I knew the stories told over night fires well. They were a people of mysticism and ritual, their marks holding the secrets and stories of their ancestors. They lived in the fog of the headlands, the borders of their territories drawn with stone statues of their god Naðr and the sun-bleached skulls and tusks of boars.

But what was a Kyrr girl doing with the Svell?

Her head tilted as her eyes narrowed at me and a sting ignited on my skin like the burn of the funeral fire. I shifted on my feet, watching her, and her brow pulled as her hand lifted, her palm pressing to her ear.

"Three days ago, a group of my people attacked Ljós. This act was taken without my consent and in direct defiance of my orders."

My eyes went back to the men in the center of the glade.

Espen stood like a statue, his gaze unwavering. "More than forty Nādhir are dead."

A long silence widened around us, and the race of my heart reignited, watching their warriors carefully.

"This is my brother Vigdis, the village leader of Hǫlkn." Bekan looked to the dark-haired man beside him who stood so rigid that he could have been carved out of stone. "We hope you will accept this offering of reparation."

Vigdis reached over his shoulder and took hold of the sword at his back. He slowly pulled it free and the sunlight caught the amber stones forged into the metal as he held it out before him.

It was a valuable weapon. Maybe the most valuable I'd ever see, with a steel blade and jeweled hilt. But offerings of reparation weren't meant to pay the value of an offense. There weren't enough precious stones on the mainland to cover the cost of forty lives. It was a symbol. And its power was entirely dependent on the honor of the one who offered it.

"Neither of us want war." Bekan stood still, waiting for Espen's answer. "Accept the offering and we both go home without another life lost."

My attention went back to the girl. She stood motionless, staring at the men in the center of the glade until a piercing call echoed overhead and her gaze snapped up to the sky, where a hawk was circling. Its wings tipped against the wind as it turned and when I looked back at her, her eyes went wide. She took a faltering step forward, her mouth opening to speak before the Tala caught her by the arm, holding her in place.

I searched the glade for what she saw, but there were only the warriors standing side by side. She was staring at Bekan.

And just as the hawk called out again, Vigdis turned to his chieftain, breaking the silence. "I love you, brother. And one day, you will understand why I've done what I've done."

He suddenly reared back with the sword, launching it forward with a snap, and it sank into Espen's stomach.

The tip of its blood-soaked blade reached out behind him where it had run him through.

My breath caught in my chest as Espen fell forward onto his knees and the wind stopped, every sound snuffed out around us. My hand drew my sword before I'd even realized what I was doing, and the sound of shouting raced through the glade. But Bekan was frozen, his hands out before him and his eyes wide with confusion. He looked from his brother to Espen and back again.

The line of Svell broke into a run, charging us, and every weapon left every sheath, blades sliding on leather in unison. Aghi called out the order and he met my eyes for only a moment before he took off in a limping run, headed straight for Vigdis, who stood over Espen's bleeding body.

I took off after him with my boots slamming into the earth as chaos broke out between the trees. Bodies slammed into each other as the two sides collided and I kept my eyes on Aghi, raising my sword as a Svell headed in his direction. I ran faster, passing the Svell and spinning on my heel as I twisted my sword in an arc around me to catch him in the gut. He tumbled into the grass and I lifted the blade before me, thick blood dripping onto the golden grass.

Aghi threw his axe behind me and it spun out ahead of us before it sank into the chest of a Svell woman, knocking her off her feet. He hobbled to her as the roar of battle swelled, his attention still set on Vigdis, who was cutting the throat of a Nādhir on his knees.

Aghi snapped his arm back, his sword slicing into the arm of a man behind him before he raised it up over his head to bring it back down into his chest. I jumped over the body as we pushed forward, staying close to Aghi's back.

Bekan pulled his sword from the side of a Nādhir and I took the knife from my belt, sliding to a stop as I aimed. I sank my arm back, the handle light in my fingers, and sent it forward, the blade flying. Bekan faltered as it caught him in the shoulder, one knee hitting the ground before he got back to his feet and ran straight for us. His sword rose behind him, launching toward me before Aghi plowed into his side, knocking the blade from his hand. He lifted his axe, but in the length of a breath, Bekan tore my knife from his shoulder and drove it forward with both hands.

Aghi doubled over and it wasn't until he hit the ground that I saw it. The handle of my knife was lodged between his ribs. I swallowed a breath as bright, sputtering blood poured from his lips and when I opened my mouth, I couldn't hear the sound of my own scream. I could only feel its burn in my throat, lighting my chest on fire as I ran to him.

I fell to the grass, catching him in my arms before he tilted forward, and his bright blue eyes looked up at me, his mouth moving around words I couldn't understand.

"Aghi." His name was strange on my broken voice and I tried to hold him up, but he was too heavy.

He sank to the ground as more blood dripped from his lips and his hands clutched onto my tunic. He pulled me down toward him, but he couldn't speak. The light was already leaving his eyes.

"Don't . . ." I whispered. But his gaze was unfocused, lifting to the sky above us.

He was already gone.

My mind tried to grab hold of it, frantically sifting through the raging flood of thoughts, but I couldn't think. I couldn't pull myself from the grass, my hands clutched so tightly to his armor that the bones in my fingers felt as if they might crack. It wasn't until the glint of a blade shone ahead that I blinked, coming back into myself.

I looked up, focusing my vision past the hot tears in my eyes, and Bekan ran before me, taking a Nādhir down with one arm, the other still bleeding badly at his side. I stood, yanking my knife from the bones in Aghi's chest and paced heavily toward the trees, headed straight for him. He didn't see me until I was already gaining on him. His axe flew at me and I sank onto my heels, letting it fly over my head before I jumped back up and bolted forward, the knife clutched tightly in my hand, slick with Aghi's blood.

I roared, the battle cry tearing from my throat as I reached him, flipping the knife in my fingers to come at him from the side. I cut into his other arm, dragging the blade down, and he fell back into the shade of the trees. Another cry broke behind my ribs as I came over him, clutching the handle with both fists as I raised it before me. I screamed as I brought it down with the weight of my whole body, plunging the blade into Bekan's heart.

His head rolled back and he gasped, coughing on the blood coming up in his throat, and I suddenly felt too heavy, the earth pulling me toward it as a whistle rang out. I looked back to the glade, where the Svell were cutting down the last of the Nādhir standing. At the very center, Espen lay in a bed of red-painted grass.

I turned in a circle, the world spinning around me. Espen was dead. Aghi . . . I tried to breathe past the strangling vision of his face going slack as he died in my arms. The breath wheezed in my lungs as more Svell came from the trees across the glade and what had just happened sank into place.

The Svell chieftain's brother had come to Ljós with a plan. We were never going to leave this glade alive.

My side hitched and I tilted, wincing against the tilt of the world around me, willing the earth beneath my feet to steady me. I clutched at my side, where a steady stream of hot blood was seeping from a cut in my armor vest I didn't remember getting. My hand slid over the wet leathers as I pressed, trying to slow it. But a guttural roar made me look up to the glade, where Vigdis was staring at me, eyes wide, as I stood over the body of his brother.

CHAPTER SEVEN

TOVA

THE MORNING FROST COVERED THE GROUND AROUND US AS we moved through the trees. It glittered in the early light, turning everything to crystal. The days had been warm and damp with the spring storms coming in from the sea, but the cold had crept in during the night.

It was a warning, just like the nighthawk.

The Svell checked their armor and weapons in silence as we lined up before the glade, where Bekan stood before the sunlit grass. I studied the serene look on Vigdis' face as he took his place beside his brother.

He and Jorrund had spent the morning speaking in hushed whispers, their breaths fogging between them as they rode side by side ahead of me. The chill crept up my spine as I watched Jorrund from the corner of my eye. There was something buried deep beneath the calm on his face.

Some unsteady, wavering thing in his eyes that I could just barely see.

Gunther took his place in front of us, leaving me for the first time since Vigdis ordered him to watch me. He'd been careful to not so much as look at me as we rode through the night, keeping his distance. The truth was that even though Vigdis had meant his presence to be a looming threat, having Gunther at my back made me feel safer. And now, as we stepped into the glade and Jorrund's smooth exterior seemed to be crumbling, I found myself taking a small step closer to where Gunther stood.

"Stay beside me." Jorrund spoke lowly in my ear.

The Svell stood like statues, their eyes watching the tree line across the glade. Jorrund's gaze was fixed on the brothers, his arms crossed over his chest and his fingers tapping his elbows nervously. He was worried. Scared, even. The weight of the rune cast had settled down on every aged bone and sore muscle in his body and it all came down to this moment.

The warriors shifted on their feet and I looked up just as movement in the shadow of the trees ahead appeared. Bekan lifted one hand into the air, mumbling something to Vigdis, whose jaw clenched as the Nādhir appeared across the stretch of dead winter grass, still half-hidden in the trees.

Bekan reached for the clasp on his chest and unbuckled it, taking the sword sheath over his shoulder and holding it out to Vigdis, but his brother only stared at him.

"You started this. Now, you're going to finish it." Bekan

looked him in the eye, his face streaked with the blood of a raven Jorrund had sacrificed to Eydis at sunrise.

Vigdis gritted his teeth, insulted. It was an order that took Bekan's rebuke even further. One that he made before the other leaders and one that Vigdis' dignity wouldn't recover from easily. It was a foolish move for the chieftain, stoking the flame of his brother's anger when he needed him most.

After a moment, Vigdis took the sword, fitting the sheath to his own back. It was Siv who didn't take her eyes from him, her lip curled over her teeth, but Vigdis didn't meet her gaze. He stared ahead to the opening in the trees, and a strange feeling pulled in the back of my mind. There were too many unspoken words between them—Bekan, Jorrund, Vigdis, and Siv. They were like steam trapped in a kettle, the lid rattling.

Bekan looked back to Jorrund before he gave the signal and we walked forward, leaving the cool of the forest and stepping into the warmth of the glade. I let my hand hover beside me, the tops of the grass pulling through my fingertips, and watched around us for any sign of the Spinners. But the clearing was quiet. And maybe that was the omen I'd missed. It was *too* quiet.

The Nādhir stopped in the center of the clearing and we walked until we'd met them, the line of Svell keeping back as Bekan and Vigdis moved ahead. They stopped before the Nādhir chieftain and a man with a braided beard the color of an autumn sunset. He let his weight sink into one leg, the other obviously weak, but he stood up tall, his chin lifted.

The two clans that made up the Nādhir were mixed together, their armor and weapons blending almost seamlessly in the line of warriors. My gaze drifted over them until it stopped on the face of a young man clad in red leathers. His dark hair was pulled into a braid over his shoulder, the stray pieces tucked behind his ears. His pale eyes were on the red-bearded man, his angled jaw tight.

But there was something strange about him. Something . . .

Bekan began to speak but a deep hum sounded in the glade, growing like a hive of bees. No one seemed to notice, their attention on the men before us, and I tilted my head, trying to listen. It reverberated like the crash of a waterfall, growing with each breath until it filled the inside of my skull.

My attention went back to the young Nādhir and as if he could feel my stare, he suddenly turned, his eyes meeting mine. A sharp prick rolled over my skin, my hands clenching into my linen skirt.

Because he didn't look away.

His stare bored into mine, making me feel suddenly unbalanced on my feet.

"What is it?" Jorrund whispered beside me, but I could barely hear him over the sound in my head.

A hissing, like water over coals. And it was getting louder. "Do you hear that?" I pressed my palm to my ear and the Nādhir's brow furrowed, his eyes falling from my face to the marks on my neck.

Jorrund's hand clamped down on my arm as Vigdis unsheathed the jeweled sword, and I pulled my gaze from the Nādhir when Bekan began to speak. But something about the look of Vigdis was wrong. The coil around his bones that had been there since Bekan reprimanded him in Liera was no longer there. He stood tall, his shoulders drawn down and his face smooth. Like the still calm that settled before death.

I tried to hear their words, watching Bekan's lips move, but the hum in the glade was now a guttural roar, drowning out everything else. When a shadow moved over the grass at my feet, I looked up to the sky, where the nighthawk was soaring over us against the glare of the sun. Its spotted feathers gleamed across its wingspan as it tilted, coming back in a circle above us.

I blinked, a sharp breath catching in my throat.

The buzzing stopped.

"The All Seer," I whispered, stepping forward.

This was wrong. Something was wrong.

"What?" Jorrund's hand found my wrist, pulling me back.

But it was too late. Sunlight gleamed on the blade of the sword in Vigdis' hands and I looked to Bekan just as Vigdis spoke words I couldn't hear. In the next breath, he was pulling the sword back behind him and driving it forward with a quick step, catching Espen's gut.

My mouth dropped open, my eyes going wide, but Jorrund was already pulling me away, walking with quick steps back toward the trees and towing me behind him.

"Wait," I cried, pulling against him as the Nādhir chieftain fell to his knees. "Wait!"

I freed my hand, pushing back into the tall grass, but Jorrund wrapped his arms around me. "Tova!"

Every blade lifted in the clearing and the full-throated screams of the clansmen ripped open the silence around us as we made it to the cover of the forest. I wrenched free of Jorrund's grasp again, turning on him. "You didn't," I whispered, searching his eyes. "Please say you didn't . . ."

But the traitorous answer was there on his face. He'd betrayed Bekan. He'd sided with Vigdis against the chieftain and sanctioned his betrayal. "You have to trust me."

"How can I?" I shouted. "Bekan trusted you and look what you've done!"

"You saw it!" His voice rose. "Destruction is coming for the Svell. We have to act. *Now.*"

I looked back to the clearing, where battle was spreading across the grass, painting everything red. Swords and axes swung and warriors fell, Vigdis driving the charge to the far side of the glade. I pressed my fingers to my lips, watching as the the fallen Nādhir chieftain stopped moving. He lay facedown, the tip of the jeweled sword reaching up to the sky from his back.

And then without even realizing it, my gaze moved away from him, looking for the young Nādhir with the pale eyes. The one who'd met my gaze. I searched the running bodies for the red leathers, but there were too many and they were moving too fast. My chest tightened around my breath as I realized he'd probably already been killed. But just as I thought it, he appeared, standing up out of the tall grass and setting his eyes on Bekan. He walked with heavy steps, blood smeared across his throat, a knife clutched in his hand.

Bekan threw his axe but missed, and the Nādhir broke into a run, launching himself forward to tear across the grass toward the trees.

The shadow of the nighthawk slid over us again.

"This is wrong," I whispered.

Bekan made it to the forest but the Nādhir was too fast. I knew what was going to happen the moment he stepped into the shade of the trees. It was too late. The Nādhir drove his knife into Bekan's arm and when he toppled backward, I closed my eyes, flinching when I heard the hollow pop of the knife plunging into Bekan's chest.

Jorrund gasped beside me, his hand flying to his open mouth.

The Svell chieftain was dead.

And when I opened my eyes, looking up to the clear blue sky, where the thin spread of clouds was pulling in delicate lines, the All Seer was suddenly gone.

Vigdis screamed in the distance, his face broken in two as his eyes found his brother. And then they were running. All of them.

And it reignited—the sound. It rose around us, filling the forest until I could feel the pulse of it under my skin.

The young Nādhir stood, his hands hanging heavily at his sides, his chest rising and falling beneath his armor vest. He took a step, hitching to one side, and when he looked down, he stilled. Blood seeped from a tear in his vest where a blade must have cut him.

He was the only Nādhir left standing and I watched the realization sink into his face, his chest heaving with breath as every Svell in the glade ran toward him. The swarm of bees in my head screamed, ringing in my ears. I pinched my eyes closed against it and when I opened them again, arrows were flying. But not from the glade. From the forest.

They dropped the Svell one by one and three riders appeared in the trees, their mouths open as they shouted at the Nādhir. He ran toward them, his hand pressed to his side, and more arrows whistled through the air as they shot them one after the other, finding their marks in the distance.

My heart stopped as my eyes landed on a set of pale hands clenched around a bow in the trees. Hands covered in black marks. I blinked, stepping forward out of a beam of bright sunlight, but this was no vision. A man covered in the marks of the Kyrr was crouched low over his horse, pulling another arrow from his back as the Nādhir ran.

I opened my mouth to call out, but no sound came. The beats of my heart tangled up, skipping so fast that my vision began to blur. The Kyrr man dropped the bow over his head as the Nādhir pulled himself up onto one of the horses and I held onto the tree beside me as they took off, disappearing into the forest.

And when I finally turned back searching for Jorrund, he stood frozen in the trees, his horrified gaze still fixed on the bloodied body of the Svell chieftain.

Lying dead at his feet.

CHAPTER EIGHT

HALVARD

EVERY SVELL LEFT STANDING RAN TOWARD ME, SWORDS AND axes swinging.

The emptiness of the forest behind me stretched in every direction. There was no way to outrun them. No way to hide. Their chieftain lay on the soft earth before me and the only answer for that was death.

But as I watched them rush toward me, I realized that it was an end I'd welcome. It was an end that the gods would favor and that Aghi would be proud of. At the very least, I'd been able to avenge him before I took my last breath. And that was something.

I stood taller despite the pain widening at my side and pulled the axe from the sheath at my back. The breath in my chest calmed, lifting in white puffs before me, the scent of soil and sap thick in my lungs.

Mýra's words came back to haunt me, the sight of her

looking up into my face finding me as clearly as if she stood before me now. She'd been right. So had Latham. And when my family made it back to the fjord from the mountain, they wouldn't find me. Like Aghi, I'd be waiting for them in the afterlife.

Just as the thought skipped across my mind, a whistle rang deep in the forest and I blinked, going still.

Vigdis and the Svell closed in on the stretch of ground between us, screaming, but arrows suddenly fell from the sky, arcing over my head and hitting their marks before me. Svell warriors hit the ground hard, sliding over the forest floor, and I turned, searching the trees.

I knew the call that echoed out, though I hadn't heard it since I was a boy. It was an old Aska battle signal. But every Nādhir who'd come with us from Hylli was lying dead in the glade behind me.

Horses appeared in the thick brush, three riders hunched over their saddles with bows lifted and arrows drawn. That's when I saw him. Asmund.

I pivoted on my feet and ran for him, the agony alive at my side piercing deeper with every draw of breath. Asmund and the raiders tore through the forest ahead, their horses kicking mud and moss behind them, and I pressed the heel of my hand into the opening of my vest, growling against the sting, running faster.

I didn't look back, weaving through the trees and pushing the swell of pain from my mind. I didn't have to look to know I was losing blood too quickly. I could feel it in the weakening of my muscles and the stuttering flicker of my thoughts. I focused on the black horse ahead, throwing myself forward with the last of the strength I had left.

An axe flew past my head from behind, slamming into a tree, and the splinters hit me in the face as I slid to a stop. Bard's horse slowed as it reached me and the bow rose before him, his back straight as he sighted down its line. He shot arrow after arrow over me as I hobbled past him, toward Asmund.

"Hurry!" He reached a hand down for me and I took his arm, pulling myself up onto the saddle behind him and throwing my leg over the horse.

In the trees ahead, the Svell chieftain's brother stood still, his fists clenched at his sides and his black eyes pinned on me as his chest rose and fell with heaving breaths.

We took off and I looked back once more to the sunlit grass where Aghi lay dead. My throat tightened and I hunched forward, the searing pain in my side pushing black into the edges of my vision. A branch caught the sleeve of my tunic, scraping against my skin as we headed into the thicker trees and the glade disappeared behind us, the Svell with it.

"How bad?" Asmund shouted over his shoulder.

"They're dead." The words boiled in my gut. "Everyone's dead."

He stiffened. "Espen?"

"Everyone."

He pulled back on the reins, slowing, and the others

rounded ahead to meet us, bows still in hand. Their faces held the same look that I imagined was on Asmund's.

Bard stopped before us. "Let me see." He pried my bloody hand from my side. "Sword?" I nodded in answer, wincing as he inspected the wound. "He's bleeding too fast."

Asmund shook his head, watching around us. "It'll have to wait. We have to go east."

"East? I have to get to Hylli," I grunted.

"You just killed their chieftain, Halvard." Asmund turned back to look at me. "By sundown this entire forest will be crawling with Svell looking for you."

"I have to—"

"We'll head east and then cut north," Bard interrupted, echoing Asmund's order.

He kicked his heel into the horse and we took off, the air turning colder as we pushed deeper into the forest. Our tracks still marked the path we'd taken to Ljós only the day before and I breathed through the burn in my eyes, remembering that moment on the trail with Aghi. A moment I would never get back.

We climbed the rise of the earth in a horizontal line until we reached the river and took the horses into the water, pushing against the current to hide our tracks. With any luck, the Svell would have lost our trail by the time they got to their horses. But luck hadn't been on our side in the glade, and I had no reason to think it would be now.

The sun was hanging above us in the sky when we finally came around the bend in the river where the raiders were camped. Bard stood on the bank ahead, Kjeld beside him, watching me as I slid down from the horse into the water. The blood from my wound clouded pink around me as I trudged up out of the cold river. But my legs gave out, my head spinning, and I fell to my knees on the sand.

"Get him up," Asmund ordered.

Kjeld and Bard took my arms, lifting me up and dragging me over the mud until we disappeared into the tall standing rocks that edged the water, where the other raiders were waiting. They stood with their arms crossed, watching silently as I worked at the clasps of my vest with numb hands, swallowing down the urge to vomit as I lifted it over my head. The gash in my side was still bleeding freely.

"What happened?" Bard looked down at me.

"Bekan's brother betrayed him." I swallowed, trying to steady my words as I got down next to the fire they'd put out that morning. The embers were still glowing beneath the thick white ash. "He killed Espen and they turned on us."

I hissed, opening the wound with my fingers and trying to see how deep the cut was, but I could barely see straight. I took my knife from my belt and raked back the cool coals, burying the blade into the ones that were still hot.

No one spoke, the reality of what had happened slowly sinking in. The Svell chieftain was dead. The Nādhir leaders murdered. If there had ever been a chance of outrunning a war, it was gone now. And from the looks on the faces of the other raiders around us, they were thinking the same.

"The Nādhir are already gathering on the fjord. They'll be ready to fight," I said between tight breaths.

"When?"

"Two days. Three. I don't know." I turned the knife over in the coals and watched the dried blood sizzle off the blade.

"We should leave the mainland," Kjeld said, looking to Asmund. "They're probably tracking us right now."

Bard's voice dropped low. "We can't leave."

"Why not? This is their war, not ours."

Bard glared at him, but he was right. As raiders, they'd left their obligations to their clans behind, but I'd known Bard and Asmund for more than half of my life. They couldn't stay in Hylli. Not after all that had happened. But they hadn't really ever left us.

"We should go. Now," Kjeld said again, turning his back to Bard. "West, deeper into the forests past Svell territory."

Asmund stared at the ground, thinking. "They won't just be looking for Halvard, Kjeld. They saw us, too."

"I can make it to Hylli on my own," I said, giving him a way out. I had no right to ask for their help. They'd come for me in the glade when they owed me nothing.

Bard straightened beside him. "And if you don't?"

"They'll be ready, with or without me."

"Espen's dead, Asmund." Bard squared his shoulders to his brother. "You know what that means. Halvard is chieftain of the Nādhir now."

I breathed through the pain winding tighter around me. He was saying aloud what I hadn't even had a chance to think. Latham, Freydis, and the other leaders would be waiting in Hylli, but Espen wasn't coming and I was the one chosen to take his place. I was the one who was supposed to lead them.

Kjeld stood back, watching us. He'd taken down the Svell and saved my life like the rest of them, but if anyone had reason to leave, it was him. He had no heritage or lost home or ancestors among the Nādhir. He was Kyrr. And he'd only found a place with the raiders because it was easier to be picked off when you were alone.

But I was the one Asmund looked to. He met my eyes over the fire pit, his lip between his teeth. "Utan."

It was the next Nādhir village pushing east toward the fjord, and I knew what he was thinking.

They were next.

"Get rid of the armor," he said, pulling the knife from his belt.

Kjeld sighed, shaking his head, but a smile spread over Bard's face. He picked up my vest from where it sat in the dirt and Asmund stepped toward me, taking the braid of hair over my shoulder. He cut it clean in one motion and dropped it beside me before he knelt down, taking my knife from the fire.

He held the glowing blade out between us.

"I won't forget this," I said, looking up to him.

He met my eyes, his voice even. "I won't let you."

I unbuckled my belt and folded it, biting down on the leather as I propped myself against the rough bark of the tree behind me. I took the knife from Asmund and marked the wound with the tips of my fingers, finding a place in the treetops to fix my eyes. I pulled a rasping breath deep into my chest before I pressed the hot blade into the wound.

I groaned, biting down hard as the skin seared and the smell of burned flesh filled the air. The sting heated the blood in my veins, the sky brightening overhead as a white light exploded in my vision and then flickered out, swallowing me in darkness.

Asmund was right.

There was no going back. Not from this.

CHAPTER NINE

TOVA

I STARED INTO THE TREES, TRYING TO CONJURE BACK WHAT I'd seen—black marks winding around wrists in the spread of a raven's wing as the man in the trees lifted his bow.

He was Kyrr. He had to be. But the Kyrr never left the headlands. I'd never seen another of my kind, not once in the years since Jorrund found me on the Svell's shore. Any pictures of them had been washed away by the storm that brought me across the fjord, only broken bits and pieces left in my memory. The sound of a woman's voice, the warm glow of firelight. The sting against my skin as someone worked at my marks with a bowl of wood ash ink and a bone needle.

I turned, looking for Jorrund, but he was watching the glade, his face pale and his mouth puckered like he was going to be sick. The sound of Vigdis' wailing echoed out around us in the silence. He sat at the edge of the trees with his brother's body in his arms, hunched over and weeping as the Svell warriors walked through the tall grass, collecting weapons and armor before dragging their own fallen clansmen into the trees to burn.

The Nādhir warriors lay in the sun, their still bodies beginning to rot. All except one.

I looked back to the trees where the young Nādhir had disappeared with the Kyrr man, his hand pressed to his side and his skin draining white. Maybe he'd be lying dead somewhere soon, too.

The blue sky where the nighthawk had appeared was now empty, not a single cloud hovering over the glade. The All Seer had seen what lay inside the heart of Vigdis and had come in warning. But the Svell didn't know the language of the future the way I did. They didn't understand that there was no such thing as a secret. The truth was everywhere. It was in everything. You only had to open your eyes to see it. The Spinners sat beneath the Tree of Urðr, watching. Listening. Weaving away at the web of fate.

Bekan's death was a punishment for Vigdis' treachery. It was a burden for him to carry for the rest of his days. Jorrund, too.

Beside me, he prayed under his breath, his eyes closed. But it didn't matter what words were spoken or what requests of their god they made. They could sacrifice a hundred oxen and fill the valley with blood. Still, they had been wrong. They'd betrayed their chieftain for their own hunger for war and there was a price to be paid for it.

The warriors looked on as Vigdis and another man carried Bekan's body into the forest with the others. The seat of chieftain now fell to him, which was perhaps what he'd always wanted. But passing the leadership of the Svell to Vigdis meant taking power away from Jorrund. And without power, there would be nothing the Tala could do to protect me. What little safety I had was now gone, and that thought terrified me.

Siv stood at Vigdis' side, waiting. She would become his second in command and the other village leaders would follow. They had to. War was coming and for the first time since the Nādhir made peace, the Svell would be forced to unify. But it would be on the battlefield.

When the Svell they'd sent out after the riders finally appeared in the trees across the clearing, the Nādhir wasn't with them. They'd lost whatever trail had been left behind and at the sight of them, Vigdis' furious stare searched the glade. "Where is she?" His voice roared and I flinched, stepping backward as his eyes found me. "Where's the Truthtongue?"

"Stay back," Jorrund whispered, stepping in front of me. "Don't say a word."

I had no choice but to listen. My hand instinctively reached up for my bow, but it wasn't there.

Vigdis stormed toward us across the grass, his hands covered in his brother's blood. His eyes set on me and the pulse beneath my skin raced, my heart coming up into my throat. "You!" he screamed, shoving Jorrund aside and snatching up my arm. He threw me back and I hit the ground hard before he came over me, taking a handful of my hair into his fist. Then I was moving, being dragged over the brittle grass. I screamed, holding onto his wrist as I skidded on the dirt behind him and the dust kicked up into the air, making me choke.

"Fire-steel! Torch!" he called out over his shoulder, and from the corner of my eye I could see Siv moving to follow the order.

"Vigdis!" Jorrund shouted behind us, but he wasn't listening.

He dropped me back on the ground and I curled into a ball, covering my head as more figures came to stand over me. A Svell man held an unlit torch before him and Vigdis struck the fire-steel. I blinked, the breath leaving my lungs as I realized what he was doing.

He was going to set me on fire.

I cried out, pulling my skirt up into my arms and running for the trees. But two hands caught hold of me, throwing me back down. "Don't!" I screamed as the fire swallowed the torch in a tangle of orange flames. "Please!"

Vigdis' fists coiled in my tunic and he pulled me to sit up, his reddened eyes leveling to mine. "You did this," he sputtered between heaving, ragged breaths. "First, Vera. Now, Bekan."

"Vigdis, please," Jorrund pleaded, his voice shaking in terror.

"Eydis has punished Bekan for not killing you when

Jorrund brought you through the gates of Liera!" He shook me. "I won't make the same mistake."

"We need to gather our warriors and meet with the village leaders." Jorrund tried to speak calmly, but his hands were trembling before him. He thought better of saying the words, but he was thinking the same thing I was. Vigdis had started the fight in the glade against Bekan's wishes. It was his own fault his brother was lying dead behind him.

"Not until I've pulled that Nādhir's lungs from his body." He glared at Jorrund, insulted.

"Their chieftain is dead and so is ours. We have to ready for war," Siv said, beside him. "This is what we wanted, Vigdis."

He dropped me, whirling on her. "*This* is not what I wanted!"

She stepped back, flinching.

Vigdis might have disagreed with Bekan, but it was apparent to anyone who knew him that he loved his brother. In his own foolishness, he hadn't accounted for losing him if he betrayed the Nādhir.

"Eydis will honor him. He will be welcomed to the afterlife," Jorrund said gently, but I could still hear the crack beneath his voice. He was scared. Not only for me—for him. He set a hand on Vigdis' shoulder but he shoved him off.

Mentioning their god would have brought Bekan pause. But Vigdis wasn't Bekan. He didn't fear Eydis the way Jorrund did because she wasn't his only god. Power and strength were what he wanted.

"Leading falls to you now, Vigdis," Jorrund tried again, appealing to his pride.

He was quiet for a moment, the heaving in his chest slowing as he stared at the ground. His hands unclenched, loosening from their tight fists. "I won't let the Nādhir go."

Jorrund nodded. "It's a debt that can be paid when we get to Hylli."

"It can't wait until then!"

"We have to move quickly. Our warriors will be here by sundown." Siv set a hand onto his arm. "By morning, we can move east. We can be in Hylli in two days and this will be over."

I looked between Vigdis and Siv, trying to think as quickly as I could. There was no escape. Nowhere to run. It was only a matter of time before Vigdis found a reason to kill me. I had to use the only power I had.

"I can find him," I said.

"What?" Jorrund's eyes widened.

"I can do it." I looked to Vigdis. He would take the first chance he got to cut my throat. I knew that. Unless he needed me. "I'll find the Nādhir." As soon as I said the words, I saw his face in my mind. Blue eyes beneath dark, unraveling hair. A gaze that didn't pull from mine. It sent the same sting racing across my skin that had been there in the glade.

"Tova, I don't think that's . . ." Jorrund stammered.

"How?" Vigdis growled.

"I know a way." It would buy me some time, but it wasn't without risk.

Vigdis' red face stared into the ground. "Alright."

"But—" Jorrund's hands lifted before him.

"You say she can see the future?" he snapped. "Then she can find the Nādhir and bring me his head. If she doesn't, I'll do what my brother was too weak to do."

Jorrund stared at him wordlessly.

"I better have his head in my hands before I get to Hylli." He turned, stalking away with Siv at his side, and I swallowed hard, my stomach turning over. The Nādhir wasn't the only blood feud Vigdis had. He blamed me for his niece Vera's death, and now his brother's. Before this was finished, my head would be in his hands, too.

Gunther stared at me, his hand on his sword and Jorrund turning to ice beside him. "What are you thinking?"

"I can find him," I said again. "You know I can find him."

"Vigdis will kill you anyway. We need you, Tova. We need you to cast—"

"The stones? You don't listen to the stones!" I flung a hand toward the blood-soaked glade, my voice rising. "You want to believe that you can carve fate into a river that leads where you want to go. It doesn't work that way, Jorrund!"

He recoiled, stepping back as if the words stung, but he didn't argue because he knew I was right. Since I was a child, he'd been trying to control everything. Bekan, me, the Spinners, the gods. It would take a lot more blood before he began to understand anything about fate.

"I know what this is about, Tova." He narrowed his eyes at me. "I saw the Kyrr man in the forest."

I stilled, swallowing hard. I didn't think he'd seen him. "This isn't about the Kyrr. It's about keeping Vigdis from killing me."

"That man was a raider."

"So?"

"So, he was probably cast out of the headlands. He won't have any more answers for you than I do."

I tried to read the look in his eyes. They betrayed more than he thought they did. He was afraid of more than just Vigdis. At times, he was afraid of *me*. And the truth was that it wasn't just the Kyrr man. It was the Nādhir. The one who'd met my gaze and didn't look away. The one that filled my head with the sound of a thousand waterfalls. The Spinners were saying something. They were speaking, and if I was going to hear it, I needed to find him.

"I'll find the Nādhir. I'll bring his head to Vigdis."

"And then?"

"And then we find a way to keep both of us alive."

CHAPTER TEN

HALVARD

THERE WERE ALREADY OVER A HUNDRED OF THEM.

We lay flat on our stomachs, watching the Svell army from the ridge high above the charred remains of Ljós. The village was no more than a blackened spot on the earth now, the trees that had once covered the roofs burned clean of their leaves. My brothers had described Hylli the same way after the Herja came, but it was a sight I never imagined I'd see.

Svell warriors young and old were clad in their leathers below, weapons strapped to their sides and their backs. They gathered around fires that snaked through the sparse trees of the eastern forest in a camp that was growing by the minute. In the distance, another trail of them was arriving from the west.

It was clear that Vigdis had planned the betrayal in Ljós. The warriors had already been called in from their villages before we ever met Bekan in the glade. It was the only explanation for how their entire army was gathering so quickly. And if they were gathering this many, they were going to push across the valley to the fjord. This wasn't about border territory or the divided leaders of the Svell. It never had been. Vigdis wanted to crush the Nādhir. And from the look of their army, he had everything he needed to do it.

I looked to Asmund and the same thoughts hung heavy on his face. Vigdis had never planned to make the offering of reparation. Just like Latham and Mýra said.

"How many more do you think are coming?" I whispered, staying close to the ground.

Asmund shook his head, his eyes running over their camp. "There are twelve Svell villages. From what we've seen of their lands, I'd say in the end they'll be at least over eight hundred strong."

There were eleven Nādhir villages, but most of them weren't as big as the Svell's. Espen had guessed we'd be able to muster only six hundred from both our territories. It wouldn't be enough.

"And there will be many more if the Kyrr are coming." I spoke beneath my breath.

"What?" Kjeld's eyes found me over Asmund's head.

"There was a Kyrr with them in the glade." As soon as I said it, the chill that had run over my skin when I saw the girl with the marks returned. The feeling of her dark eyes had been like the heat of a fire.

Kjeld glared at me. "No, there wasn't."

"She was Kyrr, Kjeld. I saw her." I'd felt her, too.

"You think they're joining with the Kyrr?" Asmund lifted himself up onto his elbows between us.

But Kjeld's gaze narrowed. "The Kyrr aren't with anyone. I'm the only one on the mainland and they would never ally with another clan."

"She had the marks. I know what I saw."

"What marks?" His voice rose. "Describe them."

"They were like yours."

"They weren't like mine," he said, gruffly, "no one's are the same. Tell me exactly what you saw."

I tried to remember, pulling the vision of her back to me from the glade. "I don't know. There was a wing on her throat. The antlers of a stag on her arm, I think."

He seemed to go suddenly still, leaning forward to listen. "What else?"

"A symbol I didn't know." I touched the center of my chest, below my neck. "Here."

His brow furrowed. "What did it look like?"

"An eye. But it was—"

His lips parted and I watched one of his hands clutch at the soil beneath him before he pinched his eyes shut, the other raking over his face.

"What is it?" Asmund watched him.

"That's not possible," he muttered.

"What's not possible?"

Asmund clicked his tongue and we looked down to see

a line of Svell mounting their horses below. I slid back slowly over the wet grass, careful not to pull at the wound on my side, and the others followed. We walked silently through the trees and I watched Kjeld stare at the ground, the stream of frantic thoughts evident on his face. He walked ahead of us until we made it back to the river where Bard was waiting with the horses. But unlike when we'd left only an hour before, he was alone.

"They're gone?" Asmund said, looking into the trees. His brother was the only raider who hadn't left.

Bard nodded in answer. "Some went up the mountain, some to the northern valley."

They would wait out the fight until it was safe to come back. And I understood why. Seeing the Svell's numbers, I was surer than ever that our chances were next to nothing.

"I'll get you to Hylli. Then I'm gone," Asmund said.

I nodded. He'd said long ago that he'd never go home again. I couldn't ask him to fight for it.

Kjeld's eyes shifted nervously, his hands fumbling over his saddlebags.

"What is it?" I eyed him.

He hooked his fingers into the strap of his saddle, pulling it tighter. "I don't know. Maybe nothing."

"Kjeld," Asmund pushed.

"I don't know how she was with them, but the Kyrr aren't allied with the Svell. I'm sure of it." He pulled himself up onto his horse, the mutter of a prayer on his breath as he pulled at the copper disc on his wrist.

Other than a few stories, there wasn't much anyone on the mainland knew about the Kyrr. Only that their people didn't come down from the headlands because that was where their god dwelled. The legend said that Naðr would never leave the frozen north, so neither would her people. Most of the Nādhir had never seen a single Kyrr in their lifetime, which made Kjeld's presence unsettling to anyone who saw him. But now there were two of his kind on our shores.

"You haven't been to the headlands in years." Asmund watched him. "It's possible they've joined with the Svell."

"I know my people." His voice rose, his gaze sharpening on Asmund.

"So, eight hundred Svell." I turned to Asmund as Kjeld kicked his horse, moving up the bank.

He nodded. "They'll want the villages. Probably settle their own people to expand their territory into the fjord."

I'd suspected the same. The Svell were already stronger in number, but they would want the lands. The fjord was a strong, resourceful position and the clans that lived farther east and south wouldn't be a threat for some time.

"They'll go to Utan next." Bard looked to Asmund.

"If Hylli has already called in their warriors, it's defenseless." I stared at the ground, imagining it. "You saw what they did in Ljós."

They would do the same to every village between here and the fjord and by the time the leaders in Hylli knew what was happening, it would be too late.

"I'll go." Bard didn't wait for an answer, pulling himself up into his saddle.

Asmund watched his brother, managing not to protest even though I could see he wanted to.

"Warn them of what's coming and send them to Möor." The mountain village would be the safest place to wait it out, and the farthest from the Svell's reach. They didn't have time to get to Virki with so many of the enemy already in the valley. "Meet us in Aurvanger. Or don't. This isn't your fight if you don't want it to be."

"I go where Asmund goes." Bard leaned forward, stroking the snout of his black horse. The worn, red Aska leathers that their father had probably taken into battle still stretched across the animal's chest. "If I'm not in Aurvanger by sundown tomorrow, leave without me."

Asmund gave him a nod and he reached down to take his arm, pulling his brother into him. I wondered if they'd ever been apart in the years since they left Hylli. We'd all been boys in Virki when the Aska and Riki fought the Herja, and they'd come back to an empty home on the fjord. Since then, it had been just the two of them.

Bard turned the horse and took off down the bank of the river, disappearing around the bend. If he hurried, maybe the Svell would find no more than an empty village when they arrived in Utan.

"How long will it take to get to the fjord?" Kjeld finally broke the silence, his fingers still wound in his bracelet.

I arched an eyebrow at him. "You're coming?"

He shrugged, holding out a handful of tree moss to me. "Where else am I going to go?"

But there was a look hidden beneath his easy eyes, a dark shadow that always seemed to be there. I'd often wondered how Kjeld ended up with Asmund. How he'd come to wander the mainland and what he'd done to be cast out from his own people. Mysteries surrounding him, the way fog shrouded the headlands. Only myths made their way down the narrow sliver of land that arched up from the mainland to the frozen north. A place where the thaw never came, the mist so thick that the blue sky was never seen.

"Thank you." I took the moss from him. "You're sure the Kyrr haven't joined with the Svell?" I asked again.

"I'm sure." He went to the water's edge, crouching down to wash up the length of his arms beneath his sleeves. The Kyrr marks were knotted so tightly that in some places, you couldn't even see the color of his skin.

I lifted my tunic, inspecting the burn at my side. The gash was closed and the bleeding had stopped, but it wouldn't protect me from the infection that I was sure would come. The tree moss would help keep it clean until I got home. I dipped it into the water to rinse it of the dirt and bark and then held my breath as I pressed it against the raw skin. The pain shot up and over my body until I could feel it in my hands, a singeing burn that made it difficult to draw another breath. I bandaged it tightly, until the sting was numbed enough to move.

"Ready?" Asmund held out the reins to me and I looked up to the horse.

Its amber hide reminded me of Aghi's horse, the color of warm sunsets over the mountain. The orange light that spilled onto the tree trunks and made everything look like it was on fire.

War is easy.

His words echoed in my mind, and I swallowed hard against the pain in my throat. He'd survived a lifetime of the fighting seasons to protect the fjord and see a new future for his people. Now, I wondered what we would say when we were reunited with him in the afterlife. If we'd have to tell him that it was all gone. The fjord. Our people. The future.

All of it.

CHAPTER ELEVEN

TOVA

GUNTHER KEPT HIS DISTANCE, RIDING BEHIND AS I LED US into the forest outside of Ljós, but I could feel his stare at my back. He and Jorrund didn't speak as we headed away from the glow of the Svell camp. It was expanding every hour as more warriors arrived from the west.

Vigdis had sent word before we'd ever even set out for Ljós, his plan to betray his brother and kill the Nādhir fully conceived since the night I'd cast the runes. I wondered what he would have done if the runes had said something different. If they'd held fortune instead of ruin. But he'd moved against Ljós before that night, and I told myself that the weight of the lives in the Nādhir village and in the glade didn't fall on me. But even if it were true, I'd still played a part. I'd justified his plan. Confirmed it. *Hagalaz* was the excuse that Vigdis needed.

We walked in silence, the sounds of night growing in the

forest as the sun began to fall. Jorrund waited in the shadows tucked under the trees, his arms tucked in his robes as the tall grass pushed and pulled around him. He didn't like the idea of summoning the Spinners, but he knew we didn't have a choice. He was too afraid to call out to Eydis after the betrayal at the glade. He'd try to earn back the honor he'd lost before he went to face his god. And the only way to do it was to be sure the Svell were the ones left standing on the bloodied earth. But Jorrund had too much faith in Eydis. The gods could be even more treacherous than mortals.

I eyed my bow, strapped to Gunther's horse beside his leg. "Do you owe Vigdis some debt, like you did Jorrund?"

He looked down at me, one eyebrow arching. "What?"

"There has to be some reason he's tasked you with watching me. And there had to be some reason you came to the beach that day seven years ago."

I watched him remember. For almost an entire year, Gunther had come to meet me in the meadow. He'd taught me how to make arrows and shoot them. He'd even made my bow. But he had never talked to me other than giving me instruction. He'd never told me why he'd agreed to help me.

"I didn't do it because I owed a debt to Jorrund," he answered, gruffly.

"Then why?"

He kicked the horse, riding past me and leaving me to walk alone. I doubted Vigdis or anyone else knew about those days in the meadow. If they did, Gunther wouldn't hold such a high ranking among the warriors. But Jorrund was good at getting people to do what he wanted. He was good at making people feel like they owed him something.

I moved slowly, watching the pattern of the thicket ahead. We were farther inland than I'd usually be when hunting for henbane, but there was no time to go back to Liera and the sun was already disappearing, cooling the forest around us. If I was going to find the Nādhir, I had to act quickly.

Vigdis' words came back to me. He'd meant what he said, but even if I did find the man who'd killed his brother, he had plenty of reasons to want me dead. I only had the time between now and then to find a way to keep myself valuable to him. After that, I didn't know what my future held. My own fate was growing dimmer by the moment.

The truth was that I understood Vigdis, even if I thought he was wrong. His zeal for his clan was pure. It ran through his veins as hot as his blood and Vera's death had struck him hard. With no children of his own, he'd lost the only soft, warm thing he'd let into his heart and it was easier to blame me than to blame Eydis. I was flesh and blood. I had a face. And most importantly, I could die.

I stopped when I saw the change in the trees ahead, where a narrow offshoot of the river wound waywardly in the dark, widening in the distance. Gunther stopped at the outcropping of stone as I pushed through the reeds. My boots sank into the softening ground and I searched the dried, dead plants of winter that were clustered along the water. If the henbane was anywhere nearby, it would be here. It was too early to find fresh blooms but last year's fallen stalks would still litter the earth.

I crouched down, digging through damp brush with my fingers and moving down the shore, my hands caked with mud. The light was almost completely gone by the time I found it. A golden bed of spent henbane peeked through a new patch of grass that reached up like fingers toward the warmth of the sun.

I raked the blades back carefully, unearthing an old straw-colored stalk lined with tight rows of seed pods. One was all I needed. I stood, pushing back into the reeds toward Gunther, and we walked back to where Jorrund waited, now almost invisible in the dark.

"I don't like this," he said, eyeing the henbane.

"I know," I whispered, walking past him.

Summoning the Spinners was dangerous, but my entire life with the Svell had been dangerous. I had never really been safe, even if Jorrund had wanted me to believe I was. So I had learned to take risks to make my existence necessary. This was no different.

The fires of the Svell camp were lit in the trees in the distance. They'd been arriving all day and by tomorrow, we'd be headed east with an entire army. Time was running out.

The meeting tent was packed full of bodies as we passed, voices booming over each other in the dark. Jorrund held open the flap of our tent and I ducked inside as he struck the fire-steel and I got to work, laying out the henbane and using my knife to cut the dead blooms from the dry stalk.

"What are you doing?" Gunther watched me warily, the light of the torch reflecting in his eyes.

"I don't know where the Nādhir is." I peeled the dried petals back and fit the tip of my blade into the pod, slicing downward in a precise line. The black round seeds glimmered beneath the husk as Jorrund came to stand over me. "So, I'm going to ask someone who does."

"There are other ways to find him," Jorrund said.

"Not this quickly." I dumped the seeds into my palm. If the Spinners had sent the All Seer, I had to believe they were trying to tell me something. That they were trying to guide me, somehow. And it wasn't only the Nādhir from the glade I wanted to find. I wanted to know more about the Kyrr I'd seen in the forest.

I stood and Jorrund held a bowl out before me, meeting my eyes. "Be careful."

I took it, not answering. I knew enough about fate to know that being careful had very little to do with living or dying. And I was still too angry with him for going against Bekan to drive away his worry.

We went back out into the crisp night air and I knelt before the nearest fire, scooping hot coals into the bowl with the blade of my knife. Jorrund's and Gunther's footsteps hit the ground behind me as I walked into the dark forest. I found a place where the moonlight spilled through the treetops and sat down, my skirt spread out around me. The coals glowed orange and red inside the bowl and I set it before me, closing my eyes and pulling in a long, steady breath.

The thoughts bled from my mind slowly, until I was left in the forest alone, only the darkness of my mind remaining. The cold of the night air wrapped around me and the rustling of leaves trailed through my thoughts until the silence settled. I opened my eyes and stared into the coals, pushing away each thought and replacing them with the sounds of the forest and the pull of the wind through the branches overhead.

I lifted my hand before me and scattered the henbane seeds onto the hot coals. Their shining hulls cracked against the heat and white smoke wound up through the dark before me like curling fingers casting a spell. I leaned over them, breathing deeply until the biting scent of it was deep in my lungs. My eyes closed against the burn in my chest and I drew another breath. The heat pushed between my ribs and I pinched my eyes closed until my hands began to feel heavy in my lap.

My head fell back and the words found my lips, the rasp of my own whispering so quiet that I could hardly hear my own voice. "I call upon the Spinners. I summon the weavers of fate."

I brought the Nādhir's face to my mind, seeing him as clearly as I had in the glade. Dark hair pulled into a haphazard braid. Deep-set eyes the color of the sea. The tingle came back up over my skin, as if I could feel him there. As if he was standing just ahead in the trees, his gaze on me.

My head swam, the earth beneath me suddenly pulling me down into it, and the white light of the moon brightened on the ground around me. I blinked, dumping the rest of the seeds onto the coals, and the smoke reignited, pulling up from the bowl in twisting pillars. I breathed it in again, but this time, I couldn't feel the burn. There was only the sweet taste of the smoke on my tongue and the faint heat lifting from the embers.

"Where are you?" I murmured, the timbre of my own voice strange.

The sound of my breath grew louder in my ears and the warmth spilled out into my body, reaching down into my hands and feet. I lay back into the dirt, my eyes fixed on the black sky, and my weight sank down into the pine needles, my palms turned up at my sides.

I tried to say the words again but my lips wouldn't move, my face numb against the cold night air when suddenly, he appeared. The Nādhir stood in the darkness before me, the shapes around him rippling like the henbane smoke until I could make out the crude gates of a small village behind him. His eyes locked on mine and I searched the black for the Kyrr. But we were alone. Just the Nādhir and I.

The dark night looked like liquid. Like we were beneath its drowning surface. The wind whipped around us as cold rain began to fall and his mouth opened, but no words came. Instead, it was the voice of the Spinners.

"Utan," they whispered, the sound echoing through the trees.

The Nādhir stared at me, unmoving until the gate melted back into a twist of dissipating smoke. It wound around him until he was gone, and in the next breath, I was alone. The cold rushed in around me and I searched the black nothingness, feeling bare in the darkness without him.

I searched for the shape of him, tried to feel the run of the current over my skin, but there was nothing. No one. Until a small flickering glow lifted overhead and I looked up, squinting against its brightening light.

There, dangling above my mind, was a soft, wavering flame. I didn't move a muscle, my breath shallow as I reached for it. Gently, as if it might disappear like the smoke.

Then, in a rush, the light flooded in a desperate, cold wave until I was covered with it.

I was underwater.

The strange, white glow cast down in beams around me, trailing beads of bubbles racing up to the surface overhead. My arms floated up before me, a cluster of yarrow marked onto one hand and a stalk of henbane on the other. They drifted, unmoving, until the blunt edge of realization lit in my mind like the cold seawater filling my chest in the silence of the deep.

I was dead. But this wasn't a vision.

It was a memory.

10 YEARS AGO

Village of Liera, Svell Territory

THE RIDER MADE IT TO LIERA BEFORE NIGHT HAD FALLEN, and by the time the sun went down, word had reached every corner of the village.

Tova followed the crowded paths with the cloak pulled up high over her head to hide her marks from the notice of the Svell that were pouring toward the ritual house. If anyone spotted her, they'd send her back to the gate. Worse, they'd beat her for coming into the village without Jorrund. But sometimes, if she was careful, she was able to disappear among them.

She slipped through the open doors silently, pressing herself between bodies until she reached the back wall, where a crude ladder reached up into the dark, smoke-stained rafters. She looked over her shoulder once before she climbed hand over hand, melting into the black that hovered over the gathered Svell, and found a place to sit on a wide wooden beam with her feet dangling in the air.

She covered her nose and mouth with the corner of her cloak. The smoke from the altar fire was thick up in the rafters, billowing up before it escaped through the opening in the roof. It stung her eyes, but from here, she wouldn't be seen. Most importantly, she could see and hear the meeting.

There had been rumors coming from the east for days about an army that attacked the Aska on the fjord. But Bekan had sent his own riders to see for themselves what had happened and in the time they'd been gone, the Svell had already split over what was to be done if it was true. Some wanted to march on the fjord before the fires could even stop burning. Others wanted to keep their years of peace intact. Even the village leaders didn't seem to agree.

The benches filled, bodies pushed into every open space in the ritual house below, and Tova watched as Jorrund came through the door with a torch, Bekan on his heels.

The crowd made way for them, the voices lowering to whispers, and Tova studied the Tala, trying to see what lay behind his focused eyes. Whatever news the rider had brought, it wasn't good.

Bekan lifted a hand into the air and the last of the whispers faded, every eye on him. His tiny daughter was cradled in his arms, her pale sleeping face flushed pink at her cheeks. Her mother had died not long after giving birth to her and instead of handing her to a nurse to raise, Bekan had taken the task up himself. Once, she'd walked into his home with Jorrund and he'd been curled up with her, asleep. Tova had decided then that she liked the Svell chieftain, even if he didn't seem to like her.

His voice rose above the sound of the fire at his back. "The Herja have attacked the fjord, taking the Aska villages. There is little left. They are now on the mountain, doing the same in Riki territory."

Tova's hands gripped the edge of the beam, leaning forward until the light from the flames below hit her face. The silence grew thin, the wind blowing against the ritual house the only sound. While some had hoped for the Aska's destruction, no one had imagined one army could take both clans. Jorrund had told her the story of the Herja, who'd come ten years earlier and attacked the fjord before disappearing. Many thought them a myth.

"Will they come here next?" a timid voice called out.

Tova looked out over the faces but whoever had asked the question didn't want to be seen. She could see the same thought in every Svell's eyes, the excitement over the possibility of war now withered into something that looked much more like fear. Hands drifted absently toward weapons or clenched into fists, and the tension pulled tighter as Bekan stepped forward.

He handed the baby girl to his brother, who stood at his side, and Vigdis took her into his arms, holding her against his broad chest.

Bekan looked out over his people, waiting for the last of

the murmuring to quiet. "If they do, we'll be ready. I want every village guarded through the night. Every warrior ready to fight."

"And Hǫlkn?" another voice shouted.

The leader of the nearest Svell village had died only weeks before. If war was coming, they wanted to know who would lead them.

Bekan's eyes went to his brother. His hair was pulled back into one long, tightly woven braid, his arms wrapped protectively around his niece. "Vigdis will take leadership of Hǫlkn."

Tova sighed in relief, and Vigdis' eyes flickered up to the rafters, where Tova was perched. She pulled her knees up into her chest, wrapping her arms around them tightly. Though she was hidden in the shadows, his frightening gaze seemed to find her, peering up through the darkness.

She pressed her lips together, the feeling of his stare crawling over her skin. The chieftain's brother hadn't taken his attention from her since she'd arrived in Liera, but now, he would take leadership of Hǫlkn, the Svell village to the north. And from there, maybe his blade wouldn't be able to find her.

Forest on the Mountain, Riki Territory

Halvard could still hear the screaming.

His numb feet dragged through the snow behind the Herja's cart as the horses walked, pulling him behind it. The rope cut into the skin around his wrists and his arms ached, the blood trailing up into the sleeves of his torn tunic. The woman tied beside him had fallen before the moon had even risen above the treetops and her lifeless body dragged over the ground beside him.

It had taken only minutes for the village of Fela to fall to the Herja in the dead of night. They'd appeared in the dark without warning, and he hadn't seen the man coming as he ran for the house across the path, where his mother was. He'd only felt wide arms wrap around his body as he was lifted up from the ground and then he was in the black forest. The sound of Eelyn's screams still rang in his ears, his name bent and broken on her cracked voice.

He pinched his eyes closed, breathing through the throbbing pain in his face. The bones in his nose were broken, the taste of his own blood still sharp on his tongue. He'd searched the ground for his brothers' bodies as the Herja pulled him into the trees, but he'd seen no sign of them. Now, he could only hope that wherever they were, they were alive. He could only hope that they weren't in the forest looking for him.

A voice called out at the back of the line and a tall Herja woman with black furs hung over her shoulders appeared, pulling another Riki woman on a rope behind her. She stepped into the moonlight and Halvard sucked in a breath when he saw the wood-beaded necklaces draped around her neck. The village Tala's face lit as she looked up to the sky, her hair falling down her back.

The Herja jerked her forward and whistled, signaling the horses to slow, and Halvard tried to meet her eyes as she was tied up beside him. But the Tala only looked up, to the stars gleaming overhead.

He opened his mouth, but before he could speak, her sharp gaze came down to meet his, silencing him. Her eyes cut to the Herja walking beside them and Halvard looked back to see more of them pouring in from the forest behind them. He wiped the tears from his cheeks with his shoulders as they lurched forward.

She waited for the last of them to pass before she finally leaned in to whisper, "It's alright."

The cart's wheels cracked over the stones buried in the snow and he tried to keep his balance, picking up each frozen foot and setting it down again as they pushed farther from Fela. He'd only ever left their village to check the nets at the river or to hunt with his brothers. Now, he wasn't sure there was even a village left to go back to. Behind them, the smoke from the fires lifted above the tallest pines and drifted into the sky. His foot caught the roots of a tree and he fell forward, crashing into the cart and losing his footing.

He tried to pull his feet back beneath him, but it was no use. The feeling had left them in the cold and the cart was moving too quickly. The Tala looked behind them before she took hold of his rope, pulling it toward her until the slack was shortened and Halvard could stand. She braced his arm as he balanced himself, a small cry slipping from his chest as he wound the length of it around his fists and tried to keep his steps in the narrow tracks of the wheels.

"Are they going to kill us?" he whispered, keeping his eyes on the ground before him.

The Tala took a few more steps before she answered, "No."

"How do you know?" He blinked, looking up to her face.

A smile pulled at the corner of her mouth and she tilted her chin up until the moonlight reflected in her eyes again. Halvard followed her gaze to the black sky, where the outline of a bird was circling far above.

"What is it?"

"The All Seer," she said.

"Is it a god?"

Her smile pulled wider. "No."

"Then what is it?"

"He's the eye of the Spinners," she said, simply.

"He's come to protect you?"

A Herja ran past them, his bloodied sword swinging at his side, and Halvard fell quiet, watching him disappear ahead.

"He's come to protect *you*," the Tala said, looking to the trees.

Halvard turned to search the darkness, the cold burning in his chest, until he caught sight of something slipping through the bits of light. His mouth dropped open, the hot tears returning as he saw Eelyn and Fiske. They ran through the trees with silent steps, tracking alongside the caravan as they walked.

And when Halvard looked back up to the sky, the All Seer was gone.

CHAPTER TWELVE

HALVARD

THE FOREST WAS QUIET, AS IF IT KNEW WHAT WAS COMING. We were only a day's ride from Hylli, but the farthest corners of Nādhir territory were already filling with Svell. The smoke from their fires reached up into the sky to the west, where they were camped at the foot of the mountains. Before the sun rose again, they would be pushing east.

Following the river meant another half day, but taking the faster route through the valley would make us easy to spot. And as long as we didn't lose more time, we would beat the Svell to the fjord. We had to.

The pain in my side deepened as the horse moved from side to side, faltering over the slick riverbed. I knew the heat swelling beneath my skin meant the wound was infected. Having a healer as a mother told me that much, but I also knew it was better to have an infected burn than a gash that wouldn't stop bleeding. If we got to Hylli in time, I'd be able to treat it before sickness could take hold and keep me from fighting. If we didn't, I'd lose my life to fever instead of battle.

I pressed my hand firmly into the old Riki armor vest that Asmund had given me to make me less recognizable to anyone we would meet in the forest. Whoever had owned it had probably died in the fighting seasons before the Nādhir made peace. My father's armor was made almost the same, except for the engraving of the yew tree on his shoulder clasps. It was the symbol that marked the blade of my axe, which had also belonged to him. Every spring, my mother opened the trunk against the wall and took his things out to oil the leathers and shine the bronze and I'd watch her, trying to remember his face. There were so many things about him that had faded, but I found myself thinking of him more and more since the day Espen told me I'd been chosen to take his place as chieftain.

I wondered what he would think. What he would say to me. I wondered if he'd be proud.

The river curved tightly around a cliff side and the moon disappeared above us. I watched the water carefully, steering the horse nearer to the bank and away from the white-capped water breaking on submerged rocks. We were moving slowly, but tracks through the forest would lead the Svell straight to us, and there was no storm breaking to cover them.

Movement in the trees caught my eye and I looked over my shoulder, pulling back on the reins. Asmund halted his horse behind me and turned, but there was nothing. Only the dark, alive with the night sounds of the forest and everything in it. A prick crept over my skin as I urged the horse forward, following after Kjeld, who was making his way around the bend.

The faint sound of a murmuring prayer on his lips drifted back to meet me. The first time I'd seen him was on the path to Fela, the mountain village where I was born. He'd just joined up with Asmund and the hollow in his cheeks was evidence he'd been starving through the winter. He didn't speak. He'd hardly even looked at me or my brothers, his attention always on the world around him. As if he could see shadows and hear voices that the rest of us couldn't. It was the same feeling that came over me watching the girl in the glade, her eyes boring into mine, her hand pressed to her ear.

Aghi told me back then to keep my distance from Kjeld. That the Kyrr were not to be trifled with. I'd heard more than one tale about what happened to anyone who trespassed onto their lands. But apart from the stories whispered about the wild clan in the headlands, Kjeld only seemed like a weary, worn down man. And in the four years he'd been with Asmund, I'd learned next to nothing about him.

"You never told me where he came from." I spoke lowly, catching Asmund's eyes in the dark.

He caught up to me, pulling the reins of his horse up higher. "He's Kyrr. He's from the headlands."

"The Kyrr never come to the mainland. In all the years

I've traveled with Aghi or taken boats out on the fjord, Kjeld is the only one I've ever seen. How did he end up here?"

"I don't know the whole story." Asmund shrugged. "In fact, I know almost nothing."

"What part do you know?"

He slowed, letting Kjeld pull farther ahead until he was almost invisible against the dark trees. "Only that I don't think he was cast out from the Kyrr like people say."

"What do you mean?"

"I mean that I think he wasn't made to leave. That he chose to."

Kjeld leaned back as the horse's gait stuttered on the slope, guiding it around the current. It didn't make any sense. The Kyrr were feared by every clan on the mainland. He couldn't have thought he'd find a new life among us. "Why do you think that?"

"Three winters ago, a man came looking for him," Asmund whispered.

"A Kyrr?"

He nodded. "He found our camp on the south side of the mountain just after the first snowfall and at first, I thought he was there to kill him. That maybe he'd come to act on a blood feud or carry out a sentence Kjeld had outrun."

"What happened?"

"He wasn't there to take him. He was pleading with him to come back."

My gaze drifted back to Kjeld. His long blond braid ran down the center of his back, the black marks spreading up out of his tunic and wrapping around his neck. He was at least the age of my brothers, probably older, and he could have a family he'd left behind in the headlands. Or maybe he was like Asmund and Bard, and left because he'd lost something.

"I couldn't hear what they were saying, but Kjeld refused to return with him. The man left and never came back."

It seemed that no one would leave their home and their people if they weren't made to, but I knew that wasn't true. It looked as if Asmund was thinking the same. He and Bard had done just that after the Herja came. Nothing made the burden of that pain easier to bear, but to some, going where no one knew the story was worth the loneliness it brought. I'd once asked Asmund if leaving the fjord had brought him peace. His answer was that it was only a different kind of pain. One that was a little easier to live with.

"Do your brothers know where you are?" Asmund asked.

"If they don't already, then they will soon."

He'd known Fiske and Iri as long as he'd known me, so he could guess what their reactions might be when they found out I'd gone. If I wasn't back in Hylli by the time they got there, they'd be scouring the forests for me, their blades soaked with the blood of every Svell they found. And Fiske's wife, Eelyn, would be with them. The only thing that burned hotter than the fury in Aghi's daughter was her love.

I swallowed hard as her face lit in my mind. When I saw her, I'd have to tell her about Aghi, and the thought almost made me hope that they would reach Hylli before me and that news of the glade would be there waiting for her.

Asmund cut to the right and I followed, watching the emptiness around us. He'd been quiet since we'd left his brother and I knew he was worried, even if he wouldn't say it. Bard was the last blood that remained of their family.

"You know you don't have to do this," I said.

"What?"

"I can get back to Hylli on my own. I'm not your chieftain."

"You're my friend."

I looked at him, but he kept his eyes ahead. After the Herja came, friends had become family because so many families were broken. But Asmund hadn't considered himself Aska or Riki or Nādhir in a long time. "You know you can stay, don't you?"

He looked up at me then, his brow pulling. "Stay?"

"You know you can come back to Hylli. Whenever you want." I wasn't giving him permission and I wasn't asking him to fight. But I wondered if he knew. If he thought he couldn't undo what he'd done. "There's a place for you, if you want it."

"I know that. But I can't go back."

He didn't look at me as he kicked his heels into the horse, riding ahead. The river curved again and we moved to the right side of the water as the left side deepened. I knew what he meant. Fighting and living were two different things. But in the span of three days, everything had changed. And I wondered if the future of the Nādhir was changing again, like it had ten years ago. Maybe we'd outwitted fate and it was coming back for us now. Maybe the gods Sigr and Thora had remembered their taste for war.

Again, the feeling of someone's eyes on me crawled over my skin and I pulled the reins back sharply, stopping. The water rippled against the horse's legs, moving around us like liquid moonlight, and I studied the forest with the breath held in my chest until my eyes caught sight of a figure in the dark. My hand lifted to my axe and I focused my eyes, watching it move in the shadows. It seemed to float, disappearing behind one tree and then reappearing behind another.

Kjeld stopped ahead, turning back.

"What is it?" Asmund called out.

"There." I pointed toward the trees, trying to focus my eyes in the dim light, and my hand fell from the handle of the axe as I realized. It was a girl.

"I don't see anything," Asmund said, his horse splashing in the water as he made his way back to me.

My lips parted, my hand winding tighter in the reins until the leather stung against my skin. It wasn't just a girl. It was the Kyrr girl, from the glade.

I watched her move slowly through the haze, her face cast to the ground before her and her hands hanging heavy at her sides. Like a spirit wandering. Like the undead souls from the old stories the Tala used to tell the children around the altar fire.

Where are you?

A voice whispered hot against my ear and I stilled, the chill in the air turning to a biting cold.

"Halvard?" Asmund set a hand on my arm and I flinched, blinking.

His uneasy eyes ran over my face.

And when I looked up again, she was gone.

"Nothing," I mumbled, shaking my head. "It's nothing."

Asmund surveyed me for another moment before he nodded and pushed past me, leading his horse to take the front of our line.

Kjeld watched me warily, reaching for the bracelet around his wrist. The copper disc shone in the moonlight. "Alright?"

"It was nothing," I said again, but to myself.

He turned, following Asmund around the cliff face, and I lifted the bottom of my armor vest, my hand going back to the bandaged wound beneath my tunic. Maybe infection was spreading faster than I thought. Or maybe it was the nights of no sleep that were casting visions in the fog. I looked back once more to the trees as the others disappeared ahead. But there was nothing. No one.

Except the heat of breath still warm against my ear.

CHAPTER THIRTEEN

TOVA

I PUSHED MY FROZEN HANDS TOWARD THE HEAT OF THE FIRE until I could almost feel its sting. My head ached, the pain of it reaching down my neck and into my shoulders and back. The henbane would take days to leave my blood, but the Spinners had given me what I'd asked for.

The vision had been clear, as if they wanted me to find him. The Nādhir from the glade was in Utan.

The flames licked up the dry wood, turning it black in the freshly dug fire pit before me. The Svell camp had expanded beyond the glade so far that I could see no end to the tents that spread into the forest. In only hours, they'd be on their way to the fjord.

Warriors from every Svell village stood together in the clearing as Vigdis recited the funeral rites for Bekan. The sound of their voices rumbled like thunder in the distance, the sacred words spoken on every tongue. I had heard the chieftain talk of his people many times, often with a conviction that seemed to rattle the walls of the ritual house. But I'd never seen them. Not like this.

Every one of them was ready for war, but no one had told them that it was Vigdis' blade that had gotten their chieftain killed and I suspected no one would. If they knew Bekan's own brother had betrayed him before a knife was driven into his chest, they may not follow him to battle. It was a secret he could trust Siv and the others who saw what happened in the glade to keep.

"Are you sure?" Jorrund leaned in closer to the fire, his eyes wide with concern. They gleamed beneath his bushy eyebrows as he studied me.

"Yes," I answered, watching the pillar of smoke lifting from Bekan's funeral fire in the distance.

The pyre was engulfed in fire and I could just barely make out the form of Bekan's body as it was eaten up by the flames. A lump curled tight in my throat and I blinked back the tears threatening to fall.

I didn't know why my heart ached at the thought of his death. Bekan had no more than tolerated me in the years since I'd come to Liera and when Vera died, he'd made no secret of the fact that he'd come to hate me. But I remembered how soft he was with his daughter. How his hand absently reached out, touching her fair hair as she stood between him and Jorrund. And even if I wasn't one of his people, I could feel the weight of what the loss meant. Something had shifted for not only the Svell, but for the web of fate. And for the first time, I was beginning to feel like a fly trapped in its threads instead of the spider walking them.

I had only summoned the Spinners once before. I'd snuck away in the early morning to burn the henbane on the same beach Jorrund had found me on. I huddled over the poisoned smoke until I was close to retching and asked the only question I'd ever had.

I wanted to know why.

Why my people had given me to the sea. Why Naðr had taken her favor from me. Why I'd washed up on the Svell shore instead of drifting out into the lonely death I'd been sent to.

That was before I knew never to ask the Spinners *why*. Because the answer was something too twisting and turning for mortal minds to comprehend. They sat at the foot of the Tree of Urðr, spinning. Always spinning. Past, present, and future all on the same loom.

They didn't answer. Instead, they gave me only darkness. Silence. I fell into the emptiness of my mind when I breathed in the smoke and when I woke the next morning, drenched by the rising tide and barely able to open my eyes, I swore I'd never ask them why again. Now, I knew only to ask them what, who, and when if I cast the stones. Because they were the only answers the Spinners would ever give to me.

"It wasn't the only thing I saw," I whispered, careful not to let Gunther hear me.

Jorrund sank down before the fire. "What is it? What did you see?"

I closed my eyes, trying to bring the vision back to my mind. "The water. A fire. I could hear . . ."

But heavy footsteps in the dirt made us both look up and I squinted against the pain that awakened in my head. Vigdis walked toward us from the glade, the fire still raging behind him. His muddy boots stopped before me, planted into the earth like the roots of a thousand-year-old tree.

"Tell me." His voice was rough, his face still streaked with dirt and soot. Siv found a place beside him.

"He's in Utan."

"How do you know?"

I pressed my palm to my forehead, breathing through the ache between my eyes. "Because I saw him."

Vigdis stared at the ground, unblinking. "Then we go to Utan."

Siv and Jorrund both looked up, surprised.

"Get them ready," he ordered.

"I'll go," Siv offered. "I'll take ten warriors and meet you before you reach Hylli."

But the edge in Vigdis' voice deepened. "We all go to Utan. Together."

The look on Siv's face turned from confusion to concern. "All of our warriors have arrived, Vigdis. We should move on the fjord and take Hylli. Now. There's no need to waste time with the border villages."

"We go to Utan. Then we go to Hylli."

"You don't need an entire army to kill one man." I stood, wavering on unsteady feet.

He turned, towering over me until I was hidden in his shadow. "Speak again, and I'll cut your tongue out," he snapped. "I don't want to only kill one man. I want him to watch us slaughter every soul in Utan before we kill him." The words suddenly took on a soft, unnerving tone.

"You asked me to find him. Not tell you which village to attack."

"There are no warriors in Utan. They've called them to Hylli." Siv seemed to agree, but Vigdis' sharp look silenced her.

Behind them, Gunther appeared the most unsettled. He stood with his arms crossed over his chest, watching Vigdis warily.

My stomach turned, my skin suddenly stinging against the fire's heat. Jorrund's arm steadied me as the glade tipped to one side and I leaned into him, almost tumbling to the ground.

"Hylli will still be there when we reach the fjord. They'll wait patiently for their deaths because they have no other choice."

He was right. There was nothing else to do unless they ran. And it wasn't likely the Nādhir would. But the expression that crossed Siv's and Gunther's faces looked as if they'd already seen more blood spilled than they wanted to. The Svell were fighters but this wasn't a generation built on battle. They'd defended their homes and their lands from raiders and thieves, but it had been more than a hundred years since they'd been at war with another clan.

Siv had taken Ljós with Vigdis and the others and she'd cut down the Nādhir in the glade. I wondered if she was willing to destroy another village of old men, pregnant mothers, and children not old enough to hold up a sword.

"We go to Utan. Now," Vigdis said again, and this time, Siv answered the command with a tight nod.

She turned on her heel and headed back to the Svell gathered before the funeral fire, and Vigdis set his attention to Jorrund. "She better be right."

Jorrund looked at me, and I could see that he was thinking the same thing. He was wondering. Doubting. He had only the power I gave him and that realization had given way to fear—something I had never really seen on the face of the old Svell Tala.

He twisted his fingers nervously into the wooden beads strung around his neck and I turned, pushing through the Svell making their way to their horses. The fire was still raging, but I could no longer see Bekan. He had disappeared, the ash floating up into the air the only thing left of him in this world.

It was an honor that the Nādhir warriors lying in the trees would never get. They'd have to rely on the sympathies of their gods and the prayers of their people to take them to the afterlife. The same fate would find the young Nādhir who'd killed Bekan, along with every living thing in Utan.

At my word.

The prophecy that had moved over my tongue. Just like the glade.

I'd only ever watched the funerals from the forest, when the people of Liera gathered to send their dead to the afterlife, and I didn't remember enough about the Kyrr to know what words they spoke or what customs they performed. I eyed the circular symbol on the inside of my wrist, tracing it with my finger. If I knew what the marks meant, maybe I would remember. Maybe the things I'd forgotten would return to me.

The smell of burning flesh and sizzling tree sap filled the air and I stood before the pyre alone, unable to feel its warmth. I was only cold. Deep inside my bones. In every shadowed corner of my soul.

The little house outside Liera didn't seem like a cage now. It seemed like a refuge. One that I couldn't reach.

My stiff muscles trembled, sending a tremor through my entire body as the poison moved deeper through my veins. Maybe this was what the undead spirits were like, the ones that filled stories. But I wondered if maybe they weren't stories after all. Maybe I was one of them. Flesh and bone on a corpse with no soul.

The weight of the rune stones hung heavy around my neck, pulling me forward, to the fire.

For a moment, I wondered if I'd even be able to feel it if I reached out and touched it. If I wrapped myself in its flames like a golden cloak. Maybe death would just feel like going home.

I watched the flecks of white ash floating up from the pyre before me, dancing in the air like lifting snowflakes, and I thought the thing I'd been so careful not to. The words I was afraid could come to life and strangle me. Make me disappear.

That I was the one who'd put Bekan on the pyre, not Vigdis. Just like Vera. And by the time the Svell reached the sea, I'd have a lot more blood on my hands.

CHAPTER FOURTEEN

HALVARD

THE FIRST TIME I'D SEEN IT, I WAS ONLY EIGHT YEARS OLD.

A rolling sea of red wildflowers burrowed up through the earth at the last of winter, bleeding into a wide stretch of the pale green valley. The evening fog pushing in from the sea hovered over it, like hands clasped carefully over the fragile wings of a moth.

My fists wound tighter in the reins at the sight.

I stopped the horse on the hill and slid down, standing waist deep in the tilting stalks of early spring blooms. My hands brushed over their tops as I walked, the smell of them bringing back countless memories of taking the path to the border villages with Aghi to trade crates of salted fish for herbs and dried venison. The valley dipped down in the center, the river slicing through it like a crack in the ice that covered the shallows of the fjord.

"Aurvanger." Asmund spoke the hallowed word softly,

looking out over the view. His own brother had died in this very field during the last fighting season our people ever fought. Only weeks later, the Herja took his parents in a raid on Hylli.

I'd heard so many stories about the battles that took the lives of the Aska and Riki for generations. Aghi had recounted the fury between the gods spilling out on the earth to my nieces over and over and I'd listen from where I sat beside the fire. Now, it was overgrown with wildflowers, making it hard to imagine death here.

"They say those flowers didn't start growing here until the Nādhir made peace." Kjeld looked over us from where he still sat on his horse.

"You sound like you don't believe it," I said.

He dropped down, pulling the water skin from his saddlebag. "Do you?"

"Yes," I answered without hesitation. I'd seen too many unbelievable things to think anything was impossible.

Asmund watched the top of the hill behind us. "We'll wait until sundown. If Bard doesn't show, we'll meet him in Hylli."

But the sound of his voice carried his worry for his brother. If Bard didn't show, there was no guarantee that we'd ever see him again. If the Svell had found his trail or caught up to him in Utan, maybe he was already dead. I could see that Asmund was thinking the same thing. His jaw clenched as he unbuckled the sheath beneath his arm.

I walked out farther until I reached the boulders that

lined the river and pulled my axe free, digging a trench into the soft earth that overlooked the water. Asmund followed me to the edge and I took one side of a large stone that was half buried in the sand. When he realized what I was doing, he took hold of the other side and we heaved it up onto the bank, setting it down on its end in the divot I'd dug. I packed the earth around the stele, stamping it down with the head of my axe, and sat back onto my heels before it. The flat side of the stone glittered in the sunlight with flecks of silver and black. It stood like a ghost in the fog before the legendary valley of Aurvanger.

A lump rose in my throat and I swallowed it down, pulling my knife from my belt. I wound my fingers tightly around its blade before I slid it against my calloused palm. The hot blood pooled in the center of my hand before I pressed my finger into it, carefully writing Aghi's name across the face of the stele. Below it, I wrote Espen's.

I opened my mouth to say the ritual words, but they didn't come. They wound tight in my chest like a fist, making it difficult to breathe.

Once, Aghi had stood on the other side of battle from my father on this very field. Then, he became a father, an uncle, a grandfather to the very people he'd spent his life killing. He'd survived a lifetime fighting an unquenched blood feud only to die at the hands of the Svell and waste away in the forest with no funeral fire to honor him as he went on to the afterlife.

But it was the death he wanted. He'd watched the clansmen he'd grown up with die protecting their people. He'd spoken the rites over their burning bodies and now, he had the same privilege, saved from the shame of dying quietly as an old man in his bed. It had been his greatest fear, being given an unworthy end.

". . . you have reached your journey's end . . ." Asmund uttered the words I couldn't, his voice trailing off in the wind.

I breathed through the pain in my throat. It had been a long time since I'd prayed to Thora or Sigr. Not because I didn't believe in them, but because I wasn't sure they listened. The will of the gods was incomprehensible, their favor ever-changing, shifting like the bending rays of sunlight that dropped through the trees. But the sound of prayer still made my chest feel hollow with memories. Because on the lips of my family, it was still alive. And in many ways, *they* had become my gods.

I'd held Aghi in my arms as the light left his eyes. I'd watched him take his last breath. And I hoped that had been enough to honor him.

I pulled the *taufr* from inside my armor vest and rubbed my thumb over its smooth surface. The etched words were barely readable now, but I had carried the stone since the day my mother gave it to me as a small boy. It was a plea to Thora. A request for protection of the one who carried it. And it *had* protected me, many times.

But it seemed as if the battle in the glade would be the last, all of its power used up. The war headed for Hylli would likely take all our lives and we would be given less than Aghi had been given in death, with no one to burn our bodies or speak the ritual words.

"What does the symbol mean?" I said, catching a tear at the corner of my eye before it could fall.

Kjeld looked up at me. "What?"

"The symbol on the girl—the eye."

"The marks are a kind of identification, they are all different for each person. But the eye is . . . Only the women in her lineage have that mark," he answered.

"Why?"

"Because it's the symbol of a Truthtongue."

I got to my feet, sliding the knife back into its sheath. "So, she's like a Tala?"

"The Kyrr don't have Talas."

Asmund looked between us. "Then what is she?"

"What do you know about the story of Naðr?" Kjeld asked.

"Not much."

He leaned into the outcropping of rock beside him. "The god Naðr had a twin sister named Lími. But Lími was fated to die. Naðr buried her sister on the headlands and swore vengeance on the Spinners for taking her life. As an offering, the Spinners gave Naðr a mortal child with the eye marked on her chest. They called her the Truthtongue and promised that every woman born into her lineage would have the ability to read the runes and see into the future.

Naðr accepted the offering and for generations, the child's descendants have led the Kyrr and cast the stones."

"You mean she can see the future," I said, studying him.

Kjeld nodded. "She's casting the stones for the Svell. It's the only reason I can think of that she'd be with them."

An uneasy silence fell between us, the wind stilling.

Asmund ran a hand through his hair, sighing. "So, are the Kyrr with them or not?"

"No. They'd never join with the Svell. They'd never join with anyone."

"Then why is the girl with them?"

"I don't know. But it means the Svell are probably even more dangerous than you think they are." He stared at the ground between us.

I tightened my fist, letting the last drop of blood fall to the earth. I had known the moment I saw her in the glade that there was something different about her. I'd felt it. And the farther from Ljós we traveled, it seemed the more I could feel her. My gaze moved up the hill, to the forest, where I'd seen her shadow in the dead of night. Only, I couldn't have.

Kjeld turned into the wind, looking out over the field. "Did you fight here? Before?"

"I was too young. I only ever waited for my father and my brothers to come home from the fighting season, wishing I was with them."

"Did they die in battle?"

"No, my father died of fever when I was six years old." I looked down to the axe in my hands, where the engraving of the yew tree looked up at me.

"And your brothers?"

I smiled. "This place gave me one of my brothers."

He lifted one eyebrow. "What do you mean?"

"And a sister. My father and my brother Fiske came home from the fighting season one year with an Aska boy named Iri who was nearly dead. I was very young. I hardly remember it, but he was gravely injured and my mother healed him, though no one believed she could. Then he became one of us. The next fighting season, both of my brothers went to Aurvanger and came home with Iri's sister. Fiske fell in love with her."

I still remembered the day Eelyn first came to our home in Fela. I'd watched her over the edge of the loft, my eyes wide. Her hair was like ice, dark streaks of blood staining her tunic, and I remember thinking that she looked like a wild animal with the firelight shining in her eyes. My mother had said she had fire in her blood. We didn't know then that the gods were going to make peace. And we didn't know that they'd use Fiske and Eelyn to do it.

"They changed the will of the gods and the fate of both our clans," I said.

Kjeld eyed me skeptically.

"You don't believe in fate?" Asmund turned to him.

Kjeld looked amused by the question. "No one can change the will of the gods."

"How do you know?"

His eyes met Asmund's and then mine for only a moment before they fell back to the water. "Because I've tried."

His voice changed, the hard edge of it fading. He reached up to the collar of his tunic, pressing his fingers to a pair of leaves at the side of his throat. They seemed to move as he swallowed hard, the glimmer of tears shining in his eyes.

"Halvard . . ." Asmund went still, his hand going to his sword as he looked up and over me, to the ridge.

I turned, searching the sky for what he saw. Over the rise of land to the south, a stretch of blue sky was visible through a break in the thick fog. There, a pillar of weak smoke drifted above the treetops.

"Utan," I whispered.

CHAPTER FIFTEEN

TOVA

THE NIGHTHAWK CALLED OUT IN THE DARKNESS OF THE forest surrounding Utan.

I stood behind the line of Svell in the silence, the sound of it crawling up my spine, its fingers wrapping around my throat like a noose and tightening.

A warning. An omen.

But we were far past any warning the gods or the Spinners could give us now. They flickered out like torches in the wind, only the scent of their smoke left behind. No one was listening.

Gunther stood at my side, his sword pulled from its sheath, his eyes on the Svell warrior in front of him.

"You have to do something," I whispered to Jorrund. "You have to stop this."

He stood beside me, the look on his face betraying his

thoughts. He knew it, in the pit of his stomach. He knew it in the shake of his bones. But beneath the murmured prayers and talk of the gods, Jorrund was a coward. He'd never speak against Vigdis. "There is nothing I can do," he said, careful not to meet my eyes.

The sharp click of tongues silenced the All Seer overhead and the Svell moved down the slope toward the village, leaving only Gunther behind. His tight gaze was pinned on the figures disappearing beneath the gate and over the fence that wound around Utan. He didn't move, his sword still clutched in his hand, and I stepped forward, watching the sight of them melt into the black.

I tried to tell myself that it was the way of mortals to find war. It was like kindling, just waiting for the smallest flame. But I couldn't squelch the soft whisper hissing in the back of my mind. The one that wondered how many Nādhir were sleeping beneath those roofs.

I looked up again to the darkening sky, but the nighthawk was gone, leaving only the faint light of the stars scattered across the expanse.

Even the All Seer didn't want to watch this.

My hands balled into fists at my sides so tightly that my knuckles felt as if they were going to crack. "We have to do something," I whispered.

"Tova . . ." Jorrund's voice pulled up in a warning I knew well.

But I didn't wait for him to finish. I stepped out from

under the trees, pulling the air deep into my lungs and my jaw dropping open to scream. But then I was tilting backward, a hot hand pressed over my mouth. I kicked as Gunther dragged me back into the shadows and dropped me hard on the ground.

"Do I need to kill you?" he asked calmly, standing over me. But even he didn't look himself. His gaze pulled back to the village, the dread of what was about to happen heavy in his eyes.

I glared up at him through hot tears, getting back to my feet. Even if I did scream, it was no use. There was no time for the people of Utan to escape. The Svell would swallow them whole and there was nothing I could do about it. In fact, I'd sent them there.

I held my breath, listening as I bit down hard on my lip, trying to keep from trembling. The silence was finally broken by the whistle of a flaming arrow cutting through the air and I turned to face Jorrund.

"There isn't a single god who looks favorably upon dishonorable killing," I said unevenly.

His eyes narrowed, his arms uncrossing. "This is war, Tova."

"That?" I raised a shaking hand, pointing toward the village at the bottom of the hill. "*That's* not war. And there will be a price to pay for it."

Jorrund looked suddenly horrified, taking a step back from me. "Is that a curse on your tongue?"

"I don't need to curse you." A single tear slid down my cheek. "The Spinners already have."

"What does that mean?" His words faltered, the fear taking hold of his voice.

"The rune cast! *Hagalaz*. Your fate has been carved into the Tree of Urðr."

"That was before the glade. Now we're set to take Hylli and the Nādhir will be gone," he said, but he was growing uneasy. He was trying to convince himself.

"You think the threat of the Nādhir is greater than the wrath of the gods?" My voice rose. "Everything Vigdis has done only *ensures* your fate. You can't erase it."

Screams tore through the forest and I cringed, a sob escaping my throat. Below, the glow of fire was spreading across Utan, lighting it like a beacon. All seven hundred and sixty warriors had been ordered to descend upon the small village and now, they were consuming it like bears after a long winter.

Gunther watched, his jaw clenched tight as the light of the fire danced on his face. The sharp clang of blades meeting found us and I sank down to the ground, wrapping my arms around my legs and burying my face into my skirts. I imagined the young Nādhir from the glade standing at the gate. Swinging his axe, his blue eyes like stars in the night. I didn't know him. I'd never seen him before that day in Ljós. But still, a feeling like I'd betrayed him sank heavily inside of me, making my stomach turn.

But it was the Spinners who'd shown me where he was. He was fated to die, too. He had to be. And I didn't know Vigdis would order the army to Utan.

"I didn't know," I cried, trying to make the words true.

But it was no use. The closeness of the forest seemed to pull away from me, leaving me alone in the dark and the feeling of a thousand eyes on me crawled over my skin like a legion of worms devouring a corpse. Because even if the All Seer wasn't watching, the Spinners were. And so were the gods. There was no way to escape their notice. Not after all I'd done.

I hadn't planned the massacre in the glade but it was my rune cast that had justified it. I hadn't ordered the Svell to Utan, but I'd summoned the Spinners to find the warrior who'd killed Bekan. I'd always known I was cursed. That something dark had marked me. It was the only reason the Kyrr would have sacrificed my life. Jorrund believed that Eydis saved me, but I knew the truth. She hadn't saved me from Naðr.

Naðr just didn't want me.

The screams softened, flickering out one by one until the silence of the night returned. Jorrund stood beside me, one hand touching my hair, but I pushed him off, getting back to my feet. We waited side by side in the minutes it took for them to lay waste to the village, until figures finally crept up the slope, moving back into the forest. The light of dusk caught the glistening of wet blood on armor and the warriors passed us, their gazes thin as they walked, the village of Utan aflame in their wake. I watched their shadows move in the trees until they were gone. I didn't want to see any more.

Vigdis and Siv were the last to appear. He marched toward us with Siv at his back, his chest heaving and his eyes cast up to me with the weight of a hundred stones. "They were waiting for us," he growled.

"What?" Jorrund spoke beside me.

"They knew we were coming. They didn't have a chance, but they knew."

Siv's gaze fell to the ground as she slid her axe back into its sheath. Even she couldn't justify the massacre.

"And he wasn't there." Vigdis lifted his hand, rearing back and swinging his arm to slap me across the face.

I fell to the ground, my hands sliding over the wet soil as my mouth filled with blood. The entire side of my face ignited with sharp pain as I looked up. He stood over me, the full fury of his stare set on my face as I spit into the dirt, wiping the blood from my lip. "He has to be. I saw it."

"You didn't see anything. You lied to save yourself," he spat.

"I swear to you," I stammered, "he's here." I went to the edge of the tree line and looked down to the village gate. It was exactly as I'd seen it in the vision. "Or, he will be. I . . ."

"At dawn, we march to Hylli. If I don't have his head in my hands, I'll take yours instead." He shoved into me as he stalked off into the darkness. "Stay with her," he barked, meeting Gunther's eyes as he pushed past him.

"I don't understand," I murmured, staring at the gate. I'd seen him there. So clearly. I'd heard the voice of the Spinners. My body still ached with the memory of it, the poison henbane throbbing beneath my skin.

"Tova, are you sure you . . ." Jorrund finally spoke.

"I saw it!" I shouted, my voice breaking.

They both looked at me, Gunther sliding his sword into its sheath. "Then, we wait."

Jorrund untied his cloak and set it onto my shoulders but I pushed him away, going to stand at the edge of the ridge alone. I didn't want his comfort. I'd just sentenced a defenseless village to die and if there was suffering to be had, I was deserving of it. The only difference between Vigdis and me was the mark of the eye on my chest.

The flames engulfed Utan below, and the bodies in the path lay still, a hollow silence falling over the cold forest. This is what Ljós must have looked like the night the Svell attacked. This is what would become of Hylli in only a matter of days, the sea inked red with Nādhir blood.

My hand went to the small leather purse against my chest, the runes tucked safely beside my heart. I wished I'd never cast them. I wished I'd never been found on that beach. A slow, frozen death adrift on the sea was better than this. It was kinder.

"If we don't find him . . ." Jorrund said gently.

"It doesn't matter," I murmured, my voice hoarse.

"What doesn't matter?"

"Any of it."

"Why are you saying that? Of course it does."

"It doesn't matter if Vigdis has my head or if the Nādhir appears and cuts my throat himself." I turned to look up at him, the tears now streaming down my face. "Because you've made me a bringer of death, Jorrund. And there's no offering of reparation for a crime like that."

"Tova." He reached out to touch me, but I stepped out of his reach.

I blinked, breathing through the pain in my jaw from where Vigdis had struck me, the iron taste of blood on my tongue. It wrapped itself around my heart and squeezed, the truth scorching inside me with the burn of a blacksmith's forge.

Hagalaz wasn't only coming for the Svell. It was coming for me, too.

CHAPTER SIXTEEN

HALVARD

I KEPT MY HEAD DOWN AS WE FLEW THROUGH THE TREES, the pounding of hooves following behind me as the horses climbed the hill.

The Svell army had marched from Ljós in a horde, leaving the ground trampled into a soft pulp beneath us. Signs of them were everywhere, scraping over the trees and dragging through the brush. Their numbers had to be greater than what we'd seen only a day before and that thought made every muscle in my body wind tight as I pushed ahead. With their warriors called to Hylli days ago, Utan would have maybe thirty or forty of our people within its gates.

Thirty people against eight hundred.

I reached back and pulled the axe from my sheath, letting it fall against my leg and urging the horse faster. We found the worn path that carved down the mountain to the fjord and I fixed my eyes on the darkness ahead, waiting for the gate to appear in the trees. But I could already smell in the air what we would find there. Blood and ash scattered over the broken, fallen remains of a quiet inland village. We were too late.

As soon as the gate came into view, I pulled back on the reins and slowed, dropping from my horse and leaving it behind as I ran on foot to the nearest thicket. The horses reared back, stamping the ground nervously with their heads craning, and Asmund and Kjeld sank down beside me as I watched the forest.

Asmund clicked his tongue before he made his way across an opening in the trees and I followed him to the brush that crested the hill, overlooking the village. I got down, tracing the path from the gate to the ritual house with my eyes. There was no movement, but bodies were strewn in every direction, fallen in the dirt and inside the open doors of empty houses. The flames still worked at some of them, filling the entire village with smoke.

I tried to shake the vision of Fela from my mind, the village I'd grown up in on the mountain. But I could still see it so clearly. The shadowed shape of the Herja spilling in from the trees. Hands dragging me into the forest, screaming. Everything burning in the snow.

Asmund's eyes flitted over the silent rooftops. "Maybe he didn't make it here," he said, almost to himself.

I was thinking the same. From the look of the fire, the Svell had attacked only an hour or two ago. Bard should have had time to warn them, but it looked as if the village wasn't empty when they'd arrived. If Bard was here, he was probably one of the bodies lying below.

"Ready?" I waited for Asmund to meet my eyes.

He answered with a jerk of his chin and Kjeld followed, not taking his gaze from the village.

I grabbed ahold of the strap of my scabbard, wincing as I tightened it around my body. It pulled at the wound below my ribs as Asmund took the bow from Kjeld and nocked an arrow, ready to cover my trail. When he gave me a nod, I stepped out from under the cover of the forest and headed across the moonlit grass. The faint sound of a wolf howling echoed in the stillness and I pushed the breath out slowly as I sank low to the ground, trying to calm my racing heart. When I reached the gate, I crouched behind the wooden post, watching.

Asmund made his way from the trees and found a place beside me, his eyes on the main path that led through the village. The mud still glistened around the army's footprints in the soft earth. Behind me, Kjeld began to pray under his breath and the name of Naðr rolled on his voice like a song.

I whistled softly and tipped my head toward the ritual house, where a trail of white smoke was still spiraling up from the roof. As he caught sight of it, Asmund stepped into the path and Kjeld followed behind him, sword drawn.

We passed the open door of a house with a smoldering fire and I looked back to Asmund. He saw it, too. The bare feet of a dead woman lay in the path, her arms clutched around a still child. A muddy axe lay beside them, her fingertips still lightly touching the wooden handle.

I gritted my teeth and ran faster, the urge to throw my axe shooting up my arm like lightning. They'd been defenseless. Helpless. The Svell had poured in from the forest in a flood and the Nādhir hadn't had a chance.

Asmund moved past me, stopping beside the huge door of the ritual house ahead. He pressed his back into the carved wood, scanning the village around us before he gave me another nod.

I took the knife from my belt and gently leaned into the heavy door until an amber crack of orange light cut through the darkness. I peered inside, where the benches were toppled, the altar fire gone out, but the coals still lit the room in a hazy glow, the smoke billowing up to the opening in the roof. I sucked in a breath and pushed it open, sliding inside with Asmund and Kjeld right behind me.

Pools of blood shone on the stone, bodies still lying where they'd fallen in the fight.

As soon as it was clear, Asmund looked to me. "They're moving fast."

"I know."

The next village was Lund. It sat on the outskirts of Nādhir territory at the base of the mountain. But if Bard hadn't made it to Utan, then he wasn't headed to Lund. And there was nothing stopping the Svell army from heading up the mountain either. The only thing we could count on was that they'd come for the fjord first and the Nādhir army would be waiting.

Asmund slid his sword back into his belt, stepping over a body and picking an axe up off the ground beside him just as a soft whistle rang outside. He pulled the blade free again, meeting my eyes.

"What is it?" I watched him think before the hint of a smile lifted on his lips.

"It's Bard," he breathed. "It's one of our calls."

I went back to the door, peering out, and Asmund came to stand on the other side. But the thick smoke hovering over the ground made it impossible to see. My fingers tightened around my knife as I pushed the door open and the ear-splitting crack of an axe hitting the wall beside me made the room spin. I whirled, lifting the blade, and behind us, a Svell warrior stood in the opening of the other set of doors, his hand still lifted from the throw.

I launched forward and ran at him, closing the distance between us in only steps and bringing my axe around me so that the blunt side of the blade caught him in the jaw. The sword fell from his hand as he tumbled backward, sliding on the stone until he rolled over the threshold, landing in the mud outside.

"Halvard!" Asmund shouted my name and I turned, searching the smoke for him.

Voices echoed in the silence and I could just barely see Kjeld swinging his sword in the path ahead, its edge catching another blade with a spark that lit the darkness. The moonlight broke through the clouds and as soon as we were out of the shadows, a Svell came from behind the next house, his sword swinging. Asmund lifted his axe, stopping the man's blow overhead, and slammed his closed fist into his face. He tilted, losing his balance, and the Svell scrambled to regain his footing before Asmund kicked him in the chest, sending him backward. But before Asmund had a chance to finish him, the man threw himself forward and the sword lifted again, ready to come down on his back.

I let the knife in my hand sink back behind my head and slung it forward, letting it fly handle over blade through the air. It hit its mark, finding the flesh between his shoulder blades, and he fell face-first into the dirt at Asmund's feet.

A strangled sound twisted on his lips as I knelt down and dragged my axe blade across his throat. His eyes blinked, his mouth falling open as he looked at me, and I didn't wait for him to die. I stood with my knife in my hand, searching the dark until I caught sight of another Svell running toward us, a sword arcing over his head. I tightened my grip around the axe and sank down into my feet, finding a center. I waited until he was only a few steps away before I heaved forward and plowed into him, sending the pointed blade of my axe into his side as he passed.

Another body slammed into me and the hilt of a sword found my face, knocking my head to the side. I brought my elbow down with a snap, catching his arm, and when his hands were loosened, I rolled, coming out from under him. The burned flesh at my side tore open and I hissed through the bone-deep pain exploding between my ribs, trying to breathe.

"Get up!" Asmund kicked the Svell's body to the side, taking hold of my vest with both hands.

As soon as I was on my feet, we ran for the gate. Footsteps punched the ground behind us and Asmund pulled the bow from his shoulder, turning. He nocked an arrow as he spun in a circle, but stopped short, his eyes going wide. Bard was running down the path toward us, one side of his body dragging and his face half-covered in blood.

Asmund dropped the bow and ran to him, taking his brother's arm over his shoulder and carrying his weight as they climbed the hill to the forest.

"You."

A soft, even voice found me, sounding over every inch of my skin in the dark, and I stopped beneath the gate, turning with my axe lifted before me. The handle almost slid from my fingers and I stilled, sucking in a sharp breath as the trees seemed to suddenly sway around me. My hand went back to the wound, now bleeding through my tunic as I blinked, but the vision didn't clear.

There, in the moonlight, the Kyrr girl from the glade stood, watching me.

CHAPTER SEVENTEEN

TOVA

There's no silence like death.

I shivered against the chill, my body still shaking from the henbane as we waited in the forest above Utan. The homes below were half-eaten up by fire now, an eerie quiet falling over what had been a village only hours ago. The Svell warriors who'd been ordered to stay back with us stalked in the trees restlessly, the tension growing with each passing minute.

"They're not coming," Gunther murmured at my back, the words sharp-edged and angry.

I ignored him, my eyes fixed on the gate. I'd seen him. I knew I had. There, beneath the arched opening in the fence that surrounded the village, the Nādhir would stand in the moonlight.

"He's not here. He never was," one of the men muttered.

The pain in my head made it hard to keep my eyes open,

every sound too loud in my ears. The trickle of the creek and the rustle of birds in the branches above us. The scrape of boots on the forest floor.

"We should be back with the others," the man spoke again.

"He's coming," I said through gritted teeth.

"When?"

I looked up to the moon hanging in the sky. "Soon." I tried to sound sure. Surer than I was.

But the truth was that I didn't know why the Nādhir wasn't there like he had been in my vision. The slow, creeping thoughts in the back of my mind whispered that the Spinners had tricked me as punishment. That they'd used the vision to bring me my own death.

Maybe they had.

I turned back to the village, where smoke still rose up from charred wood and the moonlight caught the white tunic of a woman lying dead in the middle of the path that led up to the ritual house. In my vision, I hadn't seen death. I'd only seen the Nādhir from the glade. The one who'd looked me in the eye. I swallowed hard, that same sinking feeling in the pit of my stomach returning. There was a part of me that hoped he *wouldn't* come. A part of me that was growing by the minute.

"Enough of this." The man stepped forward and caught my arm, wrenching me back to face him, and I slipped my knife from my belt, pressing the tip of it to the side of his neck.

His eyes went wide as the others moved toward me, but he lifted his hands, stopping them. He stilled, his teeth bared as he looked down at me.

"Tova, stop." Jorrund reached for the knife but I pushed him away.

"He's coming," I said again, meeting the man's eyes. "Vigdis told me to find him. That's what I'm doing."

Behind him, Gunther stared at me with surprise lit in his eyes. I'd never killed another person. I wasn't sure if I could. But I had to stay if I was going to have any chance at appeasing Vigdis.

As soon as I lowered the knife, the man shoved me hard and I slammed into the tree behind me.

"I told you." The woman beside Gunther shook her head. "We should go back."

"Not without the Nādhir," Jorrund answered, his voice lowering in warning. I wasn't the only one who'd fall under Vigdis' wrath if we came back empty-handed.

"Stop it." Gunther finally spoke from where he stood in the shadows. "All of you. We stay until dawn. If he's not here by sunup, we'll go back to the others and Vigdis can deal with her."

"Wait," Jorrund whispered, his eyes lifting over us.

I turned to see a figure moving out of the trees on the other side of the village. A man. The moonlight hit the blade of an axe at his side and he stopped at the post before two more shadows followed after him.

"It's him," I whispered.

Jorrund leaned in closer to me. "How do you know?"

"I told you. I *saw* it."

We crouched down, going silent as the three figures moved through the gate and onto the main path that led through the village.

Gunther nodded to the others and they pushed back into the forest to come from the west side, their weapons drawn out before them as the three men disappeared into the ritual house below. They moved silently down the slope and I sank beside a tree, watching them hop the fence that encircled Utan before slipping into the shadows.

I closed my eyes against the pain in the center of my forehead. The vision of the Nādhir before the gate was still sharp in my mind. His bloodied axe, his hand pressed to his side. What I'd seen had been real, but it still felt like a dream. And now that it was coming to pass, the knot between my ribs wound tighter, the prick of tears springing up in my eyes.

The sound of shouting brought me back to my feet and I searched the little bit of the village that was visible, but it was too dark. There was only moving shadow and shifting smoke. I fixed my gaze on the doors of the ritual house, my fingers tangled into one another until my fingernails bit into my skin. When another man screamed, Gunther sighed beside me.

"Go back." He looked to Jorrund. "Tell Vigdis to send more men." He ran down the slope with his sword at his side and Jorrund ran into the trees, leaving me alone.

But still, the Nādhir didn't appear beneath the gate.

My heart raced over each breath as I watched Jorrund disappear in the darkness. I looked over my shoulder, to the village. In the vision, he was there. He was right there.

I walked down the hill with my skirt twisted in my sweaty fists and stopped, almost stumbling forward as a figure burst out of the smoke. I froze, my breath bound up in my chest and I held it until it burned.

Without thinking, the word left my trembling lips. "You."

The sound that had found me in the glade crashed in my pounding head like an angry ocean, making me feel as if I was tipping to one side. I tried to steady myself, meeting his eyes and letting them anchor me. Because those same blue eyes were looking at me again. *Right* at me.

"Are you . . ." He stared at me, hand pressed into the wound at his side. Blood seeped between his fingers as he spoke between heavy breaths. "Are you really here?"

But I could barely hear him over the swarm of bees in my head. The sound swelled with each heartbeat.

"I saw you. In the forest."

I closed my eyes, wincing against the pain in my skull, and when I opened them again, the sight of him wavered.

"Who are you?" His eyes ran over my face. "What are you doing with the Svell?"

I opened my mouth to speak before I realized there really was no answer. I was a Kyrr castoff with no people and no home. I was the daughter of no one, used by a clan that I shared no blood with. There was no explanation for it. No way to make sense of it. It just . . . was.

Suddenly, he was moving, closing the distance between us and his shadow fell over me before his bloodied hands wrapped around my throat, squeezing. I lifted up onto my toes and my fingers found his wrists. I held onto him, the breath burning in my chest, and I could see that even if he didn't know who I was, he knew *what* I was. He stared at the mark below my throat, his gaze moving over my skin before he looked back up at me. I pulled at his hands, trying to draw breath, but he didn't budge. The ache in my head began to fade as I looked up into his eyes. Because they were still fixed on mine. Tears glistened at their corners, catching the moonlight, and as he pulled in a short breath, one rolled down his rough cheek.

He looked right into me as the roar of the rushing water exploded all around us, and at first, I thought it sounded familiar. Like I'd heard it before. Somewhere deep in the memories the storm that had brought me across the fjord had washed away. They took shape, curling and twisting around pieces I recognized. I blinked, trying to listen as the darkness crept in around me, his grip tightening. My hands went cold around his wrists and I searched the sounds, trying to place them.

And suddenly, it settled. It wasn't buzzing or bees or the crush of water or the crackle of ice. It was the sound of voices.

Whispers.

"Naðr."

The voices suddenly vanished, like a lit torch dropped in water, and the Kyrr man I'd seen at the glade appeared behind the Nādhir, his wide eyes set on mine.

"Stop, Halvard."

The Nādhir dropped me and I fell to the ground, choking. The burn raced down my throat as I gasped in the cold air, the feeling returning to my hands as I reached up, pulling the neck of my tunic closed.

The Kyrr man looked down at me, his breath fogging out between us. The mark of a fish wrapped around his throat, the tail disappearing into his tunic. He was older than me by many years, but the way he looked at me was familiar. It felt close.

"You know me," I whispered, studying his face. Trying to place it. Some part of me knew him, too.

"I didn't think it could be true." His voice was only a breath.

I tried to speak, but I couldn't find words. I couldn't reach the memories that were hovering above my thoughts, just out of reach. As shouting came from the forest, both men looked up, over my head.

"What couldn't be true?" I got to my feet, my fingers still cradling my aching throat.

The Kyrr man didn't answer. His eyes changed then, the sharp point of his stare softening. He looked almost . . . sad.

Voices called out in the night and I turned back to where

the Svell were coming from the trees on the other side of the village.

"Give me your axe," I said, looking to the man he'd called Halvard.

He stared at my hand outstretched before him. "What?"

"Give me your axe!" I reached up, pulling it from his grip. "You have to run."

The Kyrr man looked at me for another silent moment before he disappeared, but Halvard didn't move. The light in his eyes changed, the pulse at his neck jumping beneath the skin. "Why are you helping us?"

I looked up into his face, realizing that was what I was doing. I was helping him. Because it was one life I could save. I was suddenly overcome with a desperate need to be sure he didn't die. "Go," I whispered.

He looked at me for a long moment, swallowing hard. And in the next breath, he turned, disappearing into the trees.

I faced the village, stilling the shaking of my hands as I marched back through the gate, to the path. I searched the bodies on the ground until I found a man in a Nādhir armor vest lying facedown with long, dark hair. I took a deep breath before I rolled him over, looking down into his face. He was older than Halvard, but he'd have to do. I was out of choices. I was out of time.

I planted my feet before him, pushing every thought from my mind, the weight of the cool axe blade heavy in my open hand. The careful rendering of a yew tree branch was engraved into the shining steel and it glimmered in the faint light of the fires still burning. I pulled in a breath, my eyes fixed on the night sky. And when I lifted the axe over my head, I conjured every dark shadow within me. Every withered thing within my perishing soul. I gave myself over to that darkness. And with the cold, unbeating heart of the dead heavy in my chest, I brought the blade down.

2 YEARS AGO

Village of Liera, Svell Territory

TOVA MADE IT TO BEKAN'S HOME ON THE HILL ONLY MOments before the sun rose over the village of Liera. Her cloak was heavy and damp with the mist that whirled through the air as she'd walked the paths of the forest. But it was the uneasy ache in her stomach that made her steps falter. It had been six days since Bekan's daughter, Vera, had been bedridden with fever. And if Jorrund had summoned Tova, she must have taken a turn for the worse in the night.

She stopped before the door and drew a steadying breath before she lifted her hand to knock. Footsteps hit the floorboards inside as shadows reached across the ground in the amber light. The latch lifted and Jorrund's face appeared as the door opened, but the look on his face already held the answer she'd been called to give.

Tova lifted up onto her toes to peer over his shoulder, where Vera was tucked onto a cot beside the fire. Her gaunt face left her eyes looking hollow, one small hand set on top of the furs. Tova couldn't help but think of the tiny baby girl who'd spent her days cradled in Bekan's arms and the memory brought the sting of hot tears to her eyes.

She wound a finger around the string beneath the tunic and pulled, feeling the bite at the back of her neck. Bekan stood over his daughter, his armor gone and his clothes wrinkled. Even his braids were unraveling down his back, the darkness clinging beneath his eyes. He hadn't slept in days.

Jorrund took hold of Tova's arm and pulled her inside without a word, clearing the table and unrolling the pelt. Bekan didn't look up at her as she took the rune stones from around her neck and opened the purse. Vera's eyes weren't quite closed, only slits of reflection lighting in them. But her mouth hung open, her chest rising and falling with a slow but labored breath.

Tova didn't need to cast the stones to know what fate was carved into the Tree of Urðr for her. And she couldn't help but think again that the Spinners were cruel. Bekan had already lost his wife and now he would lose his only child.

Jorrund set a bundle of herbs into the fire pit and the smoke billowed as the healer sank down beside the cot, wiping at Vera's face. Her blond, straight hair was slicked back, falling over the edge of the cot like a curtain.

Tova clenched her hands to keep them from shaking before she poured the stones into her palm. Vera had been one of the only souls in Liera to be kind to her. One of the only Svell to not mutter threats as she passed or leave cursed charms at her door. And now, the Spinners would take even that from her.

She whispered the words on a hoarse breath, the pain in her stomach sharpening.

"Eye of the gods, give me sight."

The words rolled off her tongue as she closed her eyes, finding Vera's face in the center of her mind. Her elk-skin armor perfectly smooth, the shine of her sword at her hip. The vision felt real, and Tova wondered if it was Vera's spirit, already pulling away from her weak body. Her gray eyes looked back at Tova, the neat braids tightly pleated against her scalp.

The stones dropped to the pelt from Tova's slick fingers and she suddenly felt Bekan's gaze on her. When she looked back at him, she saw something new in his eyes. The emptiness that sank into the shadows of Vera's had found its way into Bekan's and the flicker of light made him look like a corpse. His stare bored into her, dead and brittle, and beneath it, she could see that he hated her. That he was disgusted by her. Because just as Tova didn't need to look at the stones to know, he didn't need to hear her say it.

And Tova lost not one ally that night, but two.

Village of Hylli, Nādhir Territory

Halvard stood over the deer, pulling the arrow from where it had struck between its ribs. Its black, shining eye looked up at him, reflecting the sky overhead, and he ran a hand down the arch of its neck, over its shoulder as he muttered a prayer of thanks.

It had taken hours to stalk the deer, and he'd spent most of the night crouched in the tall reeds that encircled the meadow, but he'd finally been able to take the single shot before the sun rose up over the trees. The light caught the dew on the blades of grass as he took it up onto his shoulders and started the walk back toward Hylli.

His breath fogged in the cold, but the deer's warmth took the stiff ache out of his frozen hands. The village would be full of Nādhir traveling from every village on the mountain as well as the fjord, gathering for the meeting of village leaders that was held in the Hylli ritual house every spring. It would be the first time in a year that he'd see his brother Iri, who made his home on the mountain. The birth of another child had kept him from the fjord longer than usual but they'd made the journey to stay in Hylli for the warm months, which meant that Halvard would spend more time in the forest hunting and in the water fishing to feed them all. His brothers would meet with the leaders over the next few weeks and the hill above the village would be covered in tents. The Talas would tell the stories of the gods and recount the fighting seasons that had ruled their people's lives before the peace was made. It was a time to remember the past and plan for the future. But there were many who suspected that war was coming from the west, where the Svell clan dwelled in the forested cliffs that ran into the sea.

A figure appeared in the mist ahead and Halvard stopped in the middle of the path, reaching back for his knife. But a familiar voice called his name, and the orange fox furs atop Fiske's shoulders appeared in the fog.

His hand dropped from the handle of the blade when he saw him, and Halvard tried to take apart the look on his face. But Fiske stood still, the mist moving around him, with an unreadable expression.

"What is it?" He was almost as tall as his brother now, meeting his eyes as he stopped before him, but Fiske didn't answer.

He took the deer from Halvard's shoulders and set it onto his own before he started back toward the village. "Espen is asking for you."

Halvard's brow pulled, his eyes pinned on Fiske's back as he walked ahead. "What's wrong?"

"Nothing's wrong," he answered, his voice lightening, and for a moment, Halvard thought maybe he was telling the truth.

He followed Fiske in the silence and the sounds and scents of the sea grew as they neared the village. The camped Nādhir were already awake, many of them cooking over their fires, and the smoke from the ritual house was thick and white. Fiske led him through the gate and as they passed their home, he saw his mother standing in the open doorway, her hands tangled into her apron. The same apprehensive look that had been in Fiske's eyes was lit in hers.

Halvard swallowed hard, the pulse beneath his skin

picking up until he could hear it sounding in his ears. When they reached the carved wooden doors of the ritual house, Fiske stopped, letting the deer slide from his shoulders.

"What's going on?" Halvard asked again, this time letting the fear leak out into his voice.

His brother opened the door and the heat of the altar fire came rushing out into the cold air. Inside, Espen stood before the other village leaders, waiting.

Fiske set his hand onto Halvard's shoulder, leading him down the center aisle. The Nādhir leaders stepped aside as he found a place among them, winding his fingers together at his back and trying to stand up taller before them.

"Halvard." Espen spoke first, tipping his chin up in a greeting.

Halvard nodded in return, finding the eyes of each of the leaders. But whatever was going on, they concealed it well, surveying him wordlessly.

"We have something to tell you."

He swallowed hard, unintentionally taking a small step closer to Fiske.

"You know we mortals have numbered years," Espen began. "When this life is over for me, we will need a new leader. One who can take my place as chieftain."

Halvard stared at him, a stillness settling in his bones.

"I have no sons, and I would like you to accept the responsibility."

He stepped back again but Fiske's hand pushed him forward, back into place. "I don't . . ."

"I'm not asking," Espen said, cutting him off before he could finish. "It's been decided."

"But . . ." He looked to Fiske, but he only stared ahead. "Why are you choosing me?"

Espen crossed his arms over his chest. "Because peace won't last forever. You're among the first generation of Nādhir. Your soul is good and you don't crave power. You've grown into a strong man, Halvard."

"I'm only sixteen years old." He stared at the ground, the heat burning on his face.

"I was killing Riki on the battlefield long before that age." Espen laughed. "You begin tomorrow."

He looked up. "Begin what?"

"Learning to father your people." Espen smiled, raising a hand to clap him on the arm, and the others did the same as they passed him, headed for the doors.

Halvard swallowed down the feeling of nausea, the warm air of the ritual house suddenly making him feel like he couldn't breathe.

When the doors closed, he turned to Fiske. "What did you do?"

"You think I did this?" He half-laughed, but Halvard didn't think it was funny. In fact, he was angry.

"You have to tell them they've made a mistake. You have to tell them—"

Fiske took hold of Halvard's armor and pulled him close before wrapping one arm around him. "You're afraid," he said, lowly. "That's good."

Halvard swallowed against the lump in his throat. "Fiske . . ." He searched for a way to say the words without making his brother ashamed of him.

Fiske kissed his cheek gruffly before he took Halvard's face into his hands, forcing him to meet his eyes. "I will never leave you. You know that. And when the time comes to follow you, I will."

He let Halvard go, moving past him to the doors, and when they closed, his shadow reached down the aisle, painted onto the stone. The fire blazed hot at his back and he watched the shadow waver in the shifting light before he looked up to the two faces that looked down on him from the carvings above the archway.

Thora and Sigr.

The gods of the mountain and the fjord, enemies turned allies. The mother and father of a new people. He stood, unmoving, as their gazes fell heavily upon him. And in the next breath, he dropped to his knees and begged them to change their minds.

CHAPTER EIGHTEEN

HALVARD

War is easy.

Aghi's words found me as I rode, and I remembered the way his eyes looked sad as he'd said them. But he had been wrong when he said war was easy. The faces of the dead in Utan rose up in my mind. They filled the forest around me. Strangers, but Nādhir. My people.

People I'd failed to protect.

I couldn't help but think that if Espen had survived the attack in the glade, that he would have found a way to keep them safe.

We rode for hours, through parts of the forest I'd never seen. They were places the raiders knew well, lands where no one went looking for anything. But it was Hylli that I saw all around me. I could feel it. The thought was a trail of footsteps that followed behind every thought. The wind that hit my face as I rode was the sea air coming up the cliffs.

The sound of the trees above me was the roar of white-capped waves.

Mýra would be waiting for me beneath the gate, her eyes on the stretch of earth that rolled down toward the village from the forest. If my brothers and Eelyn had made it back from Fela, they'd be standing beside her. But I wasn't there to meet them. Maybe I never would be.

I tried to draw in a breath that wouldn't come, my chest tight beneath the armor vest as I searched for the words I would need to tell them about Aghi. About Ljós and Utan and the glade. There were no words for that. There was no name for it. My family had risked everything to give me a different life than the one they knew. They'd believed that things were different now. But if I made it back to Hylli, I would be leading them right back into it.

We came up on the ridge that overlooked the river and Asmund whistled ahead, letting it ring out behind him to let us know he was stopping. The horses slowed, their gaits uneven after running all night.

Asmund helped Bard dismount and he was careful as his boots hit the ground, limping on his left leg. I came down before him, inspecting the wound. It looked like the work of a sword, one clean gash deep enough to cut through most of the muscle, but the bleeding had stopped.

Asmund helped his brother cut the wool of his pants back. "What happened?" He spoke gruffly.

Bard looked up at the sky as Asmund wiped the dirt from the broken skin. "I told them the Svell were coming, but only a few left for the mountain." He swallowed. "They didn't want to leave their homes."

I stared at the ground, my jaw clenching. They had known the Svell were coming. They knew, and still they stayed. And I wasn't sure why I hadn't known that's what they'd do. It's what my family would have done. It's what every soul in Hylli would have done.

I got down onto one knee and pulled the sides of the wound open, searching for the white bone of his leg. It was similar to the one that had given Aghi his limp in the battle against the Herja. The cut was deep, but if it was kept clean, he'd walk again.

"Here." Bard reached into his armor vest and tossed a small tin to me. "I got it from the healer in Utan for you before . . ." He swallowed the rest of the sentence.

I wondered if the healer who'd made the medicine had gone to Möor or stayed in Utan, but I knew the answer. The healer wouldn't have left the people if a fight was coming. "Thank you." I nodded, turning it over in my hand.

Asmund helped Bard to the water and he pulled the saddlebag from his horse to stitch him up. I pried off the lid of the tin to smell the sweet scent of honey and pine sap. Smells that reminded me of my mother and the sting of memory burned in the center of my chest.

Kjeld pulled up the sleeve of his tunic, eyeing a deep cut at the back of his arm and setting a piece of dry linen over it.

"You know her, don't you?" I said.

He tied off the bandage. "What?"

"The girl with the Svell. How do you know her?"

He tore another cloth with his teeth. "I didn't say I knew her."

"You didn't have to." I waited for an answer, but he ignored me, pulling the sleeve of his tunic back down. "Why did she help us? She could have called out. She could have screamed, but she told us to run."

Asmund looked between us from where he worked over Bard's leg.

Again, I waited for Kjeld to answer. But he looked straight at me, his gaze level. Whatever he knew, he wasn't going to tell us.

I unclasped my vest, pulling it over my head with my tunic, and walked straight out into the freezing water until I was waist deep, cupping handfuls of it up to scrub my face and pinching my eyes closed against the sting it shot beneath my skin. It was a welcome pain. It was better than the memory of the woman and her child lying in the open doorway. Anything was better than that.

I sank down beneath the surface and let the hum of the current drown out everything else. The sunlight cast the water into a jeweled blue and I let the air burn in my chest, my heart beating in my ears. The sound of Aghi's voice returned to me, the deep rasp of it like a fire. His clear eyes and auburn beard streaked with silver.

War is easy.

The moment we walked through Hylli's gate, the Nādhir

would look to me. But only I knew what Espen and Aghi and the others had failed to see.

They'd chosen me for peace, not war.

The aging leaders of the villages had placed their faith in me for the wrong fate. And as soon as the Svell arrived, ready and able to take everything we had, they'd know it, too.

When my lungs couldn't take any more, I shot up out of the water with a gasp. The sun was warm, the smell of winter no longer on the wind. Spring was coming. The ice was melting. And there was nothing to slow the Svell from the battle they wanted.

"We should sleep an hour." Asmund sank down at the river's edge to take a drink. He arched an eyebrow at me when I didn't answer. "You'd rather fall off your horse?"

His eyes dropped to the covered wound at my side. If I didn't clean it, I'd be half dead before the Svell arrived at the edge of our forest. But I wasn't the only one Asmund was thinking of. Bard's face was painted a pale white from the blood he'd lost. He needed rest if he was going to have a chance at making it to the fjord.

"One hour. That's it," I said.

I unwrapped the bandage beneath my armor vest carefully, wincing as I pulled the last of it back from where it was stuck to the raw, open skin. It hadn't even begun to heal, the flesh around the opening inflamed and swollen where it had torn.

Asmund pulled Bard's saddle down and dropped it in the dirt before his own and he came to sit beside me, reaching into his vest for a bundle of dried venison. Dark blood streaked two deep cuts carved into the back of his hand.

"You're hurt," I said, holding the tin of salve out to him.

"It's fine." He didn't take it, looking down at his hand as if he'd forgotten it was there. He tore a piece of the venison in two and put it in his mouth. Behind him, Bard lay back onto the saddle and closed his eyes.

He let out a long breath, chewing. "What will happen? When you get to Hylli?"

"I'm not sure," I admitted. I'd been careful not to think about it.

"They'll initiate you, won't they? As chieftain of the Nādhir?"

I leaned my elbows onto my knees, staring into the dirt. "I don't know if he'll accept me."

"Who?" Asmund's brow pulled.

"Latham."

He shrugged. "He has to."

But Latham wasn't the kind of man that could be made to do anything. After Espen, he was the oldest leader of the Nādhir and if he rejected me, I knew the others might follow. Maybe they should.

"I would understand if he didn't."

"They chose you, Halvard. They agreed."

But that wasn't what I meant and he knew it. Espen and the other leaders hadn't chosen me for this.

We sat in silence as Bard fell asleep, and Asmund watched

him, crossing his arms over his chest as he leaned back against the tree. He was worried. "Will he be alright?"

"He won't fight," I said, "but he'll be alright."

"He won't like that." He laughed.

I spread the salve over the burned skin and rewrapped it carefully as Asmund settled down to sleep and Kjeld took the place against the tree beside me, cleaning the blood from his axe.

"Who is she?" I asked again, sucking in a breath as I tightened the knot of the bandage.

Kjeld wiped the curve of the blade against the thick wool of his pants. "Someone who's not supposed to be alive."

He let the axe fall back into the sheath at his back and rolled over, and I looked up to the sky, still shrouded in thick cloud cover. We'd be back in Hylli before the day was out. Back to the salty smell of the fjord and the silvery light on the water. I tried not to close my eyes. Sleep held too many faces I didn't want to see. Voices that made my insides ache. I stared at the glitter of light on the rippling water of the river until the sun was overhead, painting everything in yellow light.

And as the warmth of the sun came, so did the remembering. It wedged its fingers inside my ribs and grabbed hold of my heart, squeezing. Because those days were gone. For all of us. So many mornings, Asmund and I had drifted out into the current as boys and thrown the nets against the wind. We'd sat around fires at night, laughing and listening to the stories my brothers told. And I wondered if this was my last story. The thought lifted like a wall of fog creeping toward me.

I was a torch in the wind.

I was flickering out.

CHAPTER NINETEEN

TOVA

THERE WERE NO OMENS FOR THIS. NO SIGNS OR RUNE STONES or prayers to be uttered.

I walked through the forest, Jorrund and Gunther at my back, with the cold weight of the head in my hands. I clutched it to my chest, the blood staining the front of my dress and the face turned up at me. Mouth open. Skin yellow and gray.

He'd known me. The Kyrr's eyes had held recognition when they met mine. I didn't know why he was on the mainland or why he was with Halvard, but he'd known me. And if he knew me, then he knew my story.

I looked down at the open eyes cradled in my arms, glad the man wasn't alive to see my face. I'd stood alone in the silent village as the Svell searched the forest, bringing the axe down before me and cutting the head from the corpse.

I would never forget that sound.

The camp was still awake when the fires came into view, the Svell feasting on the livestock they'd taken from Utan to fill their bellies for battle. Gunther opened the tent before me and I ducked inside. He hadn't spoken since we left the village and I'd noticed the strain on his face growing with each day since we left Liera. He stood beside me, his hands tucked into his vest as Vigdis looked up from where he sat over a bowl of steaming, roasted meat.

His hand froze on the spoon as his black eyes landed on the head in my hands.

The table shook as he set his hands down onto it and stood. "Is that him? The one who killed my brother?"

I pulled in a steadying breath, trying to keep from trembling. "It is."

He came around the table, taking the head from me and turning it around so that it faced him.

Really, the man looked nothing like Halvard except for maybe in the color of his hair. Even his eyes were wrong. A deep brown instead of the sparkling blue. I could still see them in my mind, filled with tears as he wrapped his hands around my throat. I reached up, gently touching the bruised skin above my collarbone. If the Kyrr man hadn't come from the forest, I wondered if he really would have killed me.

But no one looked themselves in death, and I hoped it was enough to convince Vigdis. He lifted the head before him, as if looking the dead man in the eyes. His brow furrowed as he studied it.

"They arrived in Utan in the middle of the night. He

killed two of our warriors before I took him down." Gunther spoke beside me.

I froze, looking up at his hard face, but he stared ahead, unblinking.

I'd already cut the corpse's head off when Gunther and Jorrund found me near the gate. I'd told him that I had seen one of the Svell kill him, and he didn't ask questions. He only walked into the forest without waiting for Jorrund and me to follow. Now, he was lying to Vigdis, but I didn't know why.

Vigdis let out a long breath before he set the head down onto the table beside his bowl of stew. "Make sure they're ready." He spoke to Siv, but his attention landed on me when he finally looked up. His eyes bored into mine, a fragile silence falling over the tent.

Jorrund took my arm gently, pulling me away, and I looked back once more to Gunther, who still stood before the table. He didn't look at me as Jorrund pushed the canvas open, his arm wrapping around my shoulder. "Are you alright?" He ran a worried hand over my hair and I resisted the urge to push him away.

"Am I alright?" I whispered hoarsely, stopping. "I just cut off a man's head and carried it through the forest."

"Of course. I'm sorry." He lifted his hands before him. "Who was it?" When I didn't answer, his wrinkled brow arched up over his slanted eyes knowingly. "Whose head was it?" he asked again.

I twisted my hands into my skirt. "Just a dead man in the village. I had to . . ." I swallowed, the weakness coming back into my legs. "I had to come back with something."

But the truth was that in that moment, beneath the gate with Halvard staring down into my face, I couldn't do it. There was something about him that felt too familiar. A feeling that pulled like an anchor in my chest when I saw him. If he was fated to die, he should have died in the glade. And I wasn't going to be the one to change it. Not this time. I told myself it was because I'd seen enough death, but I knew it was more than that. I didn't want the man who'd looked me in the eye to die. I didn't want to think that I'd never see him again.

Jorrund surveyed me, the worry creasing the skin around his mouth as his eyes dropped down to my throat, where I could still feel the ache of Halvard's hands. "What happened?"

I reached up, pulling the collar of my tunic up. "It's nothing," I said beneath my breath. "I need to speak with you."

His gaze flickered up to my face. "What is it?"

"I think . . ." I stopped, thinking before I said it. "I think we've made a mistake."

He looked around us warily before he put his arm back around me, leading me to our tent at the end of the row. Once we were inside, he turned to face me, lifting the torch between us. "What are you talking about?"

"It's a mistake."

"What is?"

"All of it. Utan, Ljós. Hylli. We have to stop them. We have to go back."

"Tova, you saw what the future holds. Vigdis made a difficult decision, but it was the right one."

"What if I was wrong? About the runes. About everything." I sat down on the cot, putting my face into my hands. It had been haunting me, the thought that maybe I couldn't see into the future. That maybe I didn't understand the language of the Spinners or the will of the gods at all.

Jorrund's hand landed on my shoulder and squeezed. "You weren't wrong."

"But I saw something when I took the henbane, Jorrund. Something . . ."

He crouched down before me. "What?" The firelight shifted in the wind coming in from outside and I watched his face change with it. "What did you see?"

"I think it was a memory. From before."

He stilled. "Before? You mean, before Eydis brought you to us?"

But I didn't believe that anymore, and I didn't know if he did either. It was just something he said to make sense of things that couldn't be understood. "I don't know. But I think the Spinners are trying to speak to me, Jorrund. And there's something about Halvard . . ." I called him by name without even realizing it and the word stung on my lips.

"Who?"

"The Nādhir from the glade." I looked up at him. "I

think this path is tangled with mine somehow. I think the gods will be angry with us if we don't—"

He stood. "Tova, we cannot undo what has been done. We cannot stop a war that has already spilled this much blood."

"But the gods—"

"Silence!" he roared suddenly and I flinched, recoiling. "What do you know of the gods? You're a child." He rubbed his forehead with the palm of his hand, taking a deep breath. "Remember your place, Tova. This is not for you to decide."

I stared into my folded hands, pressing my tongue to the roof of my mouth to keep from speaking. Whatever bound me to Jorrund was like the ice clinging to the shores outside of Liera, growing thinner every moment.

"You need sleep. We'll speak of this in the morning." He looked at me for a long moment before he pushed outside, taking the torch with him and leaving me in the pitch dark.

I lay back on the cot, curling onto my side. But my hands were still shaking against my chest, sticky with the dead man's blood. I could smell it. Everywhere. The stench of death and rot had clung to me in Utan and I wondered if it would ever let me go.

I pulled the vision of the water back to me. The gray deep. The stream of bubbles trailing up to the bright surface. My hands, floating out before me. And the sound. A deep hum that wrapped itself around me and pulled me down into the cold.

Until a flicker of light ignited around me. It lit the

darkness like a flash of lightning and I held my breath, waiting. My heart pounded as a flash lit behind my eyelids again and I sat up, clamping my hands to the side of the cot as another vision surfaced in the darkness.

The wavering image of a slender woman pulling long pale fingers through fire-red hair as she sat before a fire. And there was a sound. The soft, gentle hum of a song that some part of me recognized.

More fragmented pictures spilled over one another. High, jagged cliffs. Bare feet on black stone. The sharp teeth of dripping icicles clinging to the edge of a thatched roof. They loosened the seams stitched tight around the memories bound up in the back of my mind and I breathed through the pain that throbbed in my chest.

I pushed back the furs and stepped lightly across the dirt to the fire pit. Gunther's shadow was painted on the canvas, where he was posted outside my tent, and I held my breath, sinking to my knees. I didn't bother to roll out a pelt. I pulled the runes from around my neck and held them before me. Jorrund would never allow me to cast the runes by myself. He said it was too dangerous. That we needed Eydis' favor to protect me from the wicked gaze of the Spinners. But it wasn't the Svell's future I was looking into this time.

It was my own.

I emptied the pouch into my hand and my palms pressed together around them. I closed my eyes, sitting up straight with a deep, centering breath.

"Augua ór tivar. Ljá mir sýn.

"Augua ór tivar. Ljá mir sýn.

"Augua ór tivar. Ljá mir sýn."

The words rolled off my tongue, a warm tingle running over my skin.

Eye of the gods, give me sight.

For the length of a breath, I could hear another voice echoing the words. One that I knew, even if I didn't recognize it. It widened the stream of memories flashing in my mind and my own voice bled into it.

"Augua ór tivar. Ljá mir sýn.

"Augua ór tivar. Ljá mir sýn.

"Augua ór tivar. Ljá mir sýn."

I chanted, my voice deepening as I held my hands out before me and I pulled every whisper of hope and desperation from where it was hidden inside me and pleaded with it. And between the uneven beats of my heart, I let the stones fall.

The breath curled in my chest as I reached out, finding the runes in the darkness and carefully tracing their symbols with the tips of my fingers. But I needed to see them. I crawled across the floor, using a flat stone that rimmed the fire pit to push a large glowing coal onto the dirt. I rolled it before me until its light illuminated the stones just enough so that I could make them out.

Eihwaz sat in the center. The yew tree. Strength and trustworthiness. I bit down hard on my lip, my heart quickening. *Dagaz* was beside it, their sides touching. Dawn. An awakening. And to their right sat *Pethro,* the die cup and the rune of secrets.

But my gaze drifted to the corner of the spread, where one more stone was pulled up and away from the others.

Othala. The land of birth. A heritage. The story of a people.

The crunch of rocks beneath boots sounded outside and I looked up to see the shadows on the canvas moving. I frantically raked the stones together and swept them under my cot, getting to my feet as the voices grew louder.

I cursed, picking up the hot coal with my fingers and tossing it back into the fire pit with a hiss between my teeth. I pulled the furs over me just as the canvas moved and my heart slammed inside my chest as a long shadow stretched over the ground before me.

I could tell by the shape of it that it was Jorrund, his robes bundled around him. He stood in the opening of the tent silently. Maybe he'd changed his mind about what I'd said. Maybe he'd come back to apologize. But just as I was going to open my mouth and speak, he disappeared.

I let out a long breath, pinching my eyes closed against the sting on my hand where the coal had seared my skin. I rolled over, reaching beneath the cot for the rune stones and returned them to the pouch, slipping it back over my head.

Dagaz. Pethro. Othala.

It wasn't the dark fate I'd expected to see.

But it was *Eihwaz* in the center. The yew tree. And the shape of it pulled a thought like thread on a spinning wheel. It was the symbol that was marked into the skin at the hollow of my throat, above the symbol of the Truthtongue.

My mouth dropped open as I remembered, my eyes going to Halvard's axe on the ground. I sat up, reaching for it, and swallowed hard before I lifted it into the sliver of moonlight cast through the opening of the tent. I rubbed at the dried blood on the iron blade with my thumb until the shape of a branch was revealed. And not just any branch.

A yew tree.

CHAPTER TWENTY

HALVARD

THERE WERE SEABIRDS IN MY CHEST.

I could feel their wings beating behind my ribs. Their calls drifting away from shore, the sun hot on my skin even though the wind was ice.

The first time I ever saw the sea, I was eight years old. I sat on the back of my brother's horse, my fingers hooked into his armor vest as we came up over the hill and the land disappeared beneath the water ahead. I'd seen glimpses of it from up on the mountain, on the warmest days of summer when the fog was clear enough. But to see it up close, it scared me as much as it fascinated me. It was deeper than the mountain was high and it seemed to go on forever.

After only a few weeks in Hylli, the village felt like home. But the unsettling feeling of peace was something that took longer. It felt like something that couldn't be trusted. Something that couldn't be real. The holding of breath between fighting seasons had been our way of life until the Herja came and changed everything. It was hard to let go of, and I didn't know if the Nādhir ever truly had.

"Halvard."

I didn't realize I'd fallen asleep until the sound of Asmund's voice broke into the vision of the sea lit behind my eyes. I opened them to bits of purple sky poked like holes in the tree branches above and pulled in a deep breath, remembering where I was. I rubbed my hands over my face, breathing through my fingers. I hadn't slept in days, and the hunger for it made my body shake as I sat up.

Asmund stood over me, the afternoon sunlight bright behind him. "Kjeld's gone."

I looked behind me, where Kjeld had been sitting against the trunk of the tree. His saddle was missing, only the rustle of pine needles left as evidence that he was ever there.

"He was gone when I woke," Asmund said, picking up his saddle and setting it back onto the horse.

"He's superstitious." Bard leaned into the boulder beside the water, wincing against the pain in his leg. "Whoever that girl is, I think she spooked him."

"But where would he go?"

Asmund shrugged. "Maybe he'll wait out the war up on the mountain. Maybe he'll go south or meet up with the others."

I wanted to be angry, but I couldn't be. The Nādhir weren't Kjeld's people. He'd come to the mainland with nothing and even if he'd found a place among Asmund and the others, he didn't owe them anything. That's not how life among raiders worked.

Asmund and Bard readied their horses, meeting eyes over their saddles. If Kjeld was going to run, I wondered why he didn't do it after the glade. Why had he gone with us to Aurvanger? Maybe seeing the army in Utan was enough to scare him. Or maybe Bard was right and seeing the girl had driven him to leave. Whoever she was, he'd taken the secret with him, and that thought weighed more on my mind than it should have. Because even in the midst of war and all that was coming, I couldn't stop thinking about her or the way she'd looked at me in Utan as I wrapped my hands around her throat. Like she knew me, somehow.

I brushed the dirt from my pants and picked up my saddle. "You should both do the same. I can make it from here."

"We're going with you," Asmund said, waiting for me to look at him. "We're staying with you."

I buckled the straps, pulling the saddle into place. "You said you'd get me to Hylli. You nearly have."

"I want to fight with you," he said.

Bard watched his brother, a gleam of pride in his eyes. Maybe it was seeing what happened in Utan or thinking he'd lost his brother to the Svell. I didn't care why.

"If you'll have me," he added, waiting.

"We can be in Hylli in a few hours if we ride hard." I grinned. "They'll be waiting."

Asmund led the way as we pushed across the last stretch

of forest and I kept my eyes on the storm building over the fjord. In a matter of days, the rains would come and I didn't know if they'd work in our favor in battle or in the Svell's. There was only one way to win against an army like that, and it was to keep them from ever breaching the tree line above the village. But it seemed an impossible task with so few warriors. We would need the help of the gods, and I wasn't sure if they'd come when I called, the way they'd come for Espen ten years ago.

Hylli lay across the valley in the distance and I was at the foot of the mountain, stuck between dying worlds. By now, Latham would have gotten word of the Svell attack on Utan. Wherever they were, my nieces would be watching their mother and father ready their weapons the way I watched my father and brothers as a boy.

At any moment, the sea would appear beneath the sky and I would be home. I could already smell the water, mixed with the far-off rain and the new grass of early spring.

The horse picked up its pace as we made our way through the familiar land, remembering the way, and though everything within me wanted to be home, some part of me also dreaded the moment I'd walk through the gate. When we came out from under the trees, warm sunlight hit my face and I breathed through the lump in my throat. The rise of land ahead pulled down, the gray water meeting the sky, and as I came over the hill, the horse halted, hooves sliding on the damp ground.

Down the slope, all the way to the village, the Nādhir

were camped in rows of tents painted with the blood of sacrifices. The shapes and symbols of Sigr and Thora covered them, dark against the white canvas. Warriors from every village on the fjord and the mountain were waiting for the fight coming across the valley. The enormous camp covered the grass, hiding the rooftops of the village behind them.

I swallowed hard as the horn sounded, echoing up the hill and drifting into the trees behind us. We watched as bodies moved below, coming from every doorway and tent, and I pressed the heel of my boot into the side of the horse, moving down the hill slowly. Faces peered up at me, many I didn't know. But I knew the look of warriors waiting to see if they'd survive battle, even if it had never been cast upon me.

Mýra pushed through a group of men at the gate, and as soon as she saw me, she froze, dropping her hands heavily at her sides. Her lips moved around a prayer and then she was walking one foot in front of the other up the path to meet me. I swung my leg over the saddle, sliding down, and as soon as she reached me, she wrapped her arms around my neck, holding onto me tighter than she ever had.

Her words were muffled against my shoulder and I pulled back, looking down into her reddened face. Her bright green eyes were filled with tears, the darkness beneath them evidence that she'd slept little in the days since we left.

"I thought you were dead," she cried. "I thought I was going to have to tell them you were dead."

"I'm sorry." I pulled her back into me, wrapping my arms around her. "Are they here?"

"Not yet. They're coming."

I swallowed, the pain in my throat widening. "Aghi . . ."

But I could see on her face that she already knew. She nodded, wiping the tears from her face with both hands. "A man from Utan arrived this morning and told us what happened." Her voice broke. "I should have gone with you. I should have been with you."

She squeezed me tighter and I bristled, the armor vest pulling against the bandage beneath it.

"What is it?" Her hands ran over me, looking for the wound.

"It's nothing."

But she looked up at me through her eyelashes indignantly.

"Halvard!"

Latham walked up the path, clad in his armor, the thick furs on his shoulders blowing in the cold wind. Freydis was at his side, the relief not hidden on her face as her eyes landed on me. Mýra stepped aside and I walked to meet them.

Latham lifted a hand, catching my shoulder in greeting and I did the same to him. "You've heard what's happened."

"Just this morning." His jaw clenched around the words. "I'm glad to see you, Halvard." And I could see that he meant it.

Freydis lifted a hand, touching my face. "Thanks to Thora."

I swallowed hard before I spoke. "I'm sorry." I hoped they heard my meaning. That I wasn't just sorry for the loss. I was sorry that I didn't stop it. I was sorry that I'd failed to save even one of them.

"Lag mund," Latham answered and Freydis echoed, though the look in their eyes betrayed how much the pain of it struck them.

It was the way of the elders to respond to death with "Fate's hand." They'd spent much of their lives reasoning away the losses of the fighting seasons. Saying good-bye to their families and their clansmen before running into battle. They were more practiced at loss than I was.

I looked over my shoulder, searching for Asmund and Bard in the crowd. They were still mounted on their horses at the top of the hill. It had been years since the brothers had come home, and I hoped that the memories of this place wouldn't drive them to disappear the way Kjeld had.

"How long until they reach us?" Latham lowered his voice.

"They'll be in Hylli by tomorrow. We're out of time."

"Their numbers?"

A hush fell over everyone gathered around us and I tried to keep my voice even as I answered. "Greater than ours. I'd guess maybe eight hundred."

Latham looked to the ground, thinking. "The rest of our warriors will be here before morning. We'll hold the ceremony tonight." He turned back to the gate.

"Ceremony?"

He stopped midstride, looking back at me. "Espen's dead, Halvard. The place of chieftain falls to you now."

I stared at him, not knowing what to say. But he surveyed me with a look that reminded me of Aghi, a bit of humor in his eyes. Since the day they'd told me I'd take Espen's place, I'd never believed Latham supported the decision. He'd questioned me every step of the way. He'd argued with every decision. But now, in the darkest moment since the Herja came, with every eye on us, he didn't hesitate to put his trust in me.

"Come, there's much to do."

I watched him walk away, the stares of the Nādhir so heavy on me that they seemed to pin me to the ground. I couldn't move. I almost couldn't breathe.

Mýra gave me a small smile, her eyes still glistening as she held out an open hand to me. "Time to go, Halvard."

CHAPTER TWENTY-ONE

TOVA

THE EASTERN VALLEY OPENED LIKE A NEW WORLD UNFOLDING.

The sweet, familiar smell of pine faded, giving way to the cutting scent of spring, and the earth turned green beneath us as we left the borderlands. The fjord changed the land, rivers weaving like roots down the mountain on their way to the sea. It was different than the dense forests of Svell territory, where the land dropped off abruptly from crude cliffs into the wide, open water. Here, everything was hedged in, the coast curving up and around and the fjord holding Hylli like a mother holds her child.

It was beautiful.

The Svell were quiet as we moved through the fog in a dark horde of leathers and furs. Every whisper was snuffed out by the growing wind, pushing in from the sea where dark clouds gathered on the horizon. The first of the violent spring storms was on its way, just in time to wash the land of the blood that would be spilled in Hylli.

The army slowed as we reached the hill that looked out over the fjord. The mist was still thick in the air, but it was there. The village sat on the water in the distance, only barely visible over the forest where the silver sea met the land in a crooked line.

It was more like the headlands than Liera was. The memories of the place I was born were stretching into full visions more and more, and I could see them with more detail than I had even the day before. But the Kyrr were less clear, only the shape of the woman before the fire taking hold among the pictures of the village or the water. I blinked past the tears that sprang to my eyes when I thought of her. It pinched in the center of my gut, making me almost wish she hadn't surfaced from the depths of my mind. Because whoever she was, she'd probably been the one to give me to the sea. And that was a moment I was afraid of remembering.

The army slowed as we reached the other side of the hill. The tents were unrolled and the carts unloaded as the warriors settled in for a last night's sleep before war. If they won the battle in Hylli, it would be followed by smaller ones on the mountain and in the bottomlands, until they'd scoured the territory of the Nādhir that called it home.

Jorrund set the posts for our tent and I slid a corner of the canvas over them. I held it in place as he pounded a stake into the soft ground, but he didn't meet my eyes. He hadn't spoken to me since the night before, when I told him that we were wrong for the course we'd taken, and I wondered if I'd made an even greater mistake in telling him about my vision when I took the henbane. But it was hard to imagine that anything that would befall me could be worse than what had already happened. In fact, I no longer cared. The only thing that mattered to me now was keeping Halvard alive. I hadn't listened to the Spinners when I left Liera with the Svell and I wouldn't make the same mistake twice. They'd placed Halvard like a star in the constellation that made up my fate, and I would find a way to end what I'd started. I had to.

"This is an important night." Jorrund finally spoke, driving the last stake into the ground between us. "The eye of Eydis is watching and we need her favor to finish this."

I listened silently, pressing the tip of my finger against the blade of Halvard's axe at my belt.

"I know I can rely on you," he said, getting back to his feet.

He left me where I sat in the cool grass, the wind picking up the length of my skirt and lifting it into the air. I knew what he was asking. What he wanted. But I wouldn't cast the stones for him again. Not ever.

The tents popped up in neat rows on the hillside and the night fires were lit, making the camp come to life with orange light. Jorrund took a barrel from a cart as the Svell gathered in the dark, forming large rings around an open circle of green grass, and he held his hand out before me, nodding to Halvard's axe at my hip.

I gave it to him and watched as he used it to split the wood of the barrel's top and the strong smell of pitch filled the damp air. He handed the axe back to me, his attention on the ground beneath his feet as he mapped it in his mind. Once every Svell man and woman was in place, he began in the very center of the circle, tipping the barrel forward until the pine tar spilled out in a thick, steady stream. He stepped backward slowly, careful to keep the line straight, and began painting the symbol onto the grass. The Svell watched him in the growing wind as he moved left around the circle and back in, the intricate pattern visible only to him.

A larger barrel was cracked open on the back of a cart and the ale was poured until every Svell warrior had a horn to drink from. When Jorrund was finished, he stood at the north point of the hill, a lit torch in his hand. Every eye fell upon him, every word hushed as he lifted the flame to the sky.

"Eydis!" he roared, the sound muted by the howl of the wind.

I could see the trepidation in his eyes. I could hear the fear in his voice. But looking at the faces around me, I seemed to be the only one.

"We call upon you! We ask for your protection and your favor as we take the fjord!"

The wind whipped around him, the torch flame shifting violently, and every horn of ale lifted into the air except for mine. The jumbled shouts of the warriors all bled together, each man and woman calling out to an ancestor to request the use of their shield in battle.

But there was no one I could call upon. No one who was listening. Instead, I made my plea to the Spinners. I asked for their forgiveness. I begged for their help.

Every gaze cast upward to the darkening sky and they drank, ale trailing down beards and soaking into tunics. It was then that Jorrund dropped the torch at his feet and the flame caught the pitch, writhing over the grass in the paths he'd laid until the entire stave was afire.

The *Skjöldr.*

It was an ancient symbol, the shield of the fallen Svell warrior. And here, in the valley that overlooked Hylli, they were calling upon the spirits of the dead to fight alongside them on the battlefield.

Beside me, Gunther's face was illuminated by the flames of the burning *Skjöldr,* the empty horn still clutched in his hand.

"Who do you call upon?" I asked, taking a drink of the sour ale.

His expression turned suspicious at the question. "My son. Aaro."

I dropped my eyes, wishing I hadn't asked. "I'm sorry."

He said nothing, his gaze returning to the *Skjöldr.* The warriors stood around it, their horns still lifted in the air as they prayed, and I wondered if the people in Hylli could see it from the fjord.

"What village do you come from?"

"Hǫlkn," he answered, more easily.

Of course he did. Vigdis was the village leader of Hǫlkn and he'd asked Gunther to watch me because he trusted him. But even though he had the new Svell chieftain's trust, Gunther hadn't told him the truth after Utan. And though he hated me, he'd helped me before, too. There was more to his story than maybe even Vigdis knew.

"You lied last night."

He stared ahead, his face unchanging.

"Why did you tell Vigdis that you killed the Nādhir?"

A woman came by with the barrel of ale, and Gunther held out his horn for her to refill. As soon as she moved down the line, he took a long drink. "Because that's what he needed to hear. And I think you saved that boy's life for a reason."

I froze, my teeth clenched, unsure if I'd heard him right. But when I looked back up, it was clear by the look on his face that he knew what I'd done. "You saw me?"

"No, but I'm not a fool. I know the look of a man when he's been dead for hours."

"I don't understand. Why would you lie for me?"

"I didn't lie for you. I lied for them." He tipped his drink to the circle of Svell before us.

"You don't want to fight the Nādhir, do you?" I took a chance in asking it. It had been painted on his face since we'd left the glade.

"There's no need to go looking for war. War is faithful to come looking for us time and again."

"Then why are you here?"

"Because my fealty is to the Svell."

"Even if they're wrong?"

He looked down at me then, his mouth pressing into a hard line. "You know as well as I do that this started when you cast the stones."

I couldn't argue with that, but I still recoiled at the words as he said them. I felt the weight of it in every bone. And looking at Gunther now, I wondered if he felt some of that weight, too. He was the one who'd helped me all those years ago. In a way, he'd kept me alive when most others wanted me dead. Maybe he regretted it now. Maybe he was paying penance.

"I'm here to wield my blade at my clansmen's side."

"I didn't know this would happen," I said, taking another drink.

"If you can really see the future in the runes, then find a way to change it."

He met my eyes for a long moment and for an instant, I could see what lay there. The pain of someone who'd lost something. The wishing that things had turned out differently. He was old enough to be my father and I wondered if he had daughters my age at home in Hǫlkn, waiting for him. But there was also a loneliness in him that made me think that maybe he didn't.

Before I could say anything else, he moved back into the men behind him, leaving me alone. When I looked up, Jorrund watched me with the light of the fire aglow on his face.

I found the string beneath my tunic and wound my finger into it, lifting the weight of the rune stones where they hung against my chest. I wanted to believe that the fate of the Svell was carved into the Tree of Urðr and that it wouldn't change. That they'd somehow meet their end in Hylli. But I could hear it in the sudden silence of the sky. I could see it in the stillness of the Nādhir village glowing far over the forest. It didn't matter what the stones said.

Nothing was sure until death came.

CHAPTER TWENTY-TWO

HALVARD

I UNCLASPED MY ARMOR VEST AND PULLED IT OFF, DROPping it onto the table beside my tunic. The pain in my side reignited and I hissed as Mýra inspected it in the firelight. The infection had slowed, but it would be a weakness in battle. One I probably couldn't afford.

She cleaned it with a steaming cloth before she took my mother's salve from the shelf and lathered it on, not bothering to be gentle. I groaned at her touch and when I looked down, I realized she was smiling. It was a punishment for making her worry. She glared at me from the top of her gaze, securing the bandage in place.

Mýra had never been motherly in nature and though she'd had several lovers through the years, she'd never had children. Instead, she'd made my nieces her own, spending every afternoon of the last summer teaching Náli how to use a sword. Isla spent most of her days following Mýra around the village from morning to night.

I had wondered many times if losing her entire family when she was younger was the reason she'd decided never to have one of her own. But together, we'd built our own kind of family. My mother and Aghi had watched over the whole of us and I didn't know what it would feel like to sit at the table without him now.

I went to the wall and opened the heavy lid to the trunk we'd brought with us from the mountain ten years ago when we'd come to live in Hylli. My father's armor sat neatly on top of the dress clothes, the iron and dark leathers so familiar to me. I still remembered watching his body turn to ash on the funeral fire, carried away by the smoke to the next world. Most of my memories of him were like pictures half scratched out, but others were so clear. It was his face that was most shadowed. As if the only life I'd ever really lived was here, on the fjord. As if the time before that never happened.

Sometimes, I wondered if I'd even recognize him in the afterlife. But one moment had stayed with me even after so many others had disappeared. The day my father died was the day I'd first understood that death was coming for me. And I'd decided then that when it was here, I'd meet it willingly, the way he had.

I pulled the clean tunic on and took my father's armor vest into my hands, holding it before me. The leather gleamed in the low light, clean and oiled, and I fit it over my shoulders and buckled the clasps, tightening them until it pulled across my chest.

Mýra's eyes ran over me, almost sad as she stood back and surveyed me. "Let me help you."

She picked up the sheath from the table and stood up onto her toes to drop it over my head. "They would want to be here," she said, her voice strained.

"I know."

But I was glad that my mother, brothers, and Eelyn wouldn't be standing in the ritual house to see me become chieftain. I wasn't ready to face them and I didn't know if I ever would be. The story of what happened in the glade was still one I wasn't ready to tell. And more than that, my family knew me. Every fragile, unworthy thing that lay deep in my heart. I wanted to feel strong as I stood before the Nādhir. I wanted to believe that I was what Espen believed I was.

"Are you ready?" Mýra asked, brushing her hands down the sleeves of my tunic.

I nodded, taking my father's sword from the wall and sliding it into the sheath at my hip before we stepped outside. We walked through the village in silence, following the string of people already making their way to the ritual house in the dark. The drums beat like a steady heart, the glow of the altar fire blazing ahead, making silhouettes of the bodies gathered before the huge arched doorway.

"Halvard." Mýra stopped, her eyes lifted to the east.

A feeling like cold water running in my veins reached around me as I saw it. The blazing stave afire on the hill in the distance. It was the Svell.

"What is it?" She took hold of my arm.

I didn't know the symbol. The Svell were probably making sacrifices to their god in the valley, readying to march through the forest to Hylli. I shifted on my feet, the weapons at my side and at my back suddenly heavy.

"It seems wrong," I said, watching the stave glow in the darkness.

"What does?"

"To spend time on a ceremony. None of this will matter tomorrow."

"That's why we have to do it." She took hold of my vest. "If we're going to fight, we have to know that we are still who we are. If we're going to die, we have to know that we're dying for something." When I said nothing, she pulled me toward her. "What else?"

I measured the words before I spoke them. It was something I'd never said aloud, only the faintest whispers in the back of my mind daring to ask the question. "What if they were wrong?"

She stared at me, not understanding.

"What if they were wrong to choose me?"

She smiled sadly, her hand sliding into mine. "You've never seen it. You've never seen your own strength. You think that because you've never faced war that you aren't strong. You're wrong, Halvard."

She turned, pulling me with her as she walked toward the ritual house. It was already full, people spilling out the doors and into the paths that snaked through the village. They circled around the building, standing shoulder to shoulder, and at the sight of me, every voice quieted.

The drums fell quiet and I stopped, standing beneath the archway, where the carved faces of Sigr and Thora looked down on us with wide, open eyes. The heat swelled in the silence, my boots hitting the stone the only sound as we made our way down the center aisle toward the altar. Mýra's hand fell from mine before she disappeared into the crowd and ahead, Latham stood tall before the fire with the Tala and the other village leaders, their eyes fixed on me.

I took my place before them, standing with my back to the room. The warm air was too thick, my heart racing beneath the tight, woven leathers of the armor vest. A bead of sweat trailed down my brow and I resisted the urge to wipe it, my hands resting on my belt.

As the drums started again, the Tala began to sing and every voice joined him, filling the walls of the ritual house until it felt as if they were trembling around us. It was an old song, one that was engraved on the bones of the people long before they'd become the Nādhir. It told the story of the gods. Triumphs and defeats. Fate at the hands of the Spinners. The destinies carved into the Tree of Urðr. I sang the words, my voice bleeding into the others around me. Words I'd known by heart since I was a small boy.

At the sound of the Kyrr god's name, Naðr, the altar before me seemed suddenly to change, rippling in the firelight until a shape pulled together in the dim light. I could see her. The Truthtongue. The voices grew around me, making the room spin, and I closed my eyes, trying to erase the vision. But when I opened them again, she stood before the altar fire in her black linen dress, the mark of the eye on her chest wide open. Looking at me.

When I blinked again, the sting of sweat in my eyes, she vanished, and the orange light filling the ritual house returned. I looked around us, searching the sea of faces for her, but she was gone.

The Tala stepped forward, pulling a long, thin knife from his robes, and the village leaders stepped aside, leaving me to stand alone. I held out my hand and the Tala took it, lifting the blade between us. The voices continued to sing, rising louder as he shouted.

"We ask you, Thora and Sigr, to entrust your people to Halvard, son of Auben."

I closed my fingers tightly around the blade and the Tala placed a wooden bowl beneath it before he pulled the knife in one swift motion through the wound I'd cut only the day before in Aurvanger. The hot blood poured freely, trickling out between my fingers and dripping into the bowl as the voices roared around us. When it began to slow, I pulled the strip of linen from my vest and bound it around my palm.

The Tala lifted the bowl before him, chanting the ritual words before he handed it to me. I stepped forward into the line of village leaders and took my place before the multitude of warriors, all looking to me. I swallowed hard, stopping before Latham first.

He stood tall, his chin lifted.

"Latham, leader of Möor." I kept my voice even. "Will you accept me? Will you follow and fight beside me?"

He didn't hesitate, a small smile igniting beneath his thick beard as he reached up, taking the bowl from me. His eyes didn't leave mine as he raised it to his lips and took a drink, and then he was pulling me into him, wrapping his arms around me so tightly that I could hardly draw breath. I swallowed back the burn of tears in my eyes.

"I will need you," I said, before he let me go.

He nodded. "Then you will have me."

Espen had been right about him. So had Aghi. And if Latham followed me, I knew they all would.

He squeezed my shoulder before I moved to Freydis. Her pale face shined beneath a crown of red braids wound up around her head.

"Freydis, leader of Lund. Will you accept me? Will you follow and fight beside me?"

Her hands took the bowl from mine and she lifted it, taking a drink. She pulled me close, setting her chin onto my shoulder. "I will."

I moved down the line as she let me go, looking into the eyes of the men and women I'd grown up under. They were twice, some of them three times my age, and they had trusted Espen with not only their lives, but with the futures of their own families.

Now, they were trusting *me.*

As I stopped before Egil, the last village leader, a feeling like a faint whisper drew my eyes to the back of the ritual house, where the doors were still open to the night sky. And I knew before I saw. My breath caught in my chest as I found their faces among the others.

My family.

My brothers Fiske and Iri stood tall beside Eelyn beneath the archway, peering over the crowd. My mother came through the doors behind them, her eyes finding me, and her hand went to her mouth, her fingers pressed to her lips.

I swallowed hard, my hands gripping tighter around the bowl to keep it from shaking. "Egil, leader of Æðra. Will you accept me? Will you follow and fight beside me?"

He took the bowl as I looked back back to Fiske. He didn't take his eyes from mine as his lips began to move around a prayer I couldn't hear. Iri and my mother followed, but Eelyn stood frozen, the glistening of tears falling down her face visible even from where I stood. I knew that look on her, though I'd rarely seen it in the time I'd known her. She was made of iron and steel. She was the solid ice beneath my feet on the frozen fjord in winter.

But in this moment, she was afraid.

CHAPTER TWENTY-THREE

TOVA

THE *SKJÖLDR* BURNED LIKE A BEACON IN THE NIGHT.

I sat in the dirt before my cot, staring through the opening of the tent. Outside, the Svell gathered around smoking fires, drunk on ale and eating what would be for some of them a last meal. But Gunther still stood beside the door, his feet planted side by side and his shadow drawn onto the canvas.

The foul smoke of the pitch on the grass still clung to me and I could only think that Hylli would smell the same in another day. I'd stood on the hill as the sun set, watching the Nādhir village disappear beneath the fog in the distance.

I wondered if Halvard was home now. I imagined him sleeping in his bed beside his family with the warmth of the fire and the sound of the sea. But if he was home, he wasn't sleeping. The Nādhir would be preparing for a battle they couldn't win. The battle I'd brought to the fjord.

Being Kyrr on the mainland was like living as a ghost. A tormented spirit, left behind in the world of mortals to wander. When I closed my eyes, the same vision I'd had in Ljós when I took the henbane played in the darkness. The silver gray waters. The black rock that disappeared up into the mist that hovered over the sea. Careful hands working at my markings by candlelight and the soft, rasping hum of a song on a woman's breath.

Home. But even that wasn't true. Because though the marks still stained my skin, the blood that ran through my veins was a stranger to me.

Gunther's boots shifted on the rocks outside and Jorrund's voice lifted over the sound of the camp. He appeared in the opening a moment later. "Come, Tova. I need you."

But I knew what he needed. I'd known since an attack on Hylli was first ordered. He wanted me to cast the runes before battle. He wanted to paint my hands with blood again.

"No." The word was weak, and I didn't even have the courage to look at him when it fell from my lips. It was the first time I'd ever said no to Jorrund. It was the first time I'd ever denied him anything at all.

He stilled before me, speechless.

"The last time I cast the stones, you killed every man, woman, and child in the glade and in Utan. I won't do it again. Not ever. If you want to take Hylli, you'll have to do it alone."

My fingers brushed over the axe head in my lap, tracing

the shape of the yew tree etched into the shining steel. I wouldn't do it to Hylli. And I wouldn't do it to Halvard.

"Tova . . ." Jorrund struggled to keep his voice even.

"I told you." I looked up at him from the top of my gaze. "This is a mistake."

But he couldn't hear me. His face was twisted with his own thoughts, his mind racing. "I saved your life. I've treated you as my own." He murmured, "I've given you everything."

"Everything except the truth," I amended.

His lips pulled back to reveal his teeth. "What?"

"What did the Spinner tell you about me? Who am I?"

"She told me nothing about you."

"Who *am* I, Jorrund?" I pressed. "Please."

"I don't know!" He tucked his shaking hands into his robes, surprised by the flare of his own temper. He closed his eyes, breathing before he spoke again. "The only thing I know is that Eydis brought you to us. To *me*. I've told you the story."

"There's something else. Something you're not telling me. I've always known it. But I thought, in time . . . I thought I could trust you," I whispered.

"Tova." His voice softened. "Listen to me."

"No." I said the word again, and this time, it wasn't small. It filled the air between us.

A sharp glint flickered in his eyes like the strike of fire-steel. "I have done nothing but care for you since the day I found you on that half-burned boat. Your own people—"

"What?" I rasped, his words trailing off in the sudden

storm swirling in my mind. I got to my feet, my hands finding the rune stones. "What did you say?"

"I said that all I've ever done is—"

"You said half-burned boat."

"What? No, I . . ." He stumbled over the words, trying to pull them back away from me.

But it was too late. "You never told me the boat was half-burned."

"I've told you about the boat a hundred times."

"You just said it was half-burned when you found me. You never told me that before."

"What does it matter?" He flung a hand at me. "Your people didn't want you, Tova. They cast you off."

But something about those words didn't feel right anymore, even though I'd said them a thousand times myself. I closed my eyes, seeing the water again. The silver stream of bubbles. A string of bones glittering in sunlight.

That felt real.

I held my hands out before me, my palms down so that the marks were between us.

Yarrow and henbane. Life and death.

I blinked, sending one hot tear down my cold cheek. If the boat was burned, it wasn't holding a ritual sacrifice. It was a funeral boat. It had to be. The Kyrr hadn't cast me out. They hadn't given me up as an offering to Naðr.

"I wasn't a sacrifice." I said it aloud, like an incantation.

Jorrund's jaw clenched, his voice tightening. "What are you talking about?"

"It was a funeral boat, wasn't it?"

"It wasn't burned, Tova. I said that by mistake. *I* burned the boat. Don't you remember?"

I did remember the flames on the beach. But I knew Jorrund's face. Every wrinkle. Every edge of expression. It was the only face that ever dared to look into mine until the day I saw Halvard in the glade. And I could see the lie there more clearly than I'd ever seen it before. A broken smile lifted on my lips.

I walked toward the opening of the tent but he stepped in front of me, his hands raised before him. "I'm sorry. Please, we have to—"

"Move." I leveled my eyes at him, my voice dropping low.

"Tova . . ."

I went around him, and Gunther looked up, watching as I walked straight for the forest. Jorrund called out, his voice echoing in the camp, and when I heard the sound of boots, I looked back to see silhouettes moving toward me. I picked up my skirts, clutching them to my chest, and ran into the trees. My breath fogged out in bursts and I tried to focus my eyes to see, but it was too dark. The shapes moved in the fog, making me feel like I wasn't running in one direction. The forest whirled around me and I slammed into the trunk of a tree, my sleeve tearing as it caught on the bark. I ripped it free and didn't look back as the voices drew closer, running with the glow of the camp behind me until I was wrenched back and I hit the ground hard.

A man's face appeared over me before he bent down low, lifting me back to my feet. He didn't even look up as a sob cracked in my chest. His hand took hold of the neck of my tunic and he pulled me back toward the firelight. I stumbled over stones and roots until we were back in the camp, where Jorrund was waiting, Gunther beside him with an unreadable expression spread over his face.

Jorrund started toward the meeting tent and the Svell jerked me toward it, following. He shoved me inside and I toppled forward, sliding on the ground. My palms scraped against the dry, cracked mud and when I looked up, Vigdis stood before the table, his eyes cast down on me. Without pause, he took the knife on the table into his hand.

"You'll cast the stones, or you'll lose that hand." He pointed to the bloodied fist clenched in my lap. "And then you'll read them anyway."

Hot tears burned in my eyes and I sniffed them back, refusing to let them fall. Jorrund looked down at me with a strange, unfamiliar expression. Guilt. Or maybe pity. His gaze fell down to my dirty dress, my scraped hands, and for a moment, I thought he would come to me. Wrap his arms around me and say he was sorry. But he didn't.

"You're a cursed soul from a cursed people. You should have died as the gods willed it, but Jorrund and my brother were foolish and weak. You're the sickness that took my niece's life and you're the blade that took my brother's." Vigdis spoke calmly, the sound of his voice unnerving. "For as long as you are useful, I will keep you alive. The moment you fail to be of value, I will end your life and give you back to the gods."

His gaze fixed on the open collar of my tunic, where the eye was marked onto my skin. But I looked straight at him, praying that if there was any misfortune to be had beneath my gaze, that it would fall on him tenfold. I summoned the darkest work of the Spinners, imagining Vigdis dead on the battlefield, drowned in his own blood. I pulled the vision to the front of my mind, the burn of every hope inside me lighting it aflame.

As if he could hear the thoughts, he suddenly stepped back from the table and the others followed, their backs pressed to the walls of the crowded tent. Jorrund looked at me pleadingly, one hand reaching out and beckoning me forward. I gritted my teeth, one traitorous tear rolling from the corner of my eye, and stepped forward.

I pulled the stones from around my neck as Jorrund turned the elk skins over to use as a pelt. He was careful, moving slowly as if I was a bird about to take flight. But in my heart, I'd already flown away from Jorrund and every lie he'd ever told me. I was gone. And I was never coming back.

I opened the purse and my skin flushed hot under my tunic, the fury engulfing me. There was no ritual smoke, no sacred words. This time, I spoke them in my heart, with more fervor than I'd ever asked the Spinners for anything before.

Augua ór tivar. Ljá mir sýn.

Augua ór tivar. Ljá mir sýn.

Augua ór tivar. Ljá mir sýn.

Eye of the gods. Give me sight.

They filled me up, coiling around my spirit. They snaked between each bone and thought. And when I closed my eyes, it wasn't the Svell's future I asked for. It was Halvard's. I saw his face in the dark beneath the gates of Utan. I could still feel the tingle of his blue eyes on my skin, like the sting of the coal clutched in my burned fingers.

The rune stones dropped from my hand and hit the table one skittering knock at a time. I was afraid to look. Afraid to see what curse I'd brought upon him and his people. But when I looked down at the pelt, my hands froze out before me. My head tilted to the side, my fingers curling into my palms until my fingernails bit the tender broken skin.

Three stones. The first, *Sowilo.* I let out a long breath.

The sun. Victory. Honor. Hope.

I smiled, another tear falling. The rune stared up at me like a wide, opened eye.

But beside it was *Thurisaz,* the thorn. So the path wasn't clear. There would be great difficulty. And above, *Tiwaz,* the sacrifice of self.

Jorrund stepped closer, his eyes straining as he looked over the table. "This is good, isn't it?" he whispered.

I nodded. The lie was so easy to give him.

"*Sowilo.*" He pointed to the stone, smiling up at Vigdis. "Eydis will grant us victory."

"I want to hear *her* say it." Vigdis grunted, his arms crossed tightly over his broad chest.

I swallowed before I spoke, smoothing my face. "He's right."

"Because of Ljós. And Utan. You've changed our fate, Vigdis." Jorrund pressed his hands together before him, as if in prayer. "You were right."

Vigdis let out a long breath. "See, brother?" He said it so softly I almost didn't hear him, the emotion heavy on his face. He was relieved. "In the morning, we take Hylli. And the Svell begin anew."

The warriors filed outside, leaving only Jorrund and me standing before the table in the meeting tent. I stared down at the stones, feeling the weight of my own words. I'd never lied about the runes. Never, until now. I wondered if I'd broken some ancient, sacred oath or if the Spinners would curse me for it.

But in this moment, I couldn't find it within me to care.

I could feel the runes' meaning beneath my skin. I could hear it like a song. And if it was the last thing I did, I'd make sure this fate came to pass.

12 YEARS AGO

Village of Liera, Svell Territory

TOVA SET ONE FINGER ON THE RUNE STONE BEFORE HER AND slid it across the table. "*Mannaz.*"

"*Mannaz,*" Jorrund repeated, picking it up and setting it into his palm.

He studied the symbol carefully, turning it in a circle in his hand to see it from every angle. It had been almost a year since he'd brought Tova to Liera, but their lessons had only just begun. The Svell Tala wanted to know the runes the way she did. He wanted to understand them. But when the stones were cast, he couldn't see their patterns the way Tova could. He couldn't string their meanings together or fit the pieces where they belonged.

"Mankind, friends, enemies," she said, quietly, "social order."

She remembered the runes like she remembered how to buckle the bronze brooches of her apron dress or fasten her hair into the intricate braids that fell over her shoulder. She just knew. Somehow, she remembered. But when she tried to pull back the memories from before she'd come to Liera, everything was washed out. They were the crumbling edges of pictures that never came together.

Sometimes, they appeared in dreams, spinning like a wisp of smoke until they disappeared again. She'd wake with her heart racing, trying to go back. Trying to summon the vision again so that she could fit it to the other pieces that floated in her memory.

She looked down at the marks that covered her arm, winding together in a maze that she couldn't navigate. Why could she remember the runes, but not these? Why couldn't she unearth them from where they were buried in her mind?

"What is it?" Jorrund leaned forward, his voice gentle. He looked down at her with soft, slanted eyes.

"It's nothing," she answered, setting her hand into her lap and clenching her fingers into a fist. Jorrund was never cruel to her, but she didn't know how deep the well of his kindness was. She didn't want to find out.

He tilted his head curiously. "What is it, Tova?"

She thought carefully, saying the words in her head before she dared to say them aloud. She'd asked him before about her people and the place she'd come from. But Jorrund never gave her answers. He only turned her questions into something else. "Have you ever been to the headlands?"

He looked surprised by the question, his eyebrows lifting as he took his elbows from the table. "I haven't. No one has."

Tova swallowed hard, thinking that maybe she'd misread the moment. She shouldn't have asked.

"Why do you want to know?"

She picked at the unraveling linen that frayed at the edge of her sleeve.

"You can tell me." He attempted a rigid smile.

Tova studied him, trying to see beneath the look on his face. She'd learned not long after Jorrund brought her into the village that he rarely said what he meant. He was always molding the people around him. Always scheming.

"I want to go home," she whispered in the most brittle voice. It didn't matter that she couldn't remember the place she'd come from. With everything inside of her, she wanted to go back.

Jorrund surveyed her, his back straightening. "You can't go home, Tova."

The sight of him blurred in the tears springing to her eyes. "But why?"

He took a deep breath, pressing his mouth into a hard line. "I didn't want to tell you this." He paused, waiting for her to look up at him. "You didn't get lost from the headlands, *svάss*. You were sent away."

She wrung her hands beneath the table, trying to understand. "What?"

"I didn't want to tell you," he said again. "But your people . . . they cast you off."

"Cast me off." She repeated the words, as if saying them with her own lips would help make sense of them.

He leaned in closer to her. "Do you know what a sacrifice is?"

She nodded slowly.

"That's what you are. Your people tried to sacrifice you. To their god."

A sick, twisted feeling pulled behind Tova's ribs and she pressed her slick palms to her knees, trying to steady herself.

"You can never go back," he said. "If you do, they will kill you."

The tears welled in her eyes and though she swallowed down the cry in her throat, she didn't try to keep them from falling. Jorrund set the small rune stone back onto the table and slid it toward her. She stared at it.

Mannaz.

Friends. Enemies.

Her eyes flickered up to Jorrund, and she blinked, wondering which he was.

Village of Fela, old Riki Territory

Halvard stared into the pail of water at his feet, where his wavering reflection looked back at him. His eyes were red and swollen, his hair a tangled knot at the nape of his neck. He wiped the tears from his face with both hands before he opened the door, where his mother waited inside.

She looked up from where she sat beside his father's body, giving him a small smile. He'd woken in the loft to the sound of both his brothers crying, and as soon as he'd opened his eyes he'd known his father was dead. When the sun had set the night before, he'd wondered if he would go to sleep and never see him again and he was right. Having a mother who was a healer had taught him to recognize the look of death.

"Come." Inge held her hands out for the pail and he took his place at his father's side as she lifted the hot kettle from where it sat on the coals in the fire pit.

He watched her pour the steaming water into the melted snow and they each took a linen cloth, folding it neatly before they dipped it into the warm water. She dragged it over his father's shoulder and down his chest, cleaning the skin, and Halvard did the same on the other side, rinsing the cloth as he went. The sweet scent of herbs filled the house and he tried not to look up to his father's face, keeping his attention on his work. He had been sick for days, and his mother wanted him to go to the funeral fire clean. She had already set out one of his dress tunics and oiled his boots, so he would look his best when he went to the afterlife.

She finished with the washing and sat beside his body on the table, taking her time to braid his beard in elaborate strands. Halvard dropped the cloth into the pail and listened to her hum a song he'd heard her sing his entire life as she fit silver beads onto the ends of the braids and tied them off with strips of thin leather.

It seemed wrong that his father would die of sickness when he'd survived so many battles. Halvard had sat in the loft for the past three nights, begging Thora to spare his life. And as he woke that morning, he wondered if he'd ever pray to her again.

The door opened and Iri came inside, his hands and arms painted with the same gray mud that stained his tunic. Dark red cuts and scrapes traced up his skin where he'd gathered the wood for the funeral fire. Halvard waited for him to say something, but he didn't. He pulled the dirty tunic over his head, dropping it on the floor, and his blond braids fell down his back as he washed the mud from his arms silently.

Iri had come into their home mostly dead only three years before, an enemy survivor from battle. But now, he was Halvard's brother. He was Auben's son. And there was no mistaking the pain that the loss of him had struck Iri with. His shoulders shook with his silent cries as he cupped the water, washing his face.

It was almost midday when Fiske opened the door. They were dressed in their finest linen, their hair combed and braided. Fiske and Iri carried their father on a set of planks and Inge and Halvard followed. His hand fit into hers and she picked up her skirt as they made their way to the ritual house in the snow, where the village had gathered to honor Auben. He'd been born in Fela and after forty-six years of life and six fighting seasons, he'd go on to meet his ancestors in the afterlife. There, he'd wait for his wife and his three sons.

Fiske and Iri set their father's body atop the funeral pyre they'd built that morning, and then they took their places at Inge's side. Iri set a hand onto Halvard's shoulder as the Tala dropped the torch and together, they watched their father turn to ash.

When everyone had left, Halvard still stood, staring at the smoldering embers, trying to understand how his father could just be gone. He looked up to the sky, where the smoke was disappearing, imagining it taking him to the next life. But something about the thought didn't bring him the comfort it seemed to bring the others.

The crunch of boots in the snow made Halvard blink and he looked back to see Fiske coming back up the path. He pulled an axe from his back as he reached him and held it between them, the image of a yew tree engraved in the blade. It was their father's.

Halvard stared at it.

"It's yours," Fiske said, setting it into his hands.

Halvard looked up at him. "You don't want it?"

"I want you to have it."

Halvard hugged it to his chest, the weight of the iron heavy in his arms, and Fiske got to his knees before him, meeting his eyes. They were still glazed with the loss of sleep and the tears he'd shed. "It falls to me now to raise you," he said.

Halvard looked at his boots, buried in the snow between them.

"Will you trust me?" He held out an open hand.

Halvard breathed through the pain in his throat as he set his small hand into Fiske's. His brother stood, towering over him before he picked him up, and Halvard wrapped his arms around his neck, his muffled cry buried in his shoulder. And as the snow fell and the sun went down, Fiske carried him home.

CHAPTER TWENTY-FOUR

HALVARD

I WALKED THE PATH THROUGH HYLLI ALONE, STOPPING BEfore the closed door to our home in the dark, my hand on the cold latch as I listened.

I'd spent the last hours after the ceremony with Latham and the others, crowded around the fire as we talked through the battle that lay ahead. I'd tried to meet their eyes as the leaders looked to me, asking me questions about what I'd seen in the glade and in the valley. How many Svell there were and how fast they were traveling. How they'd attacked Ljós and Utan. I'd answered them, trying to sound sure.

But now, my family waited inside, their voices low around the fire. And there was no way to be strong for that moment. There was no way to tell them how sorry I was and I wondered if I would look different to them when I came through the door. If they'd see the shame of it all on me, the way they always saw everything.

I closed my eyes and swallowed hard before I pushed it open.

Fiske and Iri looked up from where they stood before the fire pit as I stepped inside, the rusted iron hinges creaking. Eelyn stood behind them, her pale eyes red and swollen. She pushed between them, walking straight to me with heavy steps until she was pressed against my chest, and I wrapped my arms around her as a soft, brittle cry escaped her lips. Fiske took the back of my neck, pressing his rough cheek to mine, and Iri did the same, putting his arms around the three of us. The familiar smell of them filled me, making my chest tight and my legs weak until they were the only thing keeping me standing.

"I'm sorry." I spoke into Eelyn's hair through a strangled whisper as she cried.

Iri squeezed tighter before he let us go and when I looked up, a tear streaked the side of his face, running into his blond beard.

"Halvard." My mother's voice sounded beside me and I looked up to see her face.

She'd been crying, but her eyes were set on me with her usual strength. Maybe because she was a healer. Or maybe because she'd lost my father so long ago. But she always seemed better able to face loss than the rest of us, her faith in the gods stronger than everyone else's combined. The silver streaked through her hair in thick, pleated strands and she smiled as she reached for me, tucking me into her with her hand stroking my hair. I kissed her cheek, trying to meet her eyes reassuringly. But I was barely holding myself together and she knew it.

"How did it happen?" Iri asked the question and everyone went quiet, waiting for my answer.

Aghi wasn't only the last of any blood family Iri and Eelyn had. He was the anchor of the one we'd all built together after the Herja came. And now, he was gone. I didn't know what that meant. What that made us.

Eelyn wiped at her face with the back of her hand before she sat down. "Were you with him?"

I nodded, trying to swallow back the tears that were brimming. I'd imagined their faces a hundred times as I told them what happened in the glade. But the pain of it was so much harsher here, outside of the walls of my mind. "He was killed in a glade outside of Ljós. Brought down by a knife in his chest." I breathed. "I was with him. I was with him until . . ." But I couldn't finish, the memory of his blue, glistening eyes on the sky so clear that it snatched the breath from my lungs.

Eelyn nodded, her hand winding tightly into her braid.

"I'm sorry," I said again, crouching down before her. "I convinced them to go. Latham and Mýra were against it, but I convinced Aghi and Espen. I was—"

"Stop, Halvard." Fiske cut me off, his voice firm. "He died honorably. That's all that matters."

Eelyn leaned forward, setting her hand on top of mine, and Iri nodded before he took a bottle of ale from the shelf on the wall and set cups onto the table. He filled them as I sat down beside Eelyn, my arm pressed to hers. My brothers took their own seats across from us and the door creaked again as Mýra stuck her head inside, a hesitant smile on her lips. She closed the door behind her and found a seat on the other side of Eelyn, sliding her arm around her waist and pouring herself a cup of ale. "Runa?"

"She stayed in Fela," Iri answered.

I was glad. Both Fiske's and Iri's children would be safe with her up on the mountain with plenty of time to leave if the Svell came. But it didn't feel like home without my nieces Náli and Isla here. And it didn't feel like our family without Aghi sitting beside us, his bad leg stretched out to the side of his stool and one elbow set on the table.

My eyes drifted to his empty seat, where I could still see him hunched over a steaming bowl of whatever my mother had made for supper. We ate like that almost every night, all of us together with the girls perched like little owls beside me.

"Tomorrow?" Fiske looked to me.

"Tomorrow. They're already camped in the valley."

"How many?" The air changed, the softness leaving their faces as it was replaced by the fight that lay deep inside them.

"We're not sure. Maybe eight hundred."

The number's weight fell heavily between us. The odds weren't good, but my brothers, Eelyn, and Mýra had faced bad odds before. When they defeated the Herja, they'd been outnumbered.

"What's our plan?" Fiske asked.

"We'll either meet them in the bottomlands or we'll try to keep them in the forest. Once they get past the tree line, they'll have the advantage and it will be a quick end." I stared into my cup. Really, it was only a matter of how long it would take them. "If we can take enough down before they reach the clearing, it will be a better fight out in the open."

I watched as Iri and Fiske both nodded in approval.

"You looked handsome up there," Eelyn said, changing the subject with a half smile almost reaching her reddened eyes.

"You looked scared. White as a goat headed for slaughter." Fiske laughed into his cup and Iri followed before I reached across the table and shoved him, sending his ale sloshing.

He tipped the cup back, still laughing.

Mýra set her chin into her hand, watching us. "Aghi would have been very proud."

"He would have." Iri refilled his cup. "It was a good death, Halvard. It was a death he's wanted for a long time."

I wanted to believe it, but only part of me did. I knew he would be proud to die for his people, but I also knew that he had more years to live. He had more to teach me.

"He felt left behind by our mother." Iri sounded suddenly tired. "When the Herja came the first time and she died in the raid, he was haunted by it. He thought he should have died protecting her. But Sigr preserved him and he'd always been angry about that. Now, he's in the afterlife with her, waiting for us." He reached across the table for Eelyn's hand and she took it, laying her head onto Mýra's shoulder.

The quiet returned until a soft rumble of thunder sounded in the distance. Before he was the man I'd met in Fela, Aghi was a husband who'd lost a wife and never found love again. He was a father who'd raised his children alone. Then, he'd helped lead both clans into one people. It was hard to imagine him as anything other than the warrior that went running to the center of battle in the glade. At times, I had wondered if Aghi and my mother would find love again in each other, but they'd both been alone too long, content with only friendship.

"I left a stele for him in Aurvanger. It's by the river." I pressed my thumb to the sore wound in my palm, reopened by the Tala's knife.

"Thank you." Iri's deep voice broke the silence.

"And I killed him," I said, "the Svell chieftain who killed Aghi. I killed him."

Fiske looked up at me then, leaning onto the table with both his elbows. There was nothing to say. It didn't lessen the blow of losing Aghi or even begin to make it right. But it was a blood feud that felt like my own. Even if our people had left those ways behind, they still lived in me. And I'd taken my first life, which had its own cost. I'd killed without even the slightest bit of hesitation or guilt. Even now, I wished I could do it again. And I wasn't sure what that meant.

I stood, setting down my empty cup before any of them

could say anything. I didn't want to talk about it, I just wanted them to know I'd done what they would have done. And I didn't want them seeking revenge for Aghi in battle when the sun rose. I wanted them to fight with the peace of knowing it was made right.

"Where are you going?" Eelyn wrapped her hand around my wrist, holding me in place.

"To walk."

She almost objected until Fiske gave her a look and she let me go. "Alright."

I unbuckled my father's armor vest, pulling it over my head and setting it on the trunk with my sheaths. The door closed behind me and I listened to the sound of my brothers' voices drift away on the warm wind as I walked up the path that led to the beach.

The stave burning on the hill in the distance had gone out, the Svell sleeping before their march down to the fjord. It was so dark that the place where the water met the black rocks was invisible, only the gleam of moonlight shining in a blade-straight line on the water.

It was the same path I'd walked for more than half of my life. The same steps I'd taken as a boy, as a young man, and now, as the chieftain of a people that didn't even exist when I was born. There was no accounting for the will of the gods or the futures that the Spinners gave to mortals. It was the reason Aghi, Latham, and Espen spoke the words *lag mund*. Fate's hand.

The battle that awaited us was only a knot in the thread

on the tapestry of our people. And though I'd known for the last two years that I'd eventually stand before them, I'd never been so aware of how incapable I would feel in the face of leading.

The Nādhir would follow me into the mist of the forest when the sun rose. And only the gods knew if we'd ever come out.

CHAPTER TWENTY-FIVE

TOVA

I DREAMED OF THE WATER.

The slice of cold against my skin and the twinkling light, dancing on the surface far above me. Slowly, it pulled farther away, growing smaller and the darkness spreading wider as I sank into the depths of the sea. And there, the woman's song found me, the lilt of a quiet, gentle hum in the emptiness.

Wake up, Tova.

I followed the drift of the voice to the fire from the fragments of a memory that always found me in sleep. The glow of it cast across my bare skin as I sat naked on a stool, a pair of hands at work on the stag's horns on my arm with a glistening needle. The shadow shifted, moving every time it came into focus, and I tried to hold it still long enough to find the pieces that fit together.

Wake up, Tova.

My eyes opened and I gasped, my lungs stiff and frozen,

as if they'd been filled with the silver seawater that surrounded me in my dream. But I was no longer sinking in the black emptiness or sitting before the fire. I was curled up beneath a bearskin in my tent with the roll of a storm growling in the distance. I was in the valley.

The repeating call of the nighthawk made me jolt and I sat up, the fur dropping from my shoulders. The camp was silent except for the slide of wind over the corners of canvas tents. Crisp night air blew in from outside and I pulled back the flap carefully until I could see the moon behind a stretch of thin clouds.

Before it, the All Seer circled overhead.

I breathed, listening to the beat of my own heart in lock step with the flap of the nighthawk's wings. The Spinners had sent him, like they always had.

But this time, he'd come for *me*.

I pulled my boots on quickly, keeping my eyes on the light casting into the tent. There was no mistaking the runes, but the future wasn't fixed. It was a thread that changed color with the shifting of the present and the past. A wave that rippled out to the vast, open sea. And if I wanted to be sure it came to pass, I needed to be there. I needed to stand before Hylli and watch the future come.

Halvard's axe hung heavily at my hip as I pulled the canvas back carefully, peering out to see Gunther at his post. He sat on an overturned crate with his knife in one hand and a whetstone in the other, sliding it down the blade in an arc to sharpen the gleaming iron. His sword was sheathed at his belt, his axe at his back. But the only chance I could take was with Gunther. I had no choice.

I stepped out into the moonlight and he went rigid at the sound, the knife turning in the light. His fingers closed tightly over the stone in his big fist and his eyes studied my bloodstained hands before they lifted to meet mine. "What are you doing?"

"I'm leaving," I answered, my gaze flitting back to the sky, where the All Seer was still circling.

"What?" He stood, hiding me in his shadow, and suddenly, he looked like one of the giants from the old stories of the gods. My heart thumped in my chest, watching the knife at his side and waiting to see if he would raise it against me. But the moments passed, the silence returning, and he didn't.

"I can end this," I whispered. "All of it."

He didn't move, except for the twitch of his hand on the handle of the knife.

"I've seen the future. You should go back to Hǫlkn. Back to your family."

His eyes narrowed. "I won't hide in my home while my clansmen fight."

I knew he wouldn't. But I didn't want to see him lying dead on the battlefield. I didn't want to stand against him or see him fall. He was a good man.

I reached beneath my sleeve and untied the bracelet around my wrist. "Then take this." I held it out to him, the copper disk heavy in the palm of my hand.

"What is it?" he breathed.

"It's a talisman. For protection." I didn't tell him that there wasn't a talisman strong enough to hide him from the wrath of the Spinners.

Gunther looked down at me for a long moment before he tucked his knife back into its sheath. He took the bracelet from my hand, turning it over in the light.

"Why did you do it?" I asked.

"What?"

"Why did you come to the beach that day?"

"Because you were a child," he said, simply.

He wasn't a warm man. There was no softness to him. But he'd been kind and he'd done what he thought was right even when no one would have agreed with him. He was maybe the only person I could trust on this side of the sea.

"I have no family left." He looked up, suddenly. "My son Aaro died in the attack on Ljós."

"I'm sorry," I whispered.

"I didn't know he was going. I didn't know what they'd planned. I have no family left," he said again.

"Then stay alive to find a new one."

His fingers closed over the talisman until it was hidden in his fist and he walked to the edge of the forest, where his horse was tied to the trunk of a wide tree. He ran a hand up its snout before he lifted my bow from the riggings and untied the quiver.

I smiled as he held them out to me, but he only stared at the ground between us as the shadow of the nighthawk swept overhead again. Its wail rang out above us as I dropped the bow over my head.

"Thank you." I reached back to feel the feather fletching over my shoulder as I secured it.

Without a word, he turned, giving me his back as he walked away. I watched him grow smaller in the low light and I held my breath as he disappeared between the tents, the lump in my throat winding tighter. I hoped it was the last time I'd ever see him. I hoped his blood wouldn't pay the debt for what I'd done.

The nighthawk cried again and I looked up, watching him tip his wings and turn to break the circle. He flew out over the forest, headed east, and I knew. The same way I knew the sound of the woman's voice in the broken memory. The Spinners had answered my prayer. They were leading me. And now it was time to follow.

I didn't look back, walking straight into the trees toward Hylli until the camp disappeared behind me, glancing up every few steps to keep an eye on the All Seer above. He flickered in and out of view, vanishing behind thick branches and then appearing again against the lambent, cloud-covered sky.

The moon's path curved overhead as the hours passed and I was swallowed up by the belly of the bottomlands, feeling alone for the first time since the Svell Tala found me on that beach. No Jorrund whispering in my ear or eyes trailing over my Kyrr-marked skin.

He would know as soon as he woke that I was gone.

He'd be frantic, afraid. And though I didn't want to care or worry for him, a very small part of me still did. He was a fragile soul, even if he didn't know it, built on the power he'd stumbled upon the day he found me. But that power was now slipping through his fingers with each breath, leaving only the man who'd lied to keep from losing his tight grip on everything around him.

I'd been a fool to believe that I belonged with Jorrund. I knew that. In fact, I'd always known. But I'd never had anywhere else to go. He'd come looking, but he wouldn't find me.

This time, I was really gone.

I walked. I walked until I couldn't feel anything. My skin numbed in the icy rain, my hair and clothes soaked through. The forest was so quiet, my footsteps pulsing in an echo against the trees as each one hit the ground. I walked until the bones of my feet ached inside my boots. Until my arms were weak from carrying the weight of my skirts. Until my eyes were so heavy that the All Seer's shape was a blur against the dark night sky. Halvard's face was the pull that swept me through the forest, coming in and out of focus in my mind. He was the one I owed something to now. The only fate that mattered.

Vigdis was right. I should have died out on the empty sea, but the Spinners had bound my fate to the young Nādhir from the glade. They'd wound our paths together for some purpose I couldn't understand. It was carved into the Tree of Urðr. Written on my soul. And it was the one thing I was going to do right. It was the one thing I was going to do on my own.

And with that single thought, I suddenly wanted to see him. I wanted to be near him, like I was beneath the gate in Utan. The whispers seemed to flutter back to life in the back of my mind, the sound of them melting into the wind and the sway of the trees.

A crack of light split the darkness ahead and I stopped, hugging my skirts tighter to my chest. The scent of the sea met me, the churn of water and the slip of cold rocks breaking the empty silence. I came through the edge of the forest, into a gust of cool, salty air. It hit my face with the moonlight and before me, the black, sleeping fjord unfurled. It foamed white on the shore, my boots at the edge of a cliff that dropped straight down to a rocky beach below. The sound of it swelled and spilled over, washing out everything else until I could feel the hiss of whispers on my skin. The click of tongues on teeth.

And I knew before I looked up that he'd be there. I knew it the way I knew the weight of the stones around my neck.

I blinked, my gaze following the edge to the feet that stood down the cliff, the moonlight on his white tunic a faint glow. It pulled around him in the wind, his hair blowing across his forehead. And when I looked up into his face, Halvard's eyes were on me.

CHAPTER TWENTY-SIX

HALVARD

I COULD FEEL HER. LIKE THE CREEP OF SILENT FOG WINDING through the trees.

The Truthtongue stood like a ghost against the night, her skin white as frost beneath her black dress. She looked down to the water below, dropping her skirts from where they were bundled in her hands, and they blew back behind her like unfolded raven's wings.

I blinked, expecting her to disappear the way she had that night in the forest. The way she had before the altar fire, the vision of her vanishing like smoke. But she didn't. She stilled before she looked up, her hands tucked against her chest as her eyes met mine. And the same feeling that had come over me in Utan returned, like needles moving over my skin. It was something I'd never felt before the day I'd seen her in the glade, but now, it was becoming familiar. It was becoming something I recognized.

I looked past her, to the trees, as I pulled the knife from my belt. "Are you alone?" My voice was lost in the wind shooting up the cliff.

She stood frozen, as if she expected me to disappear, too. "Yes," she said, stepping back from the cliff's edge.

Her eyes fell to the knife in my hand. The braids that fell over her shoulder were almost completely unraveled, the pieces falling into her face and dripping with rain. I tried not to watch the way it ran in rivulets over her skin.

The length of her dress snapped in the wind, her fingers twisting into the ends of her hair at her waist. I lifted a hand between us slowly and her lips parted on a breath as I caught her wrist and pulled her toward me. And she was real. Not like the spirit I'd seen in the forest. The back of her hand was cut through the middle of the mark of the yarrow inked there and her skin was ice cold, but she was flesh and bone before me. And still, there was something haunting about her. Something more shadow than light.

"You're really here," I said, letting go of her.

She closed her hand into a fist, covering the mark where I'd touched her with her fingers as she took a step back.

"What are you doing here?" I said, moving forward to close the space she'd put between us.

"I came to tell you . . ." But she didn't finish, her feet shifting nervously as she tucked the unwoven hair behind her ear. She pulled my axe from her belt and held it out to me. Its blade was almost completely covered in mud.

I took it, rubbing at the iron with my thumb until the engraving of the yew tree glinted.

She wrapped her arms around herself, shivering. "The Svell are coming to Hylli."

"You think I don't know that?" My voice rose over the sound of the waves crashing below and she bristled.

She turned back to face the water, hooking her hands onto the bow over her shoulder. "I'm sorry." Her lips formed the words but I couldn't hear them. She looked suddenly small. Delicate.

I sighed, letting the weight of the axe fall to my side. "Why did you help me?" I asked, my voice softening.

She looked surprised at the question, studying my face before she answered. "Because you're not supposed to die."

"If I'm not supposed to die, then I won't."

She searched my eyes, making me feel unsteady on my feet again. "That's not how fate works."

The moonlight broke through the clouds overhead, catching the eye on her chest. It stared up at me, unblinking. "Then how does it work?"

"It's always changing. Every moment. I'm trying to undo what's happened. I didn't know when I cast the stones that they would—"

"So, it was you?" I ran a hand through my wet hair, realizing that Kjeld had been right.

She said nothing, but the answer was in the way her gaze flitted back to the ground. "I didn't know."

But that wasn't good enough. An entire village was dead. Aghi was dead. "What are you doing with the Svell?"

"I'm not with them. Not anymore." Her voice faded. "I want to help you."

I tried to read the look that lit on her face. She was afraid, and even if I'd never seen war, I knew people. I didn't trust her, but the fair skin at her throat was still bruised, the welts from where I'd had my hands around her neck visible even in the darkness. She'd come here, even though I'd almost killed her only days ago.

"And I have nowhere else to go." She swallowed hard, the shame of it heavy on each word.

I blinked, the picture of her becoming instantly clearer. I could see it. There was something hollow about her. Something worn thin.

"I can help you. I can try to keep you alive."

"You can't help us." I slid my knife back into my belt and turned, starting back up the path, but she followed.

"Please." She took hold of my sleeve, stopping me, and I flinched at the feeling of her cold skin through my tunic. Her fingers wrapped around my arm and I swallowed hard, looking down into her face. The marks painted every inch of skin showing in the opening of her dress and I followed them with my eyes until they disappeared. "I want to help you." Her grip on me tightened.

"If I die fighting for my people, it will be a good death. The gods will honor it. I'll go to the afterlife with my father."

Her head tilted, her eyes glinting, as if she could see something in mine.

"I'm not afraid," I said, my voice deepening.

She stepped closer to me, her hand sliding down my arm to my wrist. "Halvard . . ." she whispered.

The sound of my name spoken in her voice made me pull free of her, my fingers twitching to go back for my knife. I didn't like the feeling it sent running through me. It sounded like an incantation on her lips.

"What's your name?"

She smiled, and a feeling like thread being pulled between my ribs made it hard to breathe. "Tova."

"Why do you care what happens to us, Tova?"

"Because our fates are bound. They're tied together," she whispered.

I'd begun to think the same thing. I didn't know why, but there was a pull between us. A draw that kept bringing me back to that moment in the glade. "What does that mean?"

She looked at me for a long moment, thinking. "I don't know. But you're not supposed to die tomorrow. I've seen it." She dropped her hand, leaving only the sting of her touch behind on my skin.

"In the stones?"

She nodded. "Yes, in the stones."

"So, you've switched sides because of what the runes told you?"

"I left the Svell because I wasn't supposed to be there.

I'm supposed to be *here.*" The tears in her eyes glimmered in the dark. "I didn't know when I read the runes that the Svell would move against the Nādhir. I didn't know any of this would happen."

"But it did."

"I know." She breathed through the hitch in her chest. "I'm sorry," she said again, her knuckles going white as her hands tangled together.

Behind her, the forest was empty. As soon as the Svell knew their Truthtongue was gone, someone would likely come looking. But by then, battle would have begun.

I stared down into the black water below, watching the water curl white before it hit the rocks and was swept back out into the sea. I had no interest in the stones or the rendering of the future. But she'd been with the Svell. She'd seen them fight and knew their numbers. I wasn't stupid enough to not accept her help.

But buried beneath those thoughts was another one that I didn't want to admit to. I didn't want to tell her to go. Now that she was here, I didn't want her to leave.

Her finger traced the line of the cut through the stalk of yarrow on her hand and I realized that she was waiting for my answer. She stood so still that it looked as if she wasn't even breathing.

Tova wasn't only trying to save me. She was trying to save herself.

"I can cast the stones for the Nādhir. I can—"

"No." I didn't let her finish.

Her brow pulled, her eyes narrowing as she looked up at me. "You don't want to know?"

"No." I turned into the wind, not waiting for her to follow. "If I'm going to fight, I need to believe that we can win."

CHAPTER TWENTY-SEVEN

TOVA

THE LIGHT OF THE SUN WAS STILL BURIED DEEP BEHIND THE horizon when Hylli came into view.

I followed Halvard up the path, my eyes on his back as he walked. He was stripped of his armor, the tunic stretched over his broad shoulders and his hair pulled back into a knot at the nape of his neck. There was a moment on the cliff when I thought he would turn me away, but the same feeling that had flooded me in Utan was now leading me into Hylli.

The shore that hugged the land looked a bit like the ones outside of Liera, but there was something different about this place. The mountain rose up before the fjord as if the gods were perched there, watching over the little village.

It was beautiful. It was a home.

I'd only heard a few stories about the gods of the Nādhir. I'd heard even less about the god of my own people, Naðr. But there were some things that were true about every god, making them all feel familiar. And Hylli felt that way. Like a place I'd somehow forgotten.

"I want to see the Kyrr who was with you in Utan," I said, quickening my steps to keep up with him.

"He's not here."

I stopped beneath the gate. "What?"

"He's gone." He finally turned to face me. "How do you know him?"

"I don't know," I answered. And if he was gone, I would probably never know. I looked up to a string of bones hung from the beam set onto the posts. They swung gently in the wind overhead. "Who was that?"

Halvard stood in the middle of the path; his eyes lifted to the arch before they fell back down to me. "The last people who tried to take this place from us."

The Herja.

He walked into the fog and I followed, the shape of houses surfacing to my left and right before Halvard stopped at a wood plank door that was windblown gray. He opened the door and disappeared inside, where the sound of voices was suddenly cut short.

Firelight spilled onto the ground before me and the smell of herbs rolled out into the night air. I stepped over the threshold carefully, looking around the large house. Two men worked over a pile of leathers at the table and Halvard picked up an armor vest from a trunk, dropping it over his tunic.

It wasn't until one of the men looked up that his hands stilled, his face half-lit by the fire. His attention went to the bow slung over my shoulder. "Who's this?" His blue eyes traced over my marks before they found my face.

"Her name is Tova."

"Are you . . . ?" His stare was more curious than fearful.

"She's Kyrr," Halvard answered, working at the clasps of his vest.

The two men looked at one another before the fair-haired one smiled and I realized that he hadn't told them about me. Or what I'd done. If he had, they would have had their swords drawn already.

A knock sounded at the door and I pressed myself to the wall as Halvard reached for the latch. "You want to help us? This is your chance."

The door swung open again and a tall, broad man with an unruly black beard stood in the mist with a few others, waiting. "Ready?" But his face changed when he saw me, his eyes widening.

"She's come from the Svell camp." Halvard tipped his chin in my direction for me to follow and we fell into step with the bodies moving quietly in the dark. "Call them up, Latham."

The black-bearded man signaled one of the others walking beside him and he disappeared before we came through the doors of the ritual house. The door slammed closed behind us and the warmth of the altar fire wound itself around me, but I was still too cold to feel it.

They gathered around a table where a map was unrolled before them, their voices all bleeding together over the sound of the fire. I found a place in the shadowed corner, my numb hands clasped before me.

"Tova." Halvard found me over the heads of the others and I stepped forward, swallowing hard. "How many Svell are camped in the eastern valley?" The others quieted as Halvard spoke and I froze as I felt the weight of their stares. They stepped to either side of the table, making room for me.

"Seven hundred and sixty," I answered, repeating the number I'd heard Siv report to Vigdis.

"Here?" Halvard pointed to a place on the map, at the edge of the forest.

"Not that close to the water." I set my hand on his and I felt him stiffen under my touch as I moved his finger north. "But they'll come from the south."

He pulled his hand from beneath mine before his fist clenched at his side.

The one he'd called Latham leaned into the table. "Forcing them to the bottomland will make it harder for them to push through."

"It will make it harder for both of us," Halvard answered.

I arched an eyebrow, watching every village leader look to Halvard as he spoke. As if he was one of them.

"Were you there when they attacked in Utan?" His attention returned to me.

I stiffened, not wanting to remember it. I wanted to erase that night from my mind the way everything else had been. I gave a single nod. "I was."

"What did they do?"

"I . . ." I stammered, unsure of what to say. Unsure of what they'd think.

This is your chance.

Halvard's words repeated in my mind.

"They stormed the village. Their warriors took down every Nādhir before they set it all on fire."

I watched Halvard flinch against the words, though he concealed it well. "How did they set it on fire?"

"Pitch arrows," I answered. I could still hear the whistle of them flying through the dark.

He looked back to the map, thinking.

Latham nodded in reply. "What do you want to do?"

My gaze tightened at the question, studying them. Latham looked up at Halvard, patiently waiting for his answer, the way Siv did with Vigdis.

I swallowed hard. He wasn't just one of them. He was *leading* them.

"Here." Halvard pointed to a dense area of forest between the fjord and the valley. "If we can keep them behind the tree line until at least half of them are dead, we will have a chance. Their arrows won't be able to reach the village from there." His hand slid to the open clearing before Hylli. "We'll keep a quarter of our warriors waiting here. The rest, to the first line in the forest."

They considered, a heavy quiet falling over the ritual house.

"What do you think?" he asked, searching their faces.

"Good." Latham nodded and the others followed. "It's good."

But there was no good plan to be made. The options were few. Keeping the fight in the forest was the best they had.

The sound of a bell rang out in the village, the sharp clang echoing around us and without pause, they moved as one toward the doors.

Halvard picked his axe up off the map, taking my arm and pulling me with him.

"You're chieftain," I said, lowly.

He let me go, fitting the axe back into its sheath. "Today I am."

"Why won't you let me cast the stones? I can help. I can—"

At that, he turned, looking down at me as the others filed out. I stilled when I felt the brush of his breath on my skin, trying not to lean into his warmth.

"I told you. I don't want to know. I trust the gods." His eyes ran over my face for a long moment, his jaw clenching. "Thank you for your help." He turned to the door. "Stay north and you should miss them."

"What?" I took hold of his vest before he stepped outside. "I'm going with you."

"Going with us?"

"I told you. I want to help."

"You did. Now go home."

"I don't have a home." My fingers dropped from the bronze clasps at his side.

His lips parted on a long breath, his gaze narrowing. "Can you fight?"

"I can shoot." I smiled, hooking my fingers into the bowstring stretched across my chest.

His eyes jumped back and forth on mine. "You know we're probably all going to die, don't you?"

I reached around him, taking the knife from the back of his belt. "I told you. You don't die today."

He crossed his arms over his chest, watching as I cut away the length of my skirts. The bell sounded again and I dropped the torn linen to the floor. I handed him the knife, and the corner of his mouth lifted, but he turned before I could see him smile.

I ran to keep up with him in the flood of warriors all headed for the gate. We reached the back of the line and I tightened the straps of the quiver and started up the hill after him. A hand lifted into the air ahead as we made it to the trees, and I saw the fair-haired man from the house waving from the front of the line. Halvard reached for him, catching his arm and taking hold of my wrist, pulling me with him as he pushed through the tightly packed bodies.

When we broke through the line, we were standing at the top of the hill, shoulder to shoulder with the others. A blonde woman and a red-haired woman stood beside them, both casting sharp glares at me.

"What's she doing here?" A man with shorn hair looked down at me with a crooked smile. It took a moment to recognize him as one of the men who'd been with Halvard in Utan.

"It's a long story," Halvard muttered, pulling his sword free.

"They aren't afraid of me." I spoke lowly beside him.

"Who?"

"All of them. Why aren't they afraid of me?"

His blue eyes were the same color as ice in the morning light. "Why would they be afraid of you?"

"Halvard!" Latham walked the line of warriors spread through the forest and Halvard signaled him with a whistle. Latham stopped before him, setting one hand on Halvard's shoulder. "On your signal."

Halvard let him go and Latham left us, finding his place down the line. We stood at the front before hundreds of warriors at our backs and spread to our left and right. Halvard's brothers both took him into their arms and kissed him before the blonde woman took hold of his armor, checking it again.

When I looked around us, every face was looking to Halvard, waiting. He took a breath before he pulled his axe free and whistled out into the forest, the sound echoing in the trees. A silence fell over the clansmen until there was only the sound of the cold, crashing waves that encircled

Hylli below. I tried not to think about what I was doing, walking into battle alongside strangers to fight the Svell. But it suddenly seemed as if it had all led to this, fate twisting and turning since that day on the beach with Jorrund. To this exact moment in time, my feet planted beside Halvard's.

The line suddenly moved forward, one step at a time, and my hand tightened around the bowstring slung across my chest, my heart racing. The trees spread out in every direction and we wove around them like a flood of water, moving through the forest as the brightening light pushed the mist through the trees ahead of us.

Halvard walked beside me, every muscle wound tight around every bone, his weapons heavy at his sides. Behind us, Hylli lay peacefully by the calm sea, but the storm was only minutes from breaking. The sharp taste of it was thick in the air.

I held on to my bow so tightly that the skin on my fingers threatened to break against it and when Halvard whistled again, the line abruptly stopped, every sound erased. He reached into his tunic, pulling a small stone from beneath his armor vest, and his thumb rubbed over its surface before he kissed it and whispered something I couldn't hear. The sound was echoed behind me, the soft, reverberating voices of the Nādhir murmuring prayers to their gods.

My face lifted to the darkening clouds and the first cold drop of rain hit my cheek. I didn't know any gods to ask for help. Even if I did, I doubted they'd come. It was the Spinners I knew, and they weren't protectors. They didn't care about the spider walking on the web of fate, but they had given me a second chance. A chance to make things right.

Instead, I prayed to the woman in my vision. I closed my eyes and conjured her. Delicate hands in the firelight and the hum of a song. Silver waters and the great statues of the headlands like giants in the fog.

The prayers faded and I opened my eyes to see shadows appearing ahead. The storm growing in the sky above us suddenly seemed to be thundering inside my chest. It snatched the breath from my lungs as a sharp sting lit there, like the tip of a knife carving the heart from between my ribs.

The Svell stretched out in the trees ahead, a never-ending line of warriors to the right and left. Their leathers blended with the colors of the forest until they were almost invisible, but the unsettled surprise was written on their faces. They hadn't expected to meet the Nādhir this deep in the bottomlands. Even if they made it to Hylli eventually, they'd do it with fewer warriors. They'd return to Svell territory dragging their dead behind them.

I blinked when a face I knew appeared among the others and I clenched my teeth, the sting of heat burning behind my eyes. In the distance, the Tala's gaze was fixed on me.

Jorrund's face twisted in fury, his teeth clenched so tightly they looked as if they may break in his mouth. Vigdis stood broad-shouldered beside him and I knew what he was thinking. That he should have killed me when Vera died. That he should have let me burn when Bekan fell in the glade. Every drop of blood spilled from here to Liera was the sea I was cursed to drown in. Somehow, Vigdis had known it. He knew that I'd bring death since the moment he first laid eyes on me.

And he was right.

CHAPTER TWENTY-EIGHT

HALVARD

THE SIGNAL MOVED THROUGH THE WIND LIKE THREAD through a needle as the Svell came into view.

The front line of their warriors stretched as long as ours, but there were rows upon rows of them waiting to press forward, toward the slope that led down to the village. Vigdis stood at its center before the others, his hair picked up by the wind, and even from this distance I could see that the blade clutched in his hand was the jeweled sword that Bekan had brought to the glade as the offering of reparation. It was the weapon that took Espen's life. The amber stone at its hilt almost seemed to glow in the palm of his hand.

I looked to Fiske and he gave me a tight nod before he slid his own sword free. I'd never seen him in battle. I'd only ever heard the stories. But looking into the face of my brother, it was as if a different person had come alive behind his eyes.

"I'm with you, brother." His deep voice carried the words in the silence and they were the only ones I needed. With Iri, Fiske, Eelyn, and Mýra at my side, I was suddenly unafraid.

Tova set her dark eyes on the Svell army. The Tala I'd seen her with in the glade stood beside Vigdis in the distance, his face full of horror at the sight of her. But she looked back at him with no expression, the bow light in her hands.

Their warriors came to a stop and Vigdis looked to the trees around us, studying the space between the two multitudes. In more than one way, meeting them in the forest gave us a disadvantage, but if fate was on our side like Tova said it was, it would be the only way to win. From the look of Vigdis, he was suspicious of the move.

I kneeled down, taking a handful of cool, damp soil into my hand and crushing it between my fingers, the feel of the earth centering me. I breathed, summoning the sight of Hylli at sunset to the front of my mind. The smell of the sea and the golden light. The sound of the water against the hull of the boat and the shells chiming in the windows. I'd been born on the mountain but I'd become a man on the fjord. Its waters flowed through my veins.

I whistled again as I stood, letting the sound ring out, and drew a last steady breath. It was the end, and I couldn't help but think it felt right. I let the weight of my sword pull me back to the battlefield and my gaze settled on Vigdis before I tipped my head back and screamed.

The rush of wind slid past me as I took off running and the war cries of my clansmen threw me forward. My feet sank into the soft ground as we wove through the trees, the Svell racing across the forest toward us. And then there was a moment of silence. A space splintered between beats of my heart, before every raging thing collided and the earth underfoot was eaten up with war.

Vigdis' towering frame ran straight for me at the front, his teeth shining as he roared. My steps hit the ground faster and I didn't slow until the glimmer of light on steel made me sink low. An axe flew over my head, catching a Nādhir woman behind me, and she was knocked from her feet, hitting the ground hard. I stood just in time to catch the man who'd thrown it with my blade, dropping him with one strike before I jumped over him. I searched the haze for Vigdis as bodies flooded around me. But he was gone, lost in the sea of battle ahead.

Fiske ran past me, his sword swinging up and over his head before it sank into the back of a Svell. The man fell at his feet and he yanked it back, spinning and taking another down with a second stroke. My eyes focused on a woman lifting a bow behind him. She sighted down her arrow at Fiske, her mouth dropping open as her fingers slid from the string.

"Down!" I ran for her as Fiske dropped to his haunches and the arrow sailed over his head and hit the Svell behind him.

She reached for another arrow but I was too close. I

brought my axe down onto her shoulder and she fell to her knees, reaching for Fiske. He toppled backward, driving his sword up to impale the woman with it. The length of the blade shone with blood as Fiske pulled it from where it was wedged between her bones and stood, heaving.

I stepped over the woman at my feet, picking up her sword with my free hand.

"Alright?" Fiske waited for me to nod before he turned back to the three warriors running toward us.

He readied, one hand hovering at his side to steady himself, and I took a step forward, pivoting on my foot to bring the axe around me with more momentum. I didn't look at the mark before it landed, relying on my aim so that I could keep an eye on the Svell woman closing in. The point of the axe blade sliced clean through the thick of the man's leg and I let the handle slide from my fingers as the woman reached me. I dropped to one knee, taking the hilt of the sword into both hands before driving it upward with a snap. It sank into the center of her chest and Fiske yanked me by my armor, pulling me up and shoving my axe back into my hands. We pushed forward, to the front line.

But before we made it, a man barreled into me, knocking me off my feet. My axe flew from my grasp and as I braced for the blow of his sword, he suddenly froze, falling to his knees before me. His hands clutched at the iron point punctured through his throat. Blood spilled out between his fingers as he clawed at the arrow.

I looked past him to see Tova, standing with her bow

lifted and her fingers curled around the next arrow's fletching. She snatched the knife from the belt of the fallen Svell at her feet, tossing it into the air, and the blade sank into the ground beside me. I rolled to the side, taking the knife into my hands, and drove it back to catch the Svell swinging at Fiske. He cried out, falling forward, and I rolled back up onto my knees, sinking the blade into his side.

When I looked back over my shoulder, Tova was gone.

Another body bolted in my direction as I yanked the blade free and I fell onto my back, lifting the knife as he came down, and it cut into him, finding the soft place below his breastbone. He landed on top of me and I looked up as two shadows slid over the ground. Fiske and Eelyn stood over me, fighting back to back. I shoved the body off of me and got to my feet. The forest was covered in fighting clansmen, their screaming muted by the roar of the storm above us.

Iri tossed my axe into the air and I caught it, using the momentum of his throw to catch a Svell woman in the arm as she reared back for a blow with her sword. She stumbled to the side and I came back with the other hand, cutting into the opening of her armor vest with the knife.

She fell as Mýra appeared behind her, blood smeared across her face like war paint. She jerked her chin to the right and I turned with the axe lifted, snapping it back before sinking it into another man's chest.

Behind him, Vigdis was pulling his sword from the body of a Nādhir, his pale face dripping cold rain.

I threw my weight forward, running as I pulled the Svell

sword from my sheath. He pivoted as the blade came down and the blow missed, catching the handle instead. I flung it back, swinging again, and the corner grazed his neck. A trail of blood spilled down over his throat, soaking into his tunic. He pressed the heel of one hand into it to stanch the bleeding and brought the sword back up, charging toward me. I caught hold of his arm, swinging him around me, and we both fell, slamming into the wide trunk of a tree.

The sword left my hand and I scrambled to my feet, coming over him before he could stand. I kicked into his side and he fell back down, groaning as he rocked onto his back, panting.

He looked up at me, his hand still pressed to the bleeding wound.

I picked up the axe, looking into his eyes. I wanted him to know it was me. I wanted him to take the memory with him to the afterlife. For the shame of it to follow him for eternity. I lifted the axe over my head, ready to bring it down, and as I pulled the breath into my chest, I froze.

The sound of a scream cut through the chaos, finding me. A voice I knew.

Eelyn.

I spun around, searching the tangle of bodies for her. She was on the ground, a Svell woman bringing her sword up with both hands.

"No!" I screamed, running as every light in the forest flickered out, only the sound of Eelyn's cries echoing in my head.

The sword came down as Eelyn bucked and it sank into her shoulder, piercing through her flesh and finding the earth. She howled, taking the woman's hair into her fist as she lifted the sword again. I took a wide step, raising the axe above my head, and threw it, my fingers sliding from the wet handle with my heart in my throat.

The sword dropped from her hand as she lurched backward and she looked down with wide eyes at the axe buried in her chest.

Eelyn sat up, taking the knife from the grass behind her and driving it into her side.

The woman dropped, sliding in the mud, and I got down onto my knees, pulling Eelyn into me.

"I'm alright," she said, but the words were broken on the growl in her throat. The opening in her shoulder was wide, the blood flowing in a steady stream down her armor. Her face was already going white.

Her arms wrapped around my neck as I lifted her from the ground and I set her back on her feet before I shoved her forward, toward an opening in the line. Behind us, Fiske and Iri were taking down a Svell and Mýra was running back into the fray.

I turned in a circle, searching for the Nādhir leathers. The ground was already covered in bodies, the Svell scattered in every direction. The clearing was illuminated with lightning behind us, where the rest of our warriors waited.

But when I turned back, Vigdis was gone.

CHAPTER TWENTY-NINE

TOVA

A CRACK OF LIGHTNING LIT THE SKY AS I PULLED THE BOW from my shoulders and ran. The deep groan of the storm rolling in from the sea unleashed the rain and it fell in thick sheets as everyone took off.

I threw one foot in front of the other as warriors passed me, their weapons raised in the air, and I pulled an arrow from my back, nocking it in one motion. I found the first Svell in my sights in the distance and let it fly. My feet slid to a stop and the Nādhir ran around me like a stone in the river. I watched the arrow pull up into the air before it tipped back down and struck the woman in the chest. She fell back, the sword flying from her hand, and the two men behind her crashed to the earth.

I turned in a circle, searching for Halvard, but he was gone, lost in the horde that filled the forest.

Everything blurred and smeared in the haze as I wiped

the rain from my eyes, the sound of war cries exploding in every direction. The storm billowed in from the sea, stronger every second. When I spotted an outcropping of boulders in the distance, I ran for it. My boots splashed in the mud as I wound around tangled clansmen, headed for the buried, moss-covered rocks. A man locked eyes with me as I passed, lunging for me, and I swung the bow back, catching him in the jaw with its end. His head whipped to the side and he faltered before a Nādhir barreled into him and they both fell, skidding over the pine needles.

I made it to the outcropping and pulled myself up over the top with sliding hands, looking down from the vantage point to see the battle stretching through the trees. I pulled another arrow from the quiver at my back, steadying myself on my knees, and sighted down the length of it for the group of Svell breaking the Nādhir line. I listened to the sound of the turning wind like Gunther taught me, measuring the arrow's path before I let my fingers slip from the string with a pop. The shot struck the shoulder of a man running toward the opening, then another, the rock anchoring below me and my breath keeping my heart from exploding in my chest.

I loosed arrow after arrow, dropping Svell as they ran. But the bow stilled in my hand, my fingers softening on the fletching when I saw a cart behind the back rows of the Svell army in the distance. It was piled high with small wooden barrels. Just like the one Jorrund had used for the stave.

And as if the Spinners wanted me to see it, a sudden flash of lightning lit one face in the fray that I recognized.

Halvard.

He plowed into a woman with a sword, knocking her down as another Nādhir plunged their blade into her chest. When he stood, his face was carved with shadows in the dim light. His brother tossed him an axe and he caught it, turning until his arm was swinging out around him to clip another Svell in the arm. The man cried out, toppling backward and Halvard finished him with one blow before he ran for the Nādhir line, where the Svell were making headway toward the edge of the forest.

They were already close. Too close.

"Halvard!" I screamed, but the sound was swallowed by the thunder. He was too far away.

A woman broke through two men fighting and followed after him, darting through the battle on his heels. She let her axe sink back behind her, ready to throw it, and my mouth dropped open, another scream trapped in my throat.

I didn't think. I pulled an arrow from my back and lifted my bow. The wind was swirling back and forth, the rain shifting with it. I nocked the arrow and stretched the string back with a steady hand. The calm fell over me, quieting the sounds of the lightning, and I closed my eyes, letting out a long, hot breath. I searched for the sound of the forest before me. The sea behind me. The storm overhead. I watched the route of the arrow in my mind.

And as another strike of lightning cracked open the darkness, I sent it into the air.

The turn of the shaft glowed like a spinning flame across the forest and it sank into the back of her shoulder. She flew forward with the force of the hit and Halvard turned, staring at the arrow in the woman's back before his gaze lifted, searching the forest until his eyes found me.

"The cart!" I pointed toward the Svell's line, screaming into the wind.

I threw my feet out, sliding down the rocks until my boots hit the ground, and took off, jumping over the fallen bodies as I pulled another arrow free.

Halvard took hold of the knife at his belt and he shouted my name as he threw it over my head. I ducked, toppling forward, and I hit the ground so hard that it knocked the breath from my lungs.

A man crashed into the mud behind me, Halvard's knife buried in his chest. He coughed blood as I pulled it free and got back to my feet. The forest turned darker with the furs and leathers of the Svell and Nādhir, the pelt of rain hitting the dead and dying as Halvard reached me, his breath fogging in the cold. All around us, Nādhir warriors were being cut down, the Svell pushing farther toward the tree line with every second that passed. Any moment, they'd be tearing down the hill to the village.

"The cart!" I shouted again.

But he didn't understand. I took the quiver from my back

and pushed it into his hands with the bow before I took his axe.

"What are you doing?" He looked at the bow, confused.

"I'm mending it," I shouted.

His eyes lifted over my head, to the Svell line. "You'll be dead before you reach it."

I smiled, lifting a hand to touch a cut beneath his eye, wiping at the blood with my fingertips. They were so blue. And still, they looked right into me, moving over my face until I could see my own reflection in them. I wanted to remember them. I wanted them to be the last thing I saw.

"I've been dead for most of my life, Halvard," I whispered.

He reached out, but I stepped back before he could touch me.

I turned on my heel and ran for the cart behind the thinning warriors in the distance, the axe heavy in my hands. A man ran at me from the side and I pushed faster, trying to get there before he did. But I wasn't fast enough. He took two steps before he collided with me and an arrow struck him in the chest, sending him backward.

I jumped over him, my arms pumping at my sides, and another man steered to head me off, an axe lifting over his head. Another arrow soared over me, dropping him in my path, and I looked back over my shoulder to see Halvard, my bow in his hands. He pulled another arrow from his back and I threw every bit of strength I had left forward as the land tipped down toward the cart.

I lifted myself over the rail and landed inside, heaving. The storm was beginning to quell, the rain softening, as I took a barrel of pitch up into my arms and threw it to the ground.

"Tova."

My hands froze on the next barrel and I could feel his stare landing hard on me before I looked up. Jorrund stood in soaked robes among the fallen bodies at the back of the Svell line, a torch in his hand. They were pushing the Nādhir back blow by blow, shortening the distance to the hill.

"Tova!" he screamed as I jumped from the cart.

The sound of Hylli's horn blared in the distance, signaling that the first of the Svell had broken through the trees. Time was running out.

Jorrund's voice echoed out again, but when I looked up, it was Vigdis who marched toward me, pushing through the back wall of warriors. In the next instant, his knife was swinging wide, catching me in the arm. I fell backward as he came over me, finding the tear in my sleeve with my fingers. Before he could bring the knife down, I rolled to my side, covering my head with my hands. The blade ripped into my other arm, the edge of the iron hitting the bone, and I cried out.

I tried to kick myself back toward the cart and Vigdis stilled suddenly, his tall frame towering over me. I stared up at him, both my hands pressing to the wounds in my arms and he turned, looking over his shoulder. My eyes went wide as the gleaming hilt of a knife came into view, buried in the back of Vigdis' armor vest. He reached behind him and tore it out, turning. And there, standing with the cold rain running over his leathers, Gunther stood, his face covered with a smear of blood.

With one quick motion, Vigdis swung his arm out in an arc, the blade slicing Gunther's throat in a clean line. I sat up, the cry trapped in my chest as the blood spilled. He fell to his knees and I lifted my eyes to the sky, swallowing down the nausea burning in my throat. He landed at my feet with a heavy thud, his hand open beside me. The talisman I'd given him was tied around his wrist.

Vigdis leaned into the cart, grasping for the wound at his back, but it was no use. The blood poured out in a thick, steady stream and after only seconds, his movements slowed, the grunt in his throat turning to a gurgle.

The moment he stopped moving, the rain stopped falling. I looked up to the gray sky, blinking. Because I knew what would be there. The nighthawk circled against the clouds, tilting in the wind.

I rocked forward onto my knees and lifted Halvard's axe over my head. The pain in my arms erupted as I brought the blade down with a crack, splintering the wood of the barrel. Jorrund still stood without moving, his mouth hanging open as I picked it up, and I snatched the torch from his hand, pushing past him. I broke through the Svell, racing toward the edge of the forest.

The barrel tipped under my arm, and I let the pitch pour onto the ground as I ran the full length of the Nādhir line.

It filled puddles, soaking into the earth, and when it was empty, I dropped it. Halvard appeared before the Nādhir, shouting orders over the strike of lightning, and I stood, waiting, as they moved into position, leaving the Svell in the trees.

Halvard's eyes found me in the chaos, and for a moment, my heart stopped beating. "Now!"

I dropped the torch at my feet.

The flame slithered away from me, shifting in the wind before the morning lit up in an amber glow. A wall of fire ignited before the tree line, the flames reaching taller than me. The Svell scrambled backward and the Nādhir followed. It was all they needed. Just a moment. A breath.

And they took it.

Halvard's brother ran past me, leaving a trail of Svell in his wake as he made his way toward Halvard. He pulled a shield up from the ground and dropped it onto the flames, creating a break in the fire, and then another.

"Go!" he roared, throwing an arm forward, and the rest of the Nādhir waiting on the slope charged. They flooded into the forest, pushing Svell back and chasing down the running warriors. Past the flames, I could see Jorrund standing over Vigdis' body, the hem of his robes heavy with mud.

Hot tears filled my eyes as I watched him, thinking he suddenly seemed so small. The man who'd raised me. Cared for me. Taught me. He'd lied and he'd used me. But he was the only father I remembered.

I opened my mouth to call out his name, but my words were cut off by the blare of the horn below. It blew in three short wails and the fighting slowed, every face in the forest turning to Hylli.

But what was there lay beyond the beach.

On the sea.

Boats as far as the eye could see were coming out of the black storm on the water. The horn blew again as they multiplied and white square sails appeared like a swirl of stars in a night sky. Lightning struck the beach and the deafening crack rang in my ears, making me feel like I was going to fall to the earth. I leaned into the nearest tree, my eyes on the water, where the carved heads of Naðr on wooden prows pushed across the water like an army of sea serpents.

The Kyrr.

CHAPTER THIRTY

HALVARD

I STOOD BEFORE THE FLAMES, THE AXE HEAVY IN MY HANDS as the Nādhir marched into the trees, pushing the Svell back. The burn of smoke in my throat raked as I turned in a circle, searching the forest for my brothers.

Ahead, two men were stalking toward me with another group of Svell at their backs. I stepped over the fading fire and readied the sword in one hand and the axe in the other as the cold rain began to fall again, washing the blood from my skin.

My steps slowed, my hands growing heavy at my sides, and the forest seemed to tilt around me. I blinked, trying to focus, pulling in a long breath and watching the width of their strides before I swung, taking both down with one clumsy turn. My hand lifted to throw the axe when a woman appeared behind them. I struck her leg and she stumbled, crashing into a tree as I drove the sword behind me. It sank into the gut of a Svell man and I kicked him from the blade.

My weight teetered forward, the last of my strength bleeding from my body and I sank to the ground, trying to catch my breath. The treetops spun overhead and I looked down to the linen of my tunic coming out from under my armor vest. It was soaked in fresh blood. My blood.

I reached beneath the leathers and touched the opened wound, where the skin had been torn back open. My hand went to the wet earth as I plunged the sword into the ground and leaned into it, trying to stand.

The glimmer of jewels shone ahead but my vision blurred. I shook my head until I could see the amber stone set into the hilt of a sword. The offering of reparation lay beside Vigdis' body in the distance. I stared at his wide frame, the side of his face pressed to the mud and his dark eyes open.

"Halvard!"

On the other side of the fire, Iri stood, watching me. Most of the warriors had pushed farther into the forest, leaving the ground littered with bodies and weapons beneath us. Iri stepped over the last of the flames and held a hand out to me. But as I went to take it, the horn in Hylli blew. The sound echoed up the hill and Iri turned back toward the village.

I dragged my feet under me, standing as the black pushed in around my mind. From above, Hylli looked empty, the last of our warriors fighting behind us in the trees. Only a few figures stood on the beach below, turned to the fog on the water.

"What is it?" Iri stopped beside me, speaking between breaths.

The ridge fell quiet, every eye turning to the sea, and I froze when I saw it, the breath binding up in my chest.

Boats.

Marked, white-sailed boats emerged from the fog like spirits, their serpent-head prows floating toward the rocky shore.

Iri muttered a curse and suddenly, my mind sharpened, my pulse evening as I searched for an explanation. It was the Kyrr. It had to be.

I took a step toward the edge of the ridge as the boats berthed on the sand one after the other. And then bodies were spilling from the wide, oiled hulls. Silver furs and twisted locks and open-throated screams covered the beach until they swallowed it whole. I watched as they tore through the village, headed for the forest, and I could see the marks. Covering every single one of them.

The Kyrr ran with their weapons drawn and painted shields lifted. They filled every path, wound around every corner, and there was a silence behind us, the echo of fighting snuffed out before the Svell retreat whistle sounded.

The painted warriors reached the hill outside the village gate and they didn't stop. More boats appeared from the wall of mist and more bodies jumped into the gray water. They flew toward us, blades shining, and I lifted my sword, sinking low into my feet to get ready. Iri did the same beside me and the Nādhir fell back to the slope, re-forming what was left of our line.

I pulled in a breath, tightening my grip on the hilt as they closed in. The Kyrr's long, twisted manes flew out behind them as they ran and I reared back, ready to catch the first one that reached me.

But they didn't.

The flood of Kyrr parted, moving around us, toward the Svell scrambling back toward the valley. I stood, lowering the sword and watching as they engulfed the forest where bodies covered the ground, as if the storm had rained down the dead. The lightning struck again, the flash blinding me, and I could feel it—the thin veil between worlds thick with spirits in the air. In a matter of seconds, the Kyrr seemed to conjure that space between life and death.

I thought I was imagining it. The Nādhir looked to me, waiting for an order, but the Kyrr weren't here for us. I walked into the trees and stopped midstride when I saw them gathering in rings in the distance.

Tova stood like a statue, her eyes wide as the Kyrr encircled her. She disappeared behind rows of warriors and her name formed silently on my lips, the sword slipping from my fingers. It hit the ground and I didn't think before I was running after them, disappearing into the mass of Kyrr.

I called her name again as I got closer and a hand caught hold of me, wrenching me back. I swung my fist, catching the man in the jaw, and he took the hit, stumbling back. But when he looked up at me, I blinked the rain from my eyes, confused. "Kjeld . . . what . . . ?"

He wiped the blood from his lip before he looked back over his shoulder toward the sound of a woman's voice shouting on the slope. I pushed past him, trying to see over the heads in front of me. The Nādhir stood holding their weapons, watching warily as a line of Kyrr marched up the path from the village gate. A woman in a red tunic appeared below it, her wide eyes searching the hill. The black pushed in again, my legs weak as the world spun around us, and I pressed my hand into the bleeding wound beneath my vest until I was groaning against the pain.

"Don't speak," Kjeld warned, meeting my eyes. "I mean it, don't say a word."

He stepped in front of me and raised a hand into the air as the swarm of Kyrr moved up the slope. The woman's white-painted face was aglow, her eyes pinned on me.

"Where is she?"

CHAPTER THIRTY-ONE

TOVA

I LOOKED INTO THE FACES OF THE KYRR AROUND ME, TREMBLING. Bone necklaces hung beneath their necks, pale gray furs draped around their shoulders over marked skin. The rain carved lines down their painted faces, making it look as if they were going to dissolve into thin air, right before my eyes. And for a moment, I thought they might. My gaze lifted to the sky and then down to my hands, and I wondered if I was dead. If I'd crossed into the afterlife.

But the feeling of eyes running over my marks brought me back and I clutched my last arrow to my chest, where my heart was pounding so hard that I could feel it in my entire body.

A woman's voice rose above the others and the flash of a red tunic appeared in the distance. She pushed through the warriors until I could see her face and I gulped in a breath, the sight of her making the tremor in my hands erupt. She stood before me, staring, her tunic turned the color of blood in the rain.

I opened my mouth to speak, but the air was trapped in my throat. My fingers wound so tightly around the arrow that I felt the tip of the head cut into the pad of my thumb.

She looked at me for another moment before she grabbed ahold of my tunic with strong hands, pulling me close as she inspected my face with narrowed, piercing eyes.

"I . . ." I whispered, but I couldn't think, my mind twisting and turning around the sight of her. Because I knew her. Somehow, I knew her.

She turned me to the side, walking slowly in a circle around me, and her scrutinizing gaze raked from my head to my feet.

"Who are you?" I dropped the arrow and pulled the sleeves of my tunic down to cover my marks, feeling naked before them.

She reached up, taking both my hands in hers, her eyes on the yarrow and the henbane. The glint of a smile lit in them as she answered. "I'm your mother, *sváss*."

The wind stopped suddenly, the storm trapped inside my head. I searched her face. But it wasn't her eyes I recognized. It was her voice. The deep, rasping sound that had been in my visions and haunted my dreams. I sucked in a breath, but before I could speak she turned, pushing back through the crowd.

"Wait!" I lunged forward, reaching for her, but two men

stepped into my path, each taking an arm and holding onto me.

I recoiled, hissing against the throbbing pain where the sword wounds were cut deep into my flesh. They were no longer bleeding, but I could see through the torn linen that they needed stitching. The men pulled me forward and my feet slid over the wet grass as we moved down the hill, toward the village.

Their grips tightened as I tried to pull free, searching the crowd frantically before I even realized what I was looking for. Halvard. But I didn't catch sight of him until we'd made it out from under the trees. He followed after us, pushing through the warriors gathered to my right. And a face I did recognize followed after him.

The Kyrr man I'd seen with him in Utan watched me. He didn't take his eyes from me as the men pulled me down the hill, toward the gate.

The village was quiet and empty and I struggled to keep up with their quick pace, their boots pounding the gravel faster than mine. Hundreds of Kyrr moved aside as the woman walked ahead, the bones around her neck jingling. She didn't look back at me as we passed through the open doors of the ritual house. I glanced back over my shoulder to where Halvard still stood beyond the gate, his face lifting above the others to see me before the doors slammed closed.

The fire blazed at the altar, lighting the dark room around us so that the white paint on the woman's face almost glowed.

I tried to wrench free of the hands again when I saw a tall man standing before the flames. The arms of his tunic were cut free so that every mark covering his thick, sculpted arms was visible. Runes, animals, symbols I didn't know. Except for one.

On the outside of his upper left arm were the antlers of a stag. And they were just like mine, their curves and points identical. I looked down to where the same symbol showed through my torn sleeve of my dress, my eyes wide.

The woman took the place beside him and the men let me go, pushing back out the doors and leaving us alone in the dark. My hands still shook as I looked up to where the sunlight spilled through the slats of the walls in sharp lines, landing on the face of the man. They both stood on the other side of the fire, staring. Their gazes ran over me, studying, and I squirmed beneath the feeling, my legs feeling too weak to hold me.

Red hair was pulled into thick, twisted locks over the woman's shoulder and beneath the marks, I could see pale, freckled skin. I swallowed hard, my eyes flitting down to my own, covered in the same spotted pattern.

When she finally spoke, I found myself holding my breath. "Tova." The accent that curled the edges of the words was different from the one I was used to. "Do you remember me?"

I looked over her face again, trying to find something familiar there. Something I knew. "I don't know," I answered, shifting on my feet. "Maybe."

But I did. Somehow. They didn't feel like strangers.

She smiled, her long fingers tangled into each other before her. "You were so small the last time we saw you. You're a woman now."

The man didn't speak. He stood a whole head taller than her, silently watching me as the woman pressed a hand to her chest. "I am Svanhild." The sound of it stung, pulling at the threads of long-dead memories. Stitches on wounds that had never healed. "This is Turonn." She looked up to the man. "We are so grateful to Naðr." Her voice broke. "For bringing you back to us."

"Do you remember?" When Turonn finally spoke, the depth of his voice filled the entire room around us. It was warm, like the feel of stone sitting in the afternoon sun. It, too, was like an echo of something I knew. "Do you remember what happened?"

I shook my head, feeling cold despite the altar fire. "I only remember waking. I opened my eyes and I was alone. I didn't know where I was because the fog was so thick and—"

"And you drifted across the fjord. Is that how you came to be with the Svell?" He seemed eager for answers, but I didn't have them. I had no idea how I'd landed on Liera's shores.

"Their Tala found me. He said that a Fate Spinner led him to the beach. That she gave me to him." Jorrund, standing in the rain alone, came back to me. The way his robes clung to him, his eyes empty.

"Of course." Svanhild smiled wider. "When Kjeld came to us and said that he'd found you . . ." She breathed through the tears in her eyes. "I knew they'd kept their promise to us."

"Who?" I wrapped my arms around myself, squeezing.

"The Spinners."

The stones pulled heavily around my neck and I reached out for the bench beside me, feeling as if I was going to fall. "But why did you . . . you sent me away."

"Sent you away?" Turonn's voice rose, the sound of anger on the words.

Svanhild silenced him with a lifted hand before she answered. "You were born our only daughter. But your fate was written on the Tree of Urðr before I ever carried you," she said. "I cast the stones to see your future when I first realized you were coming and the cast was clear. The Spinners said that you would be *Dagaz*. A new dawn. But that death was coming for you."

My shaking hand went to the center of my stomach, where the rune of *Dagaz* was marked into my skin.

"When you were only six years old, you drowned in the sea."

The gray waters. The silence. The string of bubbles racing to the surface as my hands drifted. The pieces all found me again, even clearer and brighter than they had been when I took the henbane. I imagined myself, pale and still in the funeral boat, the flames pulling in the cold wind before it disappeared into the fog. I imagined the two of them standing on the shore of the headlands in the strange light that illuminated the fragments of memory.

"We do not always understand the ways of the gods, Tova. But Naðr brought you back to us. She had a great destiny for you." Svanhild came around the fire to stand before me and her hands lifted, touching my face. "Here you are."

I looked into her dark eyes, where I could see myself. Not just my reflection. I could see parts of me there that weren't mortal. I leaned into the warmth of her, hot tears falling, and tried to swallow down the sob in my chest. I didn't remember her but maybe I did in some way. Maybe I'd only not remembered her because if I did, I'd have to feel the hole of her inside me.

This was *Othala*. The rune cast that had broken my trust in Jorrund and the last thread that tied me to the Svell. It had brought me here. To this moment.

They hadn't cast me off. Naðr hadn't forgotten me. She'd spared my life.

"They led me here, to Hylli," I whispered, my voice small. "The stones. They led me to the Nādhir. To you."

To Halvard.

She pulled me into her arms and wrapped them tightly around me. I buried my face into the thick linen of her wet tunic and cried. I let every memory come back to me. Every bit of light. Every bit of darkness. I let them pull at me like the river to the sea.

I let them take me home.

CHAPTER THIRTY-TWO

HALVARD

I PUSHED THE DOOR OPEN WITH MY HEART IN MY THROAT.

"They're alright." Fiske stopped me before I'd even made it inside, one hand catching me in the chest.

Behind him, Eelyn lay on the table, my mother working slowly at the wound carved from her shoulder into her chest. The open skin was spread wide, the white bone showing through the muscle, and she panted through bared teeth, kicking as Mýra leaned all her weight on top of her to pin her down.

"Shh . . ." She pressed her mouth to Eelyn's ear, one tear sliding down her nose.

Iri sat on the stone ledge of the fire pit, sewing up his own arm with the end of the thread between his teeth, the skin puckering with the haphazard, careless stitches. Blood covered every inch of his skin, but he was breathing. Somehow, we were all still breathing.

"I need you," my mother called over her shoulder and Fiske went to her, coming to the other side of the table. "Hold here."

He took one side of the wound into his hands and he let Eelyn gulp in a breath before he leaned into her, holding the tissue open so that my mother could clean it.

Eelyn groaned beneath his hands and I went to her, sinking down beside the table to meet her eyes.

"She's alright?" I looked up to my mother, afraid of what I may see on her face.

But she gave me a sideways smile. "Need more than a sword to take this one down, Halvard. You know that."

Fiske laughed, kissing Eelyn's forehead, but the sight of her writhing on the table turned my stomach. I didn't know how many we'd lost and I still hadn't found Latham, but my family was here, together. And I was ashamed of the relief it brought me.

"Have you seen Asmund?" I looked back to Iri.

He tied off the stitches, dropping the last bit of bloody thread into the fire. "He's alright."

I let out a long breath, pressing my forehead into my hands.

"Get the kettle." My mother kicked my boot with hers and I stood, taking the hook from the wall and fetching it from the flames. I set it onto the stool beside her where she could reach it.

"Are you going to tell us what this is with the Kyrr, Halvard?" Iri asked, coming to stand beside me. They were gathered around the ritual house in a horde, where they'd taken Tova. Every warrior waited silently, watching the village with their weapons sheathed. They didn't look like they wanted a fight, but there was no denying that from where they stood, it was a good time for one.

"I don't know," I admitted.

The Kyrr leaders had disappeared into the ritual house as soon as the Svell were gone and hadn't come out. Their boats filled the shallows, their warriors covering the beach, and a sinking feeling had pulled in my gut as I walked through the village gates. The Nādhir watched from the path and the hill, waiting their turns with the healers, and their faces betrayed the same thought that was resounding in my mind.

The Kyrr had saved us. But there was no way to know why. Or what they'd do next. They were a clan of warriors descended upon a bleeding people and if they wanted to, they could take everything from us.

"Do you think it's to do with the girl?" I didn't miss the way Fiske's gaze met my mother's.

It had to be about Tova. And Kjeld. Both of them, somehow. "Yes."

But if they'd come for more than the girl, we were ripe for the taking.

I looked down at Eelyn, running a hand over her hair. Her fair skin was more ashen than I'd ever seen it, the exhaustion glazing over her eyes. She didn't fight against my mother's hands anymore. She didn't have the strength left for that. I took a new bottle of ale from the shelf on the wall and opened it. Her shaking hand lifted to take it from me and she tipped her head back to drink.

The village was almost silent when I pushed back outside, walking up the path to the ritual house. The Nādhir were already dragging the bodies of our people down to the beach and the Svell that the Kyrr found in the forest were lined up on their knees at the top of the hill, their hands bound behind their backs. Three lines of warriors looked out over Hylli, their muddy faces watching the serpent ships that filled the cove, anchored in the calm water beneath the clearing storm clouds. A few of them already lay dead, facedown in the slick grass.

"Halvard." Freydis called to me from where she stood on the beach, her eyes reddened beneath a bleeding gash on her forehead.

Latham lay at her feet, his hands folded over his middle and his eyes closed. The wound that killed him was splayed open across his chest, his woven leather armor vest torn and unraveling in a diagonal line. I swallowed back the pain in my throat, sinking down beside him.

"The others?" I asked, wiping a streak of mud from his face with the back of my hand.

"We lost Egil, too," she answered quietly.

I set my hand onto Latham's shoulder, squeezing before I stood. I hoped it was the quick death he deserved. I hoped he was in the afterlife with my father, meeting faces of long-lost friends and telling the story of what had happened. He'd been ready to die, but I hadn't been ready to lose him. Now, I would look to Freydis and the others who were left to guide me.

The doors to the ritual house opened in the distance and from where I stood, I could see Kjeld's blond hair as he stepped into the sunlight. His eyes found me down the path before he made his way toward us.

Asmund appeared in an open doorway as I passed and I stopped to take his arm, clapping him on the back as he leaned into me. "Alright?"

"Alright," he answered, his attention on Kjeld. Together, we walked to meet him and he stopped in the middle of the trail, waiting for us.

"What is this, Kjeld?" I watched his face, looking for whatever he may not say aloud. But he looked me in the eye, standing tall before us.

"I'm sorry I didn't tell you. I had to be sure."

"Of what?"

He rubbed the place between his brows, putting the words together. "The girl—Tova—she's the daughter of the Kyrr leaders."

Asmund took a step backward, staring at him. "How did you know?"

"The marks," Kjeld answered. "I knew by her marks."

I remembered the way he reacted when I told him about

the girl in the glade and the eye inked onto her chest. The way he'd changed his mind so quickly about coming with us to Hylli and the way he'd stared at her in Utan. As if he'd seen a ghost. "You went back to tell them their daughter was alive."

He nodded. "Yes."

"And what is she to you?" My hand went on the hilt of my sword.

"What?"

"Did you use her to set right whatever made you run from the headlands?"

"She *is* the reason I left the headlands. Tova is my sister's daughter," he said, swallowing hard.

Asmund cursed under his breath, half-laughing as he looked between us.

"What are they doing here, Kjeld?" I lifted my chin to where his people were still gathered by the hundreds.

"They're here for her. For Tova."

"What else?"

I could tell by the way he pressed his lips into a flat line that he knew what I was asking. It didn't matter why they'd come. The only thing that mattered was what they'd do now that they were here.

Kjeld shook his head, looking at his boots. "The Kyrr aren't like you."

"What does that mean?" Asmund narrowed his eyes at him.

"They see the world through the omens and the runes. They don't have Talas or councils or elders, they cast the stones to consult the Spinners. There's only the stones."

I waited, trying to read him, but Kjeld never gave anything away. With him, everything was always hidden. But he'd never struck me as a liar. "What does it have to do with Tova? Why did you say she isn't supposed to be alive?"

"When my sister cast the stones and said that Tova was fated to die, I told her that I could change it. That I could make sure her future was rewritten." He paused. "It was a promise I couldn't keep. Tova drowned in the sea when she was six years old and the Spinners had their way."

The bite of cold over my skin returned, remembering the way she'd appeared to me in the forest. "Then how is she here? How did she end up with the Svell?"

"The Spinners? The gods? I don't know. When we sent her body out on a funeral boat to the sea, she was dead. I saw her. I *held* her in my arms, Halvard." He swallowed past the tears in his eyes. "She was gone."

"And you left the headlands."

He answered with a nod. "When you told me about the marks on the girl in the glade, I knew you were talking about Tova. But I had to see it for myself. I didn't think it was possible."

"And now?"

He arched an eyebrow. "Now?"

"The entire Kyrr clan is on the mainland. In my village. What happens now?"

"I don't know."

I took a step toward him. "What do you mean you don't know? You just said your sister is their leader."

He looked up at me, almost apologetic. "I told you, Halvard. They only listen to the stones."

CHAPTER THIRTY-THREE

TOVA

Svanhild set a pail down between us and dipped a clean cloth into the cold seawater. I watched her drag it down the length of my arms, cleaning around the knife wounds above my elbows and washing away the dirt and blood. As the beat of my heart slowed, the pain rose, reaching all the way down into my fingertips, the throbbing pulse of it making my stomach turn.

Hylli sat untouched outside, as if the blood of countless Nādhir hadn't just been spilled for it in the forest. It wasn't the first time many of the same warriors had fought for their home on the fjord and it likely wouldn't be the last.

I studied Svanhild's face as she worked, wondering if she planned to be an enemy or an ally. She rinsed the cloth and wiped down my arm again, until the marks that stained my skin were all visible.

"Did you do them?" I asked, trying to place her in the

vision I'd had when I took the henbane smoke. I could almost feel the warmth of the fire on my bare skin and hear the sound of a woman humming as her hands worked the bone needle over my back.

"I did."

"And they all have meaning?"

"Yes." She smiled. "Some of them are prayers, some prophecies. Some are the sacred stories of our people."

She let go of my wrist and I traced the symbols with the tip of my finger, stopping on an intricate stave below my elbow. "What does this one mean?"

Svanhild came to sit beside me, craning over my arm. "It means safety for the journey."

"And this one?" I pointed to a set of circles within one another on my shoulder.

"Blessed by Naðr."

I studied their shapes, their messages almost seeming to make them change. They were wrought with meaning, each one, but they had only ever been secrets to me. Mysteries written across my body in a language I couldn't read.

She watched me from the corner of her eye. "You still have them." Her eyes went to the opening of my tunic, where the string that held the rune stones showed.

I reached up, pulling at it until the purse was free. Its weight landed heavily in the palm of my hand.

"I made them for you when you were only a baby. Every woman in our family is a Truthtongue. All the way back to the child that the Spinners gave as a gift to Naðr as an offering. We put the stones into the boat with you when we sent it out, so you'd have them in the afterlife."

I let one stone fall into my open hand, the firelight dancing over the rune. *Othala.*

"Kjeld says you were casting the stones for the Svell," she said, leaning forward to see my face.

My fingers closed over the stone and I stared at her feet, swallowing hard.

"It's alright, Tova."

I blinked as fresh tears burned behind my eyes. "You would be ashamed if you knew what I've done."

She folded her hands into her lap, waiting.

"I knew the runes," I said. "I had a sense for them even when I first came to Liera, and when I saw that they kept me alive, I used them. But the Svell used *me,* too. I led them to attack the Nādhir in the glade and then Utan. I was the reason they came to the fjord."

"Ah, yes. It seems that way, doesn't it?"

"Seems?" I wiped the trail of a tear from my cheek. "It was my rune cast that brought them here."

She smiled again. "The fate of the Svell was carved into the Tree of Urðr long before you cast the runes. And so was yours."

"Then which comes first? The carving in the tree or the acts that shift fate?"

She laughed. "They are the same moment. We do not understand time, *svåss.* Mortal minds cannot comprehend the Spinners or their work." Her hand unfurled before me and she waited for me to set my own into it. "Before you were born, I knew that we would lose you. I didn't understand why Naðr would give you to us only to take you away. But the Spinners already knew your fate. I told Turonn that we would have you for only a little while, but my brother Kjeld—"

"Kjeld?" My eyes widened. "The Kyrr with the raiders?"

"Yes. He thought he could change your fate. And when you died, we didn't only lose you. We lost him, too. But the Spinners are *much* wiser than we are. They are expert weavers. And when the time was right, they brought you back to him so that he could keep his promise to us." She lifted a hand, catching a tear at the tip of my chin. "We gave you to the sea, Tova. But the sea gave you back."

I tried to make sense of it, looking for the pattern in my mind. But it was too knotted up. Too tangled. Something had turned the current that day. Something had woken me from death. All I thought I had understood about the Spinners and the runes was like the trickle of water from the whole of the sea. It was only now that I realized how little I knew.

But one thing was clear. It was as sharp in my mind as the sight of my mother sitting before me. I'd made a promise to the Spinners and to myself to protect Halvard and his people. And even if it meant going against the Kyrr, I'd keep it.

"What will you do now?" I asked.

She rested her head on the wall at our backs, looking down at me. "Ah, that's for the stones to decide."

"What?" The knot in my stomach tightened. If the Kyrr wanted the fjord, all they had to do was reach out and take it.

"Every moment is a possibility. The Spinners brought us here to find you. But we don't know yet what other purpose they have for us. We won't know until they tell us."

"Purpose?"

"Mortals and gods cannot be trusted to obey the warnings of the Spinners. The Nādhir should know that." Her voice trailed off.

"What do you mean?"

She sat up, leaning forward to rest her elbows on her knees as the firelight caught her eyes. "What do you know of the Herja, *svåss*?"

"That they were a demon army." The sound of the bones knocking above the gate returned to me.

"They are darker than demons, Tova. The Spinners warned Sigr and Thora that the time had come to end their blood feud. But they did not listen. So the Spinners rewrote the fate of their people on the Tree of Urðr with their blood."

The truth of it sank deep in my gut, making me feel like I was going to be sick. The Herja had almost wiped the Aska and the Riki from the earth. They'd filled the land and the water with the dead. I'd known the Spinners to be ruthless, but I had never imagined this.

"So, you'll cast the stones," I whispered.

"*You* will cast them," she said, standing.

I stared up at her, my lips parting to speak before the heavy doors creaked open and Kjeld appeared. His hair was combed back, and the sharp edges of his face looked like Svanhild's in the low light. Again, that feeling of remembering lit in the center of my chest. I'd been alone for so long, and suddenly, an entire family surrounded me.

"What is it?" The sunlight coming through the door fell on Svanhild's face.

Halvard stepped in behind him and I stood without meaning to, my fingers tightening around the small stone in my hand.

"Their chieftain wants to speak with you." Kjeld looked to Halvard.

Svanhild tilted her head to the side, eyeing him as he moved toward us. "You're quite young to be chieftain."

Halvard didn't respond, coming around Kjeld to stand before us. I waited for his eyes to meet mine but they didn't. "I want to know what you plan to do with the Svell you captured in the forest."

She picked up the bucket and poured the water into the corner of the fire pit, sending up a cloud of steam. "You want to kill them."

"I want you to release them," he said.

Her eyes snapped up, studying him, and Halvard returned my mother's gaze with an unreadable expression.

"Release them? When we set foot onto this shore, they were trying to kill you. They were trying to kill my daughter."

"They're our enemy. I'll decide what's to be done with them."

Svanhild looked amused, a bit of wonder curling on her lips. "Why would you let them live?"

"I'm not going to kill warriors with their hands tied behind their backs," he said, simply.

"Then what will you do with them?"

His chin lifted. "Let them go."

"I don't understand."

"I've seen what blood feuds do. Generations of our people gave their lives for one." He paused. "That's not how we live anymore."

I watched his face, the feeling of pride blooming in the center of my chest.

She thought for a moment before she looked to Kjeld. "Let him do what he wants with his prisoners. The rest is up to the Spinners."

Kjeld nodded in answer and Svanhild touched my arm softly before she slipped outside with Kjeld behind her. The door closed, the sunlight gone, leaving Halvard and me standing beside the fire.

"You need those closed up." His eyes fell to the cuts on my arms and the pain of them suddenly returned, coiling around me until I was trembling.

I pulled the sleeves of my tunic down to cover them. "I need to ask you something."

"What is it?" He looked apprehensive, his hand drifting to the hilt of his sword.

"There's a body in the forest that I want to burn."

He lifted an eyebrow. "Who?"

"A Svell man. He was . . . my friend. I think."

A question passed over his face like a shadow, but he didn't ask it. "Alright." His gaze went back to the door.

I knew what he was thinking. He wanted to know what the Kyrr planned to do. He wanted to know if the Nādhir were done fighting yet. "I don't know," I answered his unspoken question honestly.

I pulled in a deep breath, steadying myself as I looked up at him. The mud from the forest had been wiped from his face, but it still crept up and out of his tunic, reaching around his throat like fingers. In the firelight, I could see the pulse moving beneath his skin.

"You were right," he said, the corner of his mouth lifting. "We're not dead."

The pull of the same smile awoke on my lips and I felt the heat come up into my cheeks. "No, we're not."

"I was going to thank you." His voice dropped low.

"For what?" I asked, confused. I'd only brought darkness to him. I'd only cursed him since the day I first saw his face in the glade.

"For coming here. And for what you did in the forest."

He took a step toward me and my heart kicked in my chest, the blood running faster through my veins. I traced the shape of his eyes and the curve of his jaw with my gaze. I tried to carve into my mind a memory I'd never forget.

He came closer and I pulled the smell of him into my lungs and memorized that, too. He leaned down, hiding me in his shadow as he pressed his lips softly to the corner of my mouth. His hand wound around my waist and for a moment, I melted into him, the warmth of him flooding inside me and filling me up. And when he pulled away, the blazing fire of his touch still burned on my skin.

"You're welcome," I whispered.

He smiled, his eyes dropping to the floor, and the rough, rigid parts of him fell away, revealing a crooked smile on his lips. He turned without looking at me again and stopped before the door, his hand on the latch. And just as I thought he would speak, he pushed it open, disappearing into the light.

CHAPTER THIRTY-FOUR

HALVARD

ONE HUNDRED AND TWELVE WARRIORS LAY ON FIVE PYRES as the sun sank down the sky, disappearing behind the violet sea's horizon. The Nādhir gathered on the rocks before them were waiting, a deafening silence engulfing the village.

Iri and Mýra stood beside the docks, the water at their backs. I hadn't been here to see the village burn ten years ago, but they had. The same look that had been on their faces after that battle as there again now—the ashen weariness of bloodshed and the dreaded unknown of what was coming.

Our people had fought for the fjord and the mountain and they'd won. But it seemed we would never be free of enemies. My eyes went to the glow of the ritual house, where the Kyrr were gathered with their leaders. Behind us, their boats filled the shallows.

They'd wait until the fires were finished burning before they cast their stones to decide what to do with us. But before then, we had souls to send to the afterlife and for the first time, I would lead the funeral rites for the Nādhir.

Asmund joined me as I walked the path to the beach and I looked up to the hill that had been littered with bodies only hours before. The doors of the ritual house were open as we passed, and my gaze searched for Tova among the Kyrr, but there were only faces and voices I didn't know.

I hadn't meant to kiss her. I hadn't meant to even touch her. But the pull that had found me in the glade before all of this began was only growing stronger. I could feel her the way I could see her in the forest. Like breath on my skin. And when I watched her standing before the flames in the midst of battle, I'd known she was right. Deep inside me. There was some fate that bound us. Some future that lay waiting.

The Nādhir were gathered on the beach below, drinking our winter stores of ale as they waited. The calm, clear night was a gift from Sigr, the god of the fjord. The storm that had blown in from the sea was gone, but another was already gathering in the distant, darkening clouds.

Iri handed me the torch as I reached him and he tipped his chin up at me as I took it. Fiske had stayed with my mother as she worked over the intricate stitching on Eelyn's wound, but Mýra was beside him, and that was all the family I needed. She gave me a reassuring smile before I turned to face our people.

I looked out over my clansmen, all standing still in the quiet. There was nothing to say. No way to truly honor them with words. I didn't have Espen's gift to speak or Aghi's wisdom and I wouldn't pretend to. There was only the grief that followed death and the hollow place it left. There was only fate's hand and everything we would never understand about it.

The water crept up over the rocks as the tide rose behind us, the wind turning colder with the stars brightening overhead. I lowered the torch until it touched the corner of the first pyre and the flame caught, traveling over the oil-soaked bodies until it was swallowed in fire.

The Nādhir ritual words began, carried on rough, tired voices as I lit the others.

My hand stilled as the faint feeling of a gaze landed on me. I felt her again, in the shadows. Tova was almost invisible where she stood before the last pyre, her black dress hiding her in the dark. Only the moonlight on her pale skin made her marks visible.

I hadn't told anyone about the Svell man that I'd put onto the pyre at Tova's request. After the Svell prisoners were cut free and they disappeared into the forest, I'd followed her back into the trees in the setting sun. The jagged scar carved into the earth where she'd lit the pitch on fire was like an enormous, slithering snake. We found the man she was looking for beside Vigdis, and she took the bracelet from his wrist before I carried him through the village as dark fell.

She held the bracelet in her clasped hands as she stared

with an empty gaze into the flames. The blazing pyres bathed the beach in red light, only the shine of tears glistening in its reflection.

The bodies of the fallen Nādhir turned to ash on their way to the afterlife, and I prayed that the gods would see it. Sigr, Thora, Eydis, Naðr. The gods of the clans that lay farther to the east and beyond the mountain to the south. I prayed that they'd remember the stench of death that rose up to meet them. That they'd remember the way we would.

Tova stood before the fire, her dark hair pulling in the wind, her shape nothing but a black silhouette against the flames. She'd brought death to Utan and then she'd brought salvation to Hylli. Now, she'd summoned the entire clan of her people down from the north and our fates would drop from her hands.

She wiped her face with the back of her sleeve and I resisted the urge to reach out and touch her, reminding myself that she was a smoldering coal in the fire of the Kyrr. Her people had appeared in the storm and now, they stood able to take everything we'd just fought for. And after the stones fell, we could be standing on opposite sides again, her with her people and me with mine.

CHAPTER THIRTY-FIVE

TOVA

I COULD FEEL IT IN MY BONES.

The pounding rhythm of the drums came down from the village, where the Kyrr were gathered in Hylli's ritual house, and found me on the empty beach. Their voices carried out into the night with songs and I shivered in the cold as they twisted in the back of my mind, flickering dead memories back to life.

"It's time." Svanhild's deep voice found me and I turned to see her, my hands cradling my bandaged arms.

The funeral fires for the Nādhir had finished burning and the beach was dark, but the embers still glowed before the water. I'd watched Gunther burn until the last flames extinguished, wondering if he had made it to the afterlife or if Eydis would punish him for my treachery. I would never know. Wherever he was, I hoped he was with his son.

"Come, *svåss*." Svanhild fit her hand into mine and I

followed her with bare feet up to the path that wound through the dark village. The Nādhir were still drinking away the battle on the hill where tents ran in rows all the way up to the forest. Tomorrow, they'd be on their way home, back to their villages, and Hylli would empty itself of war. That's what I wanted to believe. But until the stones were cast, no one knew what the Kyrr would do. What *my* people would do.

The ritual house stood tall as we came up from the beach, the firelight spilling through the open arched doorway.

"What will they say?" I asked, my hand tightening around hers before she let me go.

"What do you want them to say?"

I knew the answer to that, but it was something I'd never say aloud. I knew better than to tempt the Spinners or to declare my own will before the gods. But the burn of Halvard's mouth was still warm on mine, and if I'd been brave enough to answer her, I would have said I wanted to stay. With him. Maybe forever.

She squeezed my hand before she let it go. The song rose louder, every head turned as Svanhild appeared before them, making her way through the crowd of Kyrr with Turonn at her side. Every man and woman stepped aside, leaving a clear path stretching out before me that led to the altar fire. As Svanhild lifted her hand, the singing voices stopped, their echo still ringing inside of me.

I pulled the purse from around my neck and the familiar weight of the runes in my hands grounded me to the earth as I stepped out of the wind and into the warmth of the ritual house. The Kyrr were packed in between the walls so tightly that there was hardly any air to breathe and the stone was hot beneath my feet. Every eye fell on me as I walked the aisle and stopped before the altar, emptying the purse into my hands.

I would cast the stones.

I would look into the future.

But this time, for my *own* people.

The drums started again, pounding in a rhythm that matched my racing heartbeat, and the sound of the voices changed, dropping low into whispers that wound through the mass of people and tingled up my spine. They were chanting. Or praying. Like the sound of water on hot coals. Like the fall of a thousand rivers over the falls.

I blinked, the realization hitting me so hard that it snatched the breath from my chest.

It was the same. It was the same sound I'd heard when I first saw Halvard in the glade. The sound that had pulled me after him, to Utan and then to Hylli. It wasn't a memory. It was a moment in the future.

It was now.

The slide of tongues over rasping words and the click of teeth swirled around me and I blinked back the tears in my eyes, Svanhild's words repeating.

They are the same moment.

Her lips moved with the others as she took a bundle of

herbs from the stone ledge and dropped them into the fire. The smoke billowed up behind us until the room was filled with it, casting everything in a fragrant haze that made my head swim. My heart slowed, the blood in my body warming.

I couldn't see him, but I could feel him.

I searched the faces for Halvard, but there were only the eyes of the Kyrr. The stinging, sweet smoke and the beat of the drums. And though I was surrounded by faces I didn't know in a land that wasn't mine, I fit into it in some way. Or it fit into me.

Turonn unrolled a fox pelt on the altar before me and my slick hands clutched tighter around the stones. There was no hiding what the runes said this time. There was no turning of minds. No Jorrund to twist fate into what he wanted. My mother and father stood beside me, waiting, and again, I looked for Halvard.

His face appeared at the back of the room, his dark hair tucked behind his ears and his bright eyes pinned on me. And the trembling that had been in my hands seemed to suddenly quiet. He tipped his chin up, as if to silently say that it was alright. That everything was going to be okay. And somehow, I believed him.

I let the sight of his face settle me before I closed my eyes, emptying my mind of every sound, every trace of light, until I was standing in the dark silence.

I pressed the stones between my palms, holding them out before me, a calm flooding into me that I'd never felt before. *This* was where I was meant to be. The boat hadn't led me to Jorrund. It hadn't led me to the Svell. It had led me here, to this moment.

Now.

"Augua ór tivar. Ljá mir sýn."

I spoke the words aloud, and they fell rhythmically into the sounds of the voices around me.

"Augua ór tivar. Ljá mir sýn!"

I said it again, louder.

"Augua ór tivar. Ljá mir sýn!"

I screamed it, my throat burning, and the words bent and broke around the desperate plea.

Eye of the gods. Give me sight.

Again, I brought Halvard to the forefront of my mind—the future I wanted to see.

The quiet wound through me and my lips parted, my breath hitching as I dropped the stones.

The drums stopped, every mouth empty, and silence fell over the ritual house as they hit the pelt one after the other, tumbling into place. I didn't open my eyes, afraid of what I may see. Afraid of what I may not. I held my breath and Svanhild's voice found me again.

"Tova," she whispered.

I opened my eyes and the firelight came flooding back, pulling me up from the darkness of my mind. I looked down, my eyes falling on the stones, where the runes looked up at me in a constellation written only for me. And for him.

The warmth of the kiss ignited on my skin again and I

reached up, touching the corner of my mouth, a tear sliding down my cheek. My mother had been right. There *was* a new beginning carved into the Tree of Urðr.

And the stones never lied. Not to me.

The Spinners were wise, but they weren't always kind. Sometimes fate was a tangled knot. Sometimes it was a noose. Or a net.

But sometimes, it was the rope that pulled you from the sinking deep.

I looked up, finding Halvard's eyes in the sea of faces, a smile breaking onto my lips. And as if he'd known it all along, he smiled back.

ACKNOWLEDGMENTS

As always, Joel, Ethan, Josiah, Finley, and River. You are the oil in my lamp and I'm never without light because of you. Also my family, who fill my life with true stories.

To my writing partner, Kristin Dwyer, this book literally would not have been written without you. Your belief in my voice and in my storytelling has pulled me through so many times, and you deserve so much more credit than I'll ever be able to give you. But also, you're the worst.

Eileen Rothschild, what an amazing gem of an editor I have in you! Thank you for trusting me to walk into the unknown with Tova and Halvard. I feel so very lucky to have you on my side. And to my agent, Barbara Poelle, you are just the most badass woman I know. Thank you for every seen and unseen thing you have done along this road.

Thank you to my wonderful publisher, Wednesday Books, and my team, Tiffany Shelton, DJ DeSmyter, and Jessica Preeg, for holding my hand along the way. My books would not be in the hands of readers if I didn't have you in my corner. It takes a village and I really, really love my village. Also a very special thank you to Kerri Resnick, designer for both *Sky in the Deep*'s and *The Girl the Sea Gave Back*'s beautiful covers. You are magic!

To my faithful beta readers, Natalie Faria and Isabel Ibanez, I am so thankful for your wisdom! Thank you for helping me find my way out of the weeds.

To Stephanie Brubaker: friend, critique partner, fellow foodie, and creator of the pronunciation guide for both books in this world. Thank you for always, always, always being there for me, rain or shine. And Lyndsay Wilkin, that writing retreat in Nevada City quite literally saved me. Thank you both for swooping in at a moment when I felt so very lost. All my love and gratitude to the bright shining light of optimism and hope who is Stephanie Garber. I am so happy that our paths crossed. Your encouragement and support throughout this process have meant more to me than you know.

To my local author gang, Shannon Dittemore, Jenny Lundquist, Joanna Rowland, Jessica Taylor, Kim Culbertson, and Rose Cooper. I couldn't ask for a better tribe of writers to drink an unspecified number of margaritas with.

To Amy, Angela, and Andrea, I just really love you. And to my high school sweethearts, Megwam, Cumulus Cloud, and Lizzard, I find endless inspiration in you and the way you see this world.